Advance Praise for
FINDING MRS. FORD

"In this absorbing debut, Deborah Goodrich Royce takes readers on a twisty, mesmerizing journey between the rarefied world of Watch Hill, Rhode Island and the warring gangsters of 1970s suburban Detroit, as a grieving widow is forced to confront the consequences of a fateful summer thirty-five years earlier. Brimming with vivid characters and emotional insight, *Finding Mrs. Ford* tackles big themes of identity, friendship, and loss, spinning out the suspense right to the last page. A total triumph."

—BEATRIZ WILLIAMS, *New York Times* bestselling author of
The Summer Wives

"In her literary debut, Deborah Goodrich Royce has given us the sort of thriller that wants to be devoured in one sitting. Written from start to finish with crisp and poignant prose, compelling characters and setting, *Finding Mrs. Ford* entertains as much with imagery as with its masterful plot twists. I couldn't put it down."

—JEANNE McWILLIAMS BLASBERG, author of *Eden* and *The Nine*

"Deborah Royce's first novel, *Finding Mrs. Ford* is a treat—an exquisitely written literary thriller that compels the reader forward right to the last page and makes one hope she is writing a second and a third novel."

—PATRICIA CHADWICK, author of *Little Sister: A Memoir*

FINDING MRS. FORD

DEBORAH GOODRICH ROYCE

Post Hill
PRESS

A POST HILL PRESS BOOK

Finding Mrs. Ford
© 2019 by Deborah Goodrich Royce
All Rights Reserved

ISBN: 978-1-64293-172-3
ISBN (eBook): 978-1-64293-173-0

Cover art by Cassandra Tai-Marcellini and Becky Ford
Interior design and composition by Greg Johnson/Textbook Perfect

"Last Dance"
Words and Music by Paul Jabara
Copyright © 1977 EMI Blackwood Music Inc. and Olga Music
Copyright Renewed
All Rights Administered by Sony/ATV Music Publishing LLC,
424 Church Street, Suite 1200, Nashville TN 37219
International Copyright Secured. All Rights Reserved.
Reprinted by permission of Hal Leonard LLC

Post Hill Press
New York • Nashville
posthillpress.com

Published in the United States of America

*To Kathy and Earl, Chuck,
Alexandra, and Tess—
thank you for inspiration
past, present, and abiding.*

FINDING MRS. FORD

SUSAN

*"The most important thing about a person
is always the thing you don't know."*

—*The Lacuna,* Barbara Kingsolver

1

Thursday, August 7, 2014
Watch Hill, Rhode Island

A single gunshot cracks the air.

Seagulls flutter and levitate above the sand as Mrs. Ford's dogs rise, barking. She, too, jumps just a little in her Adirondack chair and her feet lose their perch on the seawall. The echo reverberates across the sea and back to her at its edge. Mrs. Ford reaches down to pat the dogs.

Sound dissipates. Birds land. Dogs settle.

She doesn't know why she startles every time this happens. She should know better. She does know better. This is the eight-a.m. shot signaling the raising of the flag at the Watch Hill Yacht Club, a short distance from her house. But even after all these years, she is rattled by the sound of gunfire.

Before her is the lighthouse at the tip of the peninsula. Its lawn slopes back from verdant green to jagged rocks as it rises to meet the mound that gives Watch Hill its name. From this lookout, Americans kept vigil for English vessels in the War of 1812.

Lighthouse Point, nearly surrounded by water, is the place from which both Atlantic Ocean and Long Island Sound are visible. It is where they meet in a cocktail of currents that, with some frequency, foils even the strongest swimmer. It is the end of the peninsula, the end of the line.

Next stop: water. From here, all lands are reachable. Aim the bow of your ship east, you'll eventually hit Europe; aim it southeast, Africa. Keep going, and you'll circumnavigate the globe.

It is an early summer morning. Watch Hill is a summer town. Built by the summer people for the summer people. They came from Cincinnati, St. Louis, Detroit, these people, titans of industry from the Midwest, to Rhode Island to build their retreats, fifteen-bedroom "cottages" on this narrow spit of land. Not to Newport, Watch Hill's famous cousin to the east. Some say it was because many of them were Catholic and Newport would not welcome them. Whatever their reasons, they came. They came in the Victorian age, the Edwardian age, the turn of the last century.

Mrs. Ford is an example of those who come to Watch Hill still. She smiles to herself when she thinks of the lapel buttons that circulate in Watch Hill among the cognoscenti. Every summer they reappear, although she does not know who makes them. *I Am Watch Hill* one of them states. *I Married Watch Hill* announces another. In recent years, the Millennials have added a new twist—*I Partied Watch Hill*. Everyone knows who is who. The buttons aren't really necessary, but they serve to amuse. Mrs. Ford knows where she fits in in this button order.

The sun bounces back from the straight line of gold it casts across the bay from its low angle to her left, catching a few pale strands of hair that have escaped from her ponytail, and deepening the lines around her eyes. Mrs. Ford, whose age is somewhere in the middle years, is dressed in white jeans and dark glasses, a striped fisherman's shirt, and Keds—tribal costume of the natives.

She inhales deeply, willing the return of her equilibrium. She smells the beach roses that separate her lawn from her neighbor's, the salt of the sea, the coffee in the mug that rests on the arm of her chair. She sees her dogs sitting at her feet, patiently waiting for her to finish this morning ritual of quiet contemplation before they begin the routine much dearer to their hearts: the morning walk. With one hand, she reaches down to touch them, one sweet little doggy body after the other. She lingers there for the comfort the feel of them gives her.

Showtime.

She grabs the double lead and attaches it to her Cavalier King Charles Spaniels, but not before kneeling down to bury her face in their red and white spotted fur. They will always smell like puppies to her—sweet, salty, milky—no matter how old they get. She submits to their kisses, laughs, and gets up. She leaves her coffee and heads toward the porte-cochère of the gatehouse that marks the edge of her property.

The proscenium arch of this entrance creates an irresistible invitation for passersby all summer long. The tourists can't help themselves. Looking through the porte-cochère at the roses, the lighthouse and the sea, centered so perfectly, people wander through it, like entering the frame of a painting, to take a photograph. These trespassers alarmed her when she first came here, when she married Jack and began to spend her summers in Watch Hill. She still doesn't like finding strangers on her land, but she has come to accept the fact of them.

This morning, it is still too early for tourists. She steps out of her driveway and, as is her custom, is about to turn to the right. She almost does not see the car, non-descript, late-model American, parked to the left of her house. She starts off, the dogs are pulling her, but something makes her freeze. Some old fighter's instinct, nearly buried by years of comfort, but not quite dead.

She stops. She turns back. She considers the car.

A Crown Victoria?

The sun glints off of its windshield—mirroring back an image of the scene she already knows—the green of the trees, the blue of the sky, the silent glide of a lone, white gull. A place for everything and everything in its place.

Once again on this perfect summer day, she has conjured past ghosts come to haunt her. Deliberately, she shakes off her nerves and slackens her grip on the dogs that she has been holding back. She turns to begin her walk.

The car shifts into gear and rolls after her.

Mrs. Ford sets off at a brisk pace past Lighthouse Road. She rounds the bend and nods to the security guards who protect the pop star who lives in the old Harkness House. From the days when Mrs. Harkness invited her ballet dancers to practice here to now, when the pop star has her celebrity friends visit, that house has always attracted attention. Too much attention, she thinks. She also considers where the pop star would fit on those little Watch Hill buttons. *No category for her*, she muses.

She nears the Ocean House Hotel and pauses to take in its yellow clapboard, just now absorbing and reflecting back the morning sun. The mass of it, invisible until she clears a stand of trees and is almost upon it, never fails to surprise her. She continues along Niantic Avenue, pulling her dogs back from flattened frog bodies—frogs that should have stayed in the reeds and off the road the night before when their adventurousness betrayed them.

She doubles back on Ninigret, past the shingle houses, the turn-of-the-century cottages built for those captains of industry, long since gone from this seaside paradise. She follows Watch Hill Road to Bay Street to complete her circle.

The Crown Vic cruises several car lengths behind her. It is hard to tell if the car is following her or if the driver is simply lost. Though the summer people of Watch Hill are not disposed to ostentatious vehicles, a Crown Victoria would not be typical. It could belong to a day-tripper in search of beach parking or a gawker, ogling the fancy houses. The color of the car is too neutral to name—something of a beige leaning to grey—champagne, you might call it euphemistically. Mrs. Ford, having stifled her own anxiety, hardly notices it. The dogs are focused forward on passing butterflies and the occasional squirrel; they are no help to their mistress.

She continues along the quay. As she passes, boats barely move in the bay, their halyards flap in the slight breeze with an occasional soft clang of a bell. There is not much surf on this still day, but the vague whisper of water hitting the sand can be heard on the other side of the cabanas that line Napatree Point. Later in the day, the noise level will rise as the carousel organ cranks up, children squeal, parents scold, dogs bark.

But not yet.

The morning sky sparkles. There is no fog at all and the air is crisp, giving a feeling of September. New York's Fishers Island is visible, as is

Stonington, Connecticut. From other angles, Montauk and Block Island wink in the distance. The peninsula of Watch Hill affords views of many approaches. But this morning, Mrs. Ford is not looking.

She and the car, some distance behind her, advance down Bay Street, the commercial district. Its shops are unopened. She passes St. Clair Annex, a lone hive of activity, serving pancakes, eggs, and bacon. The menu hasn't changed for generations, with the exception of the egg-white omelet, a solitary nod to modern dietary concerns. The hungry wait outside for tables. As she moves through the crowd, children tug on parents' sleeves, asking if they might pet her dogs. Parents, in turn, ask Mrs. Ford. "Of course," she says. "They are friendly."

Farther along, Mrs. Ford stops at the kiosk of the Flying Horse Carousel. The horses hang motionless, real horsehair manes, genuine leather saddles, exactly where they were abandoned by a traveling carnival in 1879. Next to the kiosk, newspapers lie bundled. She has to wait a minute or two until the clock strikes nine, for an adolescent to arrive and cut the plastic that binds the stack. The girl hands her the top copy, mounts the rest in the newspaper rack and throws open the ticket window, signaling the start of a new day at the beach.

Mrs. Ford glances at headlines, skimming over words—Jihadists, ISIS, Mosul, Yazidis, Chaldeans, Kurds. She tucks the paper and its warnings from far-away-places firmly under her arm to continue on her way.

The Crown Vic waits, moving only when she does.

Mrs. Ford, the dogs, and the car continue up the road in a gap-toothed caravan. Seconds after she has turned into her driveway, unleashed her dogs, and followed them onto the lawn, the Crown Victoria rolls through the porte-cochère. It crunches tentatively up the gravel drive and stops. Two men in dark suits emerge.

Wrangling a crab claw from the mouth of a dog, for one final moment, Mrs. Ford remains innocent. She does not see them yet. It is only when she hears one of the men say, "Susan Ford?" that she freezes, just for an instant, before she rises and turns to face them.

She drops the crab claw, wipes her hand on the edge of her folded newspaper and finds her voice. "Yes. May I help you?"

"FBI, ma'am." He flashes a badge. "We'd like to ask you a few questions."

At this, Susan Ford casts a quick glance over her shoulder at the lighthouse, the lookout point. She does not make a motion to retreat, but the sharp turn of her head betrays her longing to flee. She considers, for one frantic moment, heading in the opposite direction, toward the water and away from these men. But she does not do so. Instead, she looks back at them and smiles.

"Please come in," she says, her composure regained—she hopes—before its loss was visible. "I'll make some tea."

And just as if they were expected guests, she leads them to the door of Gull Cottage, her pretty shingle house by the sea, as a sudden gust tips over the cup she had left on the arm of her chair.

2

Susan closes the door behind her and turns to face her visitors. The dogs bolt, as one, past the men's legs, headed for the kitchen and their water bowls. Dropping the leash and newspaper on a bench, she motions with her left hand. "After you," she says, allowing the FBI agents to precede her into the living room so that her body does not obscure the full view of the sea beyond.

The effect is dazzling. Light glints off of the water and streams through the un-curtained windows at the far end. The walls, covered with intricately coffered paneling, are painted glossy white. There are ceiling beams, three-foot deep doorways, and floors of highly lacquered wood, like that used by boat builders. The layers of varnish must number in the dozens. Teak, mahogany, and fir fill the room and the subtle variations of color and grain draw the eye from one to the other.

Susan's husband, Jack, spent six years building the house, re-working every architectural detail to perfection. His fondness for interior windows is in full play in this room with views open to the dining room, sunroom, even to the master bedroom upstairs through a startling window cut into the ceiling. Good furniture, good rugs, and good pictures are casually, though meticulously, placed. The focal point, jutting out from the wall opposite the water, is a ship's figurehead: a dark-haired woman, leaning out above the mantle, her gaze fixed inscrutably on the sea.

The FBI agents have stopped short, as Susan knew they would. The subtle details are overwhelming and difficult to absorb on first look. Susan recognizes, from her own original visit to the house in the early months of dating Jack, that people are both amazed and humbled to come upon such a wonder. It is like boarding a yacht from a century past that has taken root on dry land, while the figurehead looms, pointing them in the direction of the water, beckoning them to turn the wheel and head out to sea.

Susan gives the agents a moment to take it in. When she senses that they are sufficiently intimidated, she speaks.

"Please take a seat. I'll ask Helen to bring us some tea."

"No tea, ma'am."

"Are you sure? It really is no problem. I'll just…"

"No tea."

"Of course. No tea. Why don't you sit here?"

Susan directs the men, both of them, to a sofa facing the water. She takes her place on a blue and white striped armchair looking back at them. Sitting together on the sofa is awkward and each of the agents must readjust his posture, crossing and re-crossing his legs in an effort to find distance from his partner. They squint to see Susan with the halo of sunshine backlighting her form. She has regained control of the situation. As she has learned from her husband over the years, she says nothing. "Let the other person feel uncomfortable," Jack always told her. "Wait for him to talk. Just wait."

Susan waits.

Just as the agents seem to have found their least uncomfortable positions, both dogs bound into the room, onto the sofa and onto the men, making them begin the process all over again. The taller man casts a glance at Susan in search of an intervention, but she continues to sit, unperturbed.

"What are their names?" ventures the tall one. Maybe he'll play good cop. The other one is as silent as Susan. He'd have been a good match for Jack.

"Calpurnia and Pliny."

"What kind of names are those?"

"Pliny the Younger was married to Calpurnia. She was his third wife. He was the nephew of Pliny the Elder. Roman Senator. Pompeii," she waves her hand and trails off, effectively concluding the subject.

"Weird names for dogs."

"My husband loved history. We call them Cal and Plin."

Finally, the short guy speaks. His cadence and grammar are more formal than his partner's. "Mrs. Ford, we're here to talk to you about Samuel Fakhouri. We'd like to ask you some questions."

"Samuel Fa...?" Susan looks from one to the other. "I'm not sure I know who that is."

"Samuel Fakhouri. F-a-k-h-o-u-r-i."

"Thank you for the spelling."

"Any time. Thank *you* for the Roman history. Always nice to meet a classicist."

Susan turns her eyes to him. This one is definitely bad cop. "I don't believe I know anyone by that name. Maybe you could give me some more information as to why you think I might know Mr...."

"Fakhouri."

"Mr. Fakhouri. Yes. I'm not sure I can help you. I'm certain I don't know anyone by that name," she asserts for the third time, her face as impenetrable as the ship's figurehead on the wall.

"That's odd, Mrs. Ford, because he knows you."

Susan lets out a laugh. A small laugh mixed with an exhalation. But definitely a laugh.

"Is that amusing, Mrs. Ford?"

"I don't mean to be rude but I'm rather busy this morning, so perhaps..."

"Samuel Fakhouri was picked up by our agents yesterday. He'd flown from Baghdad to Istanbul to Toronto to Boston, and we got him in a taxi on his way to see you. We're pretty sure it was you he meant to see, because we found your name and address on a paper among his possessions. Does that trigger any memories, Mrs. Ford?"

3

Monday, June 11, 1979
Suburban Detroit

Susan opened her eyes to dim light. Dust motes floated in an elongated triangle of sunlight slanting down from a window above her. Panic lapped her consciousness as she remembered that she had fallen asleep in the basement. What time was it? She sprang from the sofa and fell hard on her knees on the linoleum. Pins and needles attacked the foot she must have had tucked up under her, leaving it dead asleep. She hauled herself up, hopped the rest of the way across the floor, and did a one-footed jump up the steps.

In the kitchen, she was relieved to see that it was only 6:54 a.m. She would not be late for her first day of work. She held the coffee pot under the sink, scooped grounds into the percolator basket, fastened the parts together, and plugged the thing in.

"Dad!"

No sound.

"Daddy!"

Nothing.

Susan moved down the back hall to wake her father and get him propped up on some pillows. She guessed this wouldn't be a day that William Elton Bentley would be getting out of bed.

After her shower, she wiped condensation from the mirror and took a good, long look at herself. Her face looked flushed in heat that was already sultry and she had a crease running down her right cheek. She had to stop sleeping on that old couch.

Back to the kitchen to grab two mugs—cream and sugar for her father, sugar only for her—then down the hall to the bedroom where her father had dozed off again.

"Hey, Daddy. Rise and shine." Susan swept back the curtains and opened the window a few notches more. "Here's your coffee."

Elton opened his astonishingly blue eyes. Cornflower blue, her mother had called them, but Susan found them bluer than that. Despite his age and his infirmities, he still had some set of peepers. Susan's eyes were brown like her mother's—a living reminder blinking back from her own reflection.

"Did you breathe all night?" he asked. Susan's father greeted her practically every morning of her life with this inanity and it always made the two of them laugh.

"I think so, Daddy. I'm still here. How about you? Are you getting up today?"

"God willin' and the creek don't rise." He winked at his little girl.

"I'm starting work today, Dad. At Winkleman's. The ladies' boutique."

"That's fine, Susie Jo." Her father was truly the only person on the planet that Susan would permit to address her this way. "Don't let it distract you from your goals, though."

"I won't, Daddy. This is just a summer job."

This year would be Susan's last at Lake Erie College in Painesville, Ohio, a small liberal arts institution that had seen better days. The charismatic Dr. Paul Weaver, its president of twenty-five years, had recently retired, and the grandiose perks of his tenure—a college yacht, a box at the Cleveland orchestra—were quickly disappearing. But the Academic Term Abroad, mandatory for all juniors, carried on. This had drawn Susan to Lake Erie and, afterwards, the memory of her junior semester in France—her first trip abroad—was planted in her mind as her North Star, guiding her toward the future. She most definitely had her goals.

"Good girl." He reached out to give her his cup. "I might need to rest a spell. I'm feelin' pretty tuckered already."

"Are you sure, Daddy? It's pretty early still." But she could see that he'd made up his mind.

In her bedroom, Susan nibbled on toast and stepped into the outfit she had laid out the night before. A crisp white A-line skirt and a red silk ascot blouse with a bow that she meticulously tied at the neck. This style of top had become so popular of late that everyone called it the "working girl blouse." Well, that's what she was this summer.

She slid her feet into red cork T-strap platforms, leaned over her make-up mirror to brush on some mascara and lip gloss, gave her short blond hair a tousle, and pinched both cheeks, hoping the blood flow would smooth out that crease.

"I'm going!" she called to the silent house and gently closed the door behind her.

Her tiny *Le Car* sat in the driveway. As far as she knew, it was the only car in the neighborhood that hadn't been made in Detroit. Renault's newest model had captivated her from the moment she'd first seen it advertised and she had spent two years saving to buy a used one. In bright yellow, with a thick black stripe and the words, *Le Car*, boldly scrawled along both sides, everything about it charmed her. It was small in contrast to the Cadillacs her parents had favored. It drove hard, unlike the cushioned ride of the Buicks and Lincolns of their friends. And it was French, which symbolized everything that Susan hoped to become.

She revved the engine and set off for Winkleman's.

Deftly, she maneuvered into the parking lot of Tech Plaza. Her mother had told her that JFK had visited this shopping strip on his campaign trail in 1960, though it was hard for her to imagine a president—even a presidential candidate—coming to Warren, Michigan now. What middle-class dream had Warren symbolized then? Today, Susan could only see its sameness, its monotonous stretches of razor-straight streets, all named for girls like her—Darlenes and Lindas and Marshas.

Susan's reverie was shattered by the bleat of a car horn. She slammed on her brakes—though she couldn't have been going more than twenty—as a bedraggled white Corvette streaked across her path.

"Hey!" Susan shouted.

But the car was no longer in earshot.

Her composure shaken, Susan followed her new employer's instructions and parked at the back of the lot. Unfolding herself from her car, she flattened her skirt with her hands, and tightened the bow of her blouse. Then she started—feet turned out, shoulders back and head held high, like the dancer she was—toward the neat row of shops. As she neared the front, she noticed the same Corvette parked askew and straddling two spaces.

"Hi!" A girl popped out of it and spoke directly to Susan. She was the most beautiful girl that Susan had ever seen.

"You cut me off back there," Susan said, instantly embarrassed by her tone. "I mean, you drove right in front of me."

"Oh my God! I'm so sorry!" the girl effused. "I was changing the radio station and I didn't see you and then you were just there like a turtle in the road."

"What?"

"I'm Annie Nelson! I'm starting work at Winkleman's today!"

Susan couldn't help but stare. The girl wore a knock-off of the Diane Von Furstenberg wrap dress—its V cut low in the front—and chunky Candies heels, made of wood with only a thin strip of leather to hold them on. Her chestnut hair was softly curled and hung down to the middle of her back. Slightly taller than Susan, with a more curvaceous figure and very long legs, she had eschewed stockings to leave them bare. That was uncommon.

"You're going to work at Winkleman's?" Susan parroted back.

"Yeah! You too?"

"Uh. Yes."

"First day?"

"Yes."

"Me too! That means we'll be best friends."

It was a ridiculous thing to say. She had practically run Susan over and now she was prattling on about being best friends.

"You know, we're supposed to park at the back." Susan heard herself sounding peevish again.

The girl—Annie—didn't seem to notice Susan's foul mood. "What's your name?" she asked.

"Susan Bentley."

"Do you always wear your hair so short?" she said as she pointed a finger.

Self-consciously, Susan touched her head. She had recently shorn her blond hair after seeing Jean Seberg in a French class screening of *Breathless*. Boyish, her father had called it, but she was attempting to look gamine.

Before she could stop herself, her hand slipped down to her cheek to feel if the sleep-crease was still there. Annie's beauty was unnerving.

"I like it."

"What?"

"Your hair! It looks good with your brown eyes."

Susan stared at this outrageous girl. Annie's eyes were hazel, with a slight tilt upwards at the outer corners. Her brows were dark, with an arch that was peaked just outside the irises, her nose strong, her lips full. Her features shouldn't have all worked together, but they did. Taken as a package, which is the only way you can take someone, Annie was impossibly beautiful.

But it was Annie's movements, her body language that held Susan's attention. She moved in staccato, fluttery bursts, like she wasn't fully in control of her own trajectory. To a particular type of man, Susan guessed, Annie might have looked as if she were in need of rescue—as if strong arms could just reach out and grab her, keep her from falling over her own two feet.

Suddenly, in a gesture that might have struck Susan as overly familiar, if it weren't for Annie's disarming persona, she held out her hand to Susan. "Wanna go in together?"

Susan looked around for an alternative. Seeing none, she cautiously linked arms with Annie, a girl so exotic to Susan that she might as well have been an ostrich taking form on the asphalt today.

Together, Susan and Annie finished the walk into Winkleman's, plunk in the middle of Tech Plaza—that shining star of Warren's past that could not have augured its future.

4

"Annie?" Susan called out, as she tidied the area around the cash register—clipping receipts, piling loose hangers, dropping pens in their cup. Ten days into the job, their manager had run to the bank and left the two of them in charge of the store. "It's been quiet for an hour now. Let's go back and clean up the dressing rooms before Nancy comes back."

"Ugh," grunted Annie, who was trying on scarves in front of a mirror. "Do we have to?"

"It'll go faster with the two of us doing it. We'll hear the chimes if anyone comes in."

"You're so sensible, Susan. I bet you make your bed every morning."

"I…" Susan caught herself answering seriously. "Okay, I'm a bore. But, c'mon. Let's go."

"You're not the bore. This job is the bore."

"The pay's not bad."

"The pay's not great."

"Why don't we debate this while we hang up clothes?"

"Okay. You win."

Susan and Annie marched in tandem to the back of the store. Inside the dressing rooms of Winkleman's were five separate cubicles. The biggest, with three-way mirrors and a carpeted drum on which to stand, was

18

spacious enough for a seamstress to work her magic. Cleaning up these fitting rooms was to be their final duty of the day.

And a long day it had been.

From matrons to teens, there had been a steady stream of customers since morning. Winkleman's was every female's go-to stop, especially in summer when teenagers were out of school. The boutique carried the finest clothes in Warren and its air conditioning—which most of Warren's look-alike ranch houses did not have—was a draw.

"What a day," Susan said. "I'm exhausted."

"All those pimply teenagers!" Annie chimed in. "You have to watch them like hawks. Most of them have sticky fingers."

"Annie!"

"It's true! C'mon, Susan."

"Have you ever shoplifted?" Susan asked.

"Me? I try anything once. Twice if I like it."

"Three times to make sure."

"What?"

"Mae West." Susan looked closely at Annie to make sure she wasn't pulling her leg. "You're quoting her. I was just finishing the quotation."

"I am? I thought I made that up."

"Not really. No."

Annie burst out laughing. "You're pretty useful to have around!"

"Ha ha," Susan said dryly. "You said we were best friends the first day we met."

"I'm clairvoyant."

"You're definitely something," Susan said as she pushed open the doors to the dressing rooms, one by one. "Look at this! Aren't you amazed by the mess?"

"Um, no." Annie trailed behind.

"Well, the sooner we clean up, the sooner we're out." Susan grabbed a pile of rejects from the floor of the first cubicle and thrust it at Annie. She scooped up another pile and walked to the rolling rack at the end of the hall.

"How do you hang this stupid thing?" Annie struggled to attach a one-shouldered dress to a hanger.

"Here," Susan took it and revealed the hidden straps meant to hold the dress to the hanger. "I'm just saying I wouldn't leave clothing all over the floor in heaps."

"I would. Everybody would. Look around, Susan. Everybody does."

"I see that. But I always hang everything up. I mean, I don't actually take it back to the racks. I'm not that fussy."

"Who, you? You're not fussy at all! Here, you finish this." Annie dropped the mustard-colored cowl neck sweater that she'd been turning around, trying to determine which end was up.

Susan struggled with it for a moment then shrugged. "I can't hang up this thing either." She gave up the hanger and opted to fold it for shelving.

"I'm bored. Wanna play Truth or Dare?" Annie asked, in a burst of energy. "I'll go first!"

"What?"

"I pick Truth," Annie answered herself. "Okay. Three years ago, for senior prom, I bought a dress at this very Winkleman's and returned it the next week."

"After you wore it?"

"Yes, Susan, after I wore it. How about you?"

"How about me what?"

"Tell me something."

"Like what?"

"Like a Truth or Dare something."

"I'm not really sure I want to play this game."

"Oh, come on!"

"I don't think so."

"Just pick truth. It's easier. You only have to tell me one little secret."

"Oh, all *right*. But you have to promise not to tell anyone."

"Honest Injun," Annie held up her right hand in a scout pledge.

"Well," Susan hesitated and sat on a stool, holding the folded sweater on her lap, smoothing it flat with her palms. "When I got to college, there was a party the first night. I put on a sweater like this one—a cowl neck—except it was black. It felt strange, like it didn't sit right on my body. The seams in the sleeves kept twisting around my arms. And, I

20

hadn't remembered the neck being ribbed. The whole time I was talking to people I tried not to fidget. But when I came home I saw what I'd done. I'd worn the sweater upside down." Susan trailed off and lapsed into silence. She gave the cowl neck sweater one final press, rose and placed it on the top shelf of the rack.

"That's it? That's your big secret?"

"It's just that I'd never met these people before and I came to an event with my clothing *upside down*."

"I don't really get the big deal. I bought a dress, wore it and then returned it. Although I did manage to wear it right side up," Annie said as she cracked up laughing.

"I don't know. I just felt awkward."

"Yeah, I get that part. But, so what?"

Susan had revealed something of herself in the story and had expected Annie to understand it without explanation. It had been a little test, which Annie seemed to be failing.

"Well, I thought it was clear." Susan watched herself now, taking a risk, knowing she was putting herself out there, in front of Annie, a wild card. "I just felt foolish in front of everyone."

Annie reached out and touched Susan's shoulder. "It's okay. I feel foolish all the time."

The doorbell chimed.

"Oh geez! I hope it's not another customer!" Susan said as she moved toward the front.

"Hey!" Annie blurted. "Wanna go to Sanders? It's Friday night and I have nowhere to go. Might as well eat ice cream!"

Annie, Susan recognized, had just done a generous thing. Maybe Annie had passed the test, after all. Maybe Susan could risk just a bit more. "Sure," Susan replied. "I'd like that."

5

Thursday, July 12, 1979

Inexorably, like a waterfall eroding rock, the full throttle rush of Annie worked to soften Susan's reserve. Perhaps because of the amplitude of God's gifts to her, Annie exuded no competitive edge. She seemed to genuinely like Susan, which made it impossible for Susan not to like her. Despite their differences, and those certainly outweighed their similarities, Susan was drawn to the pure incandescence of Annie Nelson. She wasn't sure why Annie was drawn to her.

Just this afternoon, they'd gone back to Sanders.

An old-fashioned soda fountain with swiveling stools, Sanders was famous for its hot fudge cream puff. One single cream puff covered the plate, filled with an enormous scoop of vanilla ice cream, all of it slathered in hot fudge. It was large enough to share but Annie and Susan each ordered her own.

"God, this is good!" Annie said with her mouth full. "What's the matter? Don't you like yours?"

"I do." Susan picked up her spoon. "Do you know what this is called in France?"

"I'm sure you're going to tell me."

"A *profiterole*. Isn't that a great word?"

"It's a beautiful word but I'm not gonna remember it."

"I told you I lived there, right?"

"Yes, Susan, you did."

"You should go. I think you'd really like it. You're already so free and easy."

"That's me. Miss Easy Breezy!"

"It's a good thing."

"My stepfather doesn't think so."

"It's hard to convey what it was like there, Annie. I lived in a sixth-floor walk-up, and every day, I came home from classes and trudged up those stairs. There was only one toilet on each floor and everyone on the floor shared it. The shower was two flights down and the *whole* building shared that.

"I was in shock the first time I saw it. There was a little drippy faucet in the middle of a big tiled room. The water never even got hot. My room was freezing, too. I had to sleep in pajamas, a sweater, and socks. I never got warm the entire time I was there. But I loved it!"

"Can I eat yours?" Annie asked as she fixed her eyes on Susan's barely touched plate.

"Sure," Susan said, pulling herself out of her memories. She passed her plate across the table. As Annie reached out to take it, her sleeve slid up her arm, revealing a nasty contusion. "What happened to you?" Susan gasped.

"What?" Annie yanked down her sleeve and took another bite of cream puff.

"Your arm, Annie! That bruise is horrible! Do you want me to look at it again? Maybe put something on it?"

"No! God, Susan, it's just a bruise. Don't be so dramatic."

"It's…I'm sorry." Susan had a squeamish feeling of wandering into taboo territory. "I…uh…what happened?"

"I walked into a door. You've seen me walk. I'm clumsy."

"Oh. Well, can I do something?"

"I said no. Anyway, back to Paris. Your description doesn't sound very pleasant."

Susan studied Annie who kept her eyes fixed on her plate. It was unmistakable that the subject was firmly closed. Finally, she continued,

"Well, that's probably not the adjective I'd choose. I think we Americans overrate the pleasant. Yes, certain aspects of life were less convenient there. But convenience isn't all it's cracked up to be. Anyway, I loved it. I wanted to stay forever."

"Do you really talk like that?"

"Like what?"

"*We Americans overrate the pleasant*?"

Susan reddened. "I don't mean to sound pretentious. It's just that it was all so different from here. I mean, look at this. This shopping center, this parking lot." Susan gestured toward the seemingly endless expanse of parked cars.

"I get it. I'd like to get out of here too. I think what you've done is pretty amazing! Kinda free and easy." Annie winked at her.

She laughed uneasily. "That's probably the first time I've ever been called that."

"I don't know," said Annie. "Still waters run deep, right?"

Susan smiled, but she could not lose the image of that enormous bruise on Annie's arm.

* * *

Hours later, Susan remained unsettled. She paced the floors of her family's house, avoiding the boards that creaked. Slumber eluded her, and her book had lost its appeal. Elton had long been asleep, if he'd ever even been awake. Nights at home were the hardest. Mother gone. Father going. Susan felt like the last man standing at the station, the train chugging off in the distance. And now, Annie had entered her life, like an apparition in a gothic novel.

She shook off that dramatic thought and wandered into the living room where she clicked on the TV.

"Good evening. This is Bill Bonds with Action News. First up, we go to Chicago where a bizarre event is still unfolding at this hour. In a baseball-double-header with the Detroit Tigers, a promotional stunt by White Sox management has turned violent.

"'Disco Demolition Night' they called it and disc-jockey, Steve Dahl, was hired to deliver it. In a season of sluggish ticket sales, they wanted to fill Comiskey Park. Dahl enlisted an 'Anti-Disco Army' to do it. Admission was set at ninety-eight cents plus one disco record, which Dahl promised to blow up on the field between games.

"Expected turn-out of twenty thousand people was quickly surpassed. Current estimates range from fifty to ninety thousand individuals converging in and around the stadium.

"From the start, the rambunctious fans threw records at the players, but the Tigers won Game One, four to one. Between games, Dahl blew up the crate of records, did a victory lap, and left the stadium.

"Then pandemonium broke out. As clean-up began, the crowd poured onto the diamond. For forty minutes, the scene was chaos. Rampagers ripped bases out of the ground, climbed poles, and worsened the damage already done by the explosion.

"Traffic is currently at a standstill in the immediate vicinity of the stadium. Game Two has been postponed and there is talk of the White Sox being asked to forfeit it. American League President Lee MacPhail will issue his ruling in the morning. Stay tuned for our Action News follow up tomorrow."

What on earth did it mean?

Susan stared at the screen, steeped in her own isolation. Culture wars and violent protests in Chicago—like her life back in Paris, her life with her family, life in general, she might add—it was all out of reach to her here, in the dark, all alone.

6

The telephone shrilled from the wall in the kitchen. Susan tossed her book, jumped out of bed and tore down the hall to answer it. She didn't know why she was running. If she missed it, they'd certainly call back.

"Hello?" she panted.

"Hey. It's Annie. I know you're off today, but can you meet for a drink later?"

"No ice cream?"

"You never eat yours and I end up eating two. Anyway, I have something I need to tell you. How about Reggie's at three after I finish work?"

Susan agreed and returned to her reading, but thoughts of their date kept surfacing. What could Annie possibly *need* to tell her?

Susan arrived early and shifted her weight on the sidewalk. Across from her was the General Motors Technical Center, namesake of her workplace, Tech Plaza. The place made her think of her mother.

Maggie had always tried to lend significance to their little corner of the world. After World War II, she had recounted in one of her stories, General Motors hired Eero Saarinen to carve a sleek creative hub out of the farm fields to the north of the city. President Eisenhower had even presided over the grand opening.

No one else remembered any of this. The denizens of the neighborhoods that spread for miles around his minimalist campus had not heard

26

of Mr. Saarinen and would not know his neo-futuristic design if it were sitting in their backyards. Which, as Susan could tell them, it was.

Opposite was a lunch place called Reggie's. It was a dark, windowless box. Serving GM executives, from noon to three it teemed with diners, drinkers, and smokers, most of them male. Susan found it an odd choice to meet, but she turned to go inside.

The last of the men were trailing out, back to their desks for the few remaining hours of the day. They lingered in the foyer, blinking in the light as the door opened, back-slapping and making plans for fishing trips and football pools. Adjusting her eyes to the gloom, Susan paused. A cluster of jacketless, loose-tied men moved past her. One of them, she really couldn't tell which one when she whipped her head around to look, actually pinched her bottom.

"Excuse us, darlin'," said one, smiling broadly.

"Smile, sweetie," directed another. "You'll look much better if you smile."

Susan loathed the way men commanded women to smile after an idiotic or lascivious remark. She imagined women, the lot of them, walking around grinning like a bunch of simpletons, grinning when insulted, grinning when pinched. And men receiving these smiles as their birthright.

Annie arrived to break Susan's reverie. In her usual high spirits, she flung open the door, banging it back on its hinges. The noise turned every head, but it was Annie who kept them all staring. Annie, of course, was smiling. No one needed to tell her to. And she didn't look like an idiot. She looked radiant and young and alive. The men were speechless with admiration. Annie clattered past them in her Candies.

"I'm sorry I'm late! I counted my drawer out wrong, but Nancy helped me get it straight. Let's sit down." She looped her arm through Susan's.

"It's all right. I just arrived," Susan explained as the they made their way to a table.

Annie sat down with a plop. "Okay, what would you like to drink? My treat. I'm having cranberry juice, but you have a drink. I drink cranberry juice all the time. My doctor says it's good for my kidneys."

"What's wrong with your kidneys?"

"Oh, you know." Annie waved a hand then fiddled in her purse for some lip-gloss, which she applied to her mouth at the table.

Susan could not imagine Annie having anything wrong with her at all. She watched her closely and uttered the thought that had been percolating since she had met Annie a month ago. "You remind me of my mother."

"I can't believe you just said that to me!"

"I meant it as a compliment. My mother was glamorous."

"If I said that someone reminded me of my mother, they should take it as a major insult. Wait, what do you mean, *was*?"

"Oh. My mother died when I was fifteen. I don't really like to talk about her very much." Susan rose to take off her sweater. "It's kind of hot in here, don't you think?"

"Not really. No."

"I guess I had to think about it for a while." Susan hesitated before going on. Annie, uncharacteristically for her, allowed Susan her moment. "Anyway, my mother laughed a lot, like you. She was loud, like you. She was carefree, like you. She was just a lot like you. Or, I should say, you're a lot like her."

"Okay. I guess I'm not gonna throw a drink at you. It sounds like you liked your mom."

"I did. I loved my mother."

"Hey! Guess what? I got a job!" Annie really could change on a dime. Right now, though, Susan was thankful for the lifeline out of a painful subject.

"Annie, you *have* a job."

"No, but I got a *better* job. That's why I wanted to meet you—I want you to get a job there too!"

"Where?" Susan had no idea why, but her nervous hackles were rising.

"It's a disco called Frankie's. Have you been there? It's amazing—all silver and black and shiny! And the tips are really good because the girls wear these outfits that look like suits but with the legs out. Kinda like

Saturday Night Fever with a vest and shirt and tie. Did I mention the tips?" Annie wrapped up her soliloquy breathlessly.

"What'll you ladies have? We're closing soon, so make it quick," said their waitress, clearly displeased to see them at the end of the lunch shift. Having met the last bunch of customers on their way out, Susan could certainly sympathize.

"I'll have cranberry juice with lots of ice and she'll have a Black Russian," Annie ordered for them both.

"Annie, I don't want a Black Russian. I'll have coffee."

"You sure? I thought you'd like that, foreign traveler that you are," Annie winked at her. "How about a White Russian? That's lighter 'cause it has cream."

"Yes, I'm sure. No Russians," she laughed. "Just coffee."

"Fine," huffed the waitress, already walking away.

Susan turned her attention back to Annie. "A disco? That's funny. Did you see the news last night? That weird thing in Chicago?"

"I'm not really a news kinda girl. C'mon, Susan, come work at Frankie's with me."

"I don't even know what you're talking about. What kind of job is it?"

"Cocktail waitress! I heard they were looking and I went over and met the boss and he hired me right then. He asked if I have any cute friends who want jobs too. You have to be attractive to work there."

"We practically just started at Winkleman's! I mean, Nancy's a nice boss and the hours aren't bad and—I don't know, Annie."

"Oh, come on, Susan! This'll be fun! And it'll give you much more money to go back to college this fall."

"A suit with no pants? What do you mean, no pants?"

"They're not naked! They wear pants, but they're like bathing suit bottoms."

"That sounds horrible."

"It's not. Plus, the boss is really nice. His name is Frankie too. Just like the disco. And he's sexy." It was evident from the way Annie threw out this information that she considered it bait.

"Won't your parents object? My dad'll think this is really a bad idea."

Annie looked at Susan and, for the first time in the few short weeks of their acquaintance, Susan saw her effervescence dim. "I don't live with my mother and stepfather. We don't really get along. I live with my grandmother and she doesn't ask me a lot of questions."

"Oh." Susan sat back in her chair. She thought about what Annie had just revealed about her family. She thought about her own family—her father, old, sick, and in bed. Her mother, gone six years now. She thought about her boyfriend, Todd—correction: her ex-boyfriend, Todd. Who was in her life to care if she worked in a disco? Her father, surely, but, to be honest, he wouldn't need to know. He was probably a lot like Annie's grandmother—there but not really there. Not fully aware of Susan's comings and goings anymore. What was the difference between her family and Annie's? Probably not much.

Susan recognized the tightening stomach, the flush and tingle of rising adrenalin that was taking hold of her, and she acknowledged her familiar companion—fear. She looked at Annie, sitting across from her, appearing utterly fearless. Was she? Or was she just able to mask anxiety? Fear is an emotion that is doled out unevenly. Susan had always grappled with an overabundance of it.

She remembered lying in bed one night as a little girl. Her parents had music playing down the hall—*Moon River*—its plaintive chords of loss and longing evoking in her a sensation of dread. Really, it was unmasked fear. Right then, she knew that her father would die while she was still young. The fact that her mother went first was a shock. Susan's mother was decades younger than her father. It made no sense, but it had happened. The thing she had feared hadn't happened yet, though she knew it was on its way. The thing she hadn't had imagination *enough* to fear had happened anyway.

What difference did her instincts make?

Susan recognized that Annie's proposal was a bad idea—uncertain, if not outright risky. In spite of that, or perhaps because of it—to counter her fear, to win against it—Susan said yes. The only reason she listened to Annie that day, got in her car, drove to a disco, and got herself hired as a cocktail waitress was *because* she was afraid to do so. It was really as simple as that.

Annie and Susan quit Winkelman's, their nice boss, Nancy, their day-time hours, their safe routines—and they did it badly. Required to show up at Frankie's that very weekend to train as waitresses, they left Nancy in the lurch, with no notice of their departure. Susan felt bad about this behavior, but she did it. She was conscious that she was disappointing Nancy but, somehow it seemed that Annie was held less accountable. Annie laughed and kissed Nancy on the cheek, hugging her as she went. Susan followed sheepishly behind, knowing she was doing the wrong thing for the wrong reason and doing it all the same.

7

Thursday, August 7, 2014
Watch Hill

Susan shifts to the left in her armchair and changes the cross of her legs. She smiles at the FBI agents—a tight, closed-mouthed smile.

"Do I need a lawyer?" she asks. "Iraq? FBI? This sounds much too serious for a summer morning in Watch Hill."

"That's up to you, Mrs. Ford," replies the tall one. "But it never hurts to talk to an attorney."

Susan looks from one to the other, working a little harder to maintain the appearance of casual control. "Might I ask your names?"

The taller one responds again. "Yes, of course. Here are our cards. FBI, Boston Field Office."

Susan takes two cards handed to her by the one man. "Special Agent DelVecchio? Special Agent Provenzano?"

"I'm DelVecchio," the shorter one says, "and he's Provenzano."

"Yes, well, process of elimination."

"You're funny, Mrs. Ford."

Again, Susan smiles. "Excuse me for a moment." And she goes with the dogs on her heels.

In the kitchen, Susan allows her brightness to ebb. She sits to place her call, hovering her hand over the cradled receiver like a psychic

32

reading vibrations. Helen, Susan's long-time Filipina housekeeper, stops what she is doing to watch her.

"You okay, Mrs. Ford?" she asks. "Do you need something?"

"What? Yes, of course. I'm just making a call here. I'm fine." Susan picks up the receiver to dial.

* * *

She returns to her morning visitors, leaving the dogs in the kitchen. In the dining room, she halts her step. Through one of Jack's interior windows, she has a neatly framed view of the men in the living room. Unaware of her presence, Provenzano and DelVecchio sit waiting. Provenzano fiddles with his phone, checking messages or sending texts. DelVecchio takes a moment to brush some dog hair from his pants legs, then picks at little strays which he flicks to the Heriz rug. They don't speak to each other.

"Quiet in here." Susan enters the room. "Was there anything else regarding Mr.....?"

"Fakhouri," answers DelVecchio. "Chaldean name. You're from Detroit, right?" He does not wait for an answer. "Lots of Chaldeans in Detroit. Interesting group. In the news quite a bit this summer, over in Iraq. Forced out of Mosul by ISIS. Because they're Christians. Catholics. That's what I find interesting. Not Orthodox, but Catholic. I'm Catholic, too, but I thought everyone in the East was Orthodox. That's before I got into this line of work."

"Glad to see our government agents are so well informed."

"Oh yes, Mrs. Ford, we're informed. We study up on current events. We find it pertinent to our line of work."

"We'll be in touch, Mrs. Ford," says Provenzano—the tall one, ever polite—as he awkwardly rises. "We look forward to seeing you again, very soon."

DelVecchio gets up as well. "You have an interest in Roman history. I understand that. Me, I like Seneca."

"Forced to commit suicide by Nero, wasn't he?"

"Yes, Mrs. Ford, he was. Nero didn't trust him. Thought Seneca was conspiring to kill him. Didn't go well for Seneca, though, that suicide. Slit his veins, swallowed poison, lots of steps that didn't quite do it. Like when the Russians tried to kill Rasputin. Shot, strangled, poisoned, thrown in the River Neva. Turns out he had water in his lungs, so he was alive through the whole ordeal. Didn't die 'til he hit the river."

"Come on." Provenzano puts an end to his partner's intellectual stunts. "Time to go."

"What an interesting subject," Susan says. "You must be fun at a dinner party—so much trivia at your disposal."

DelVecchio adds a coda. "We see patterns in our field. There's nothing new under the sun. Ecclesiastes."

Susan looks him straight in the eye. "I'll try to remember that."

She turns and proceeds toward the front door, through the beautiful and gleaming room, past the paintings, the antiques, over the Oriental rug and the huge hearth of the fireplace. She walks under the imposing figurehead, high on the wall, whose expression has not changed in two hundred years and is not about to do so now, despite the antics of the humans below her.

Susan continues up three short steps into the entry hall and back down three more to the front door, up and down in the many-leveled house that Jack built. She resolutely grabs the handle, gives it one hard turn, and pulls.

"Goodbye, then," she says crisply.

"Goodbye, Mrs. Ford," says DelVecchio. He adds a courtly flourish. "Until we meet again."

Provenzano nods and utters a clipped, "Ma'am."

Then—at last—they are out.

Susan closes the door softly. She exercises restraint. She has been practicing self-control for thirty-five years and is not about to relinquish it now, when all evidence tells her she needs it most. She stands at the mullioned glass panel to the left of the door, from which she has a view of the driveway. She watches the men walk slowly to their car.

They pause and turn back. From where they are standing, Susan knows, they have a full view of the panorama. Gull Cottage to the right, her neighbor's house, Neowam, on the left, the sweep of lawn rising in a gentle mound before dropping down to the seawall of large, weather-rounded stones. Then the sea beyond, calm, just as it was when Susan left the house to take her walk this morning, barely a whitecap breaking the surface. In the middle distance, the sailboats motoring out from right to left, out of the harbor on their way to the Atlantic, beyond the lighthouse. Far away, the big ships, the containers, crossing the horizon—carrying Africa, China, South America—past the cottages of Watch Hill, past Susan and the men from the FBI. To the left, the lighthouse, standing, light revolving, day and night, from red to white, from white to red. No sound on this fogless day.

The men can't help but look, like children at a puppet show, at the boats traversing the stage on horizontal tracks, before they turn and continue to their car. Doors slam, one after the other. Slam, slam, in quick succession. Provenzano is behind the wheel, on the far side of the car, just out of Susan's sightline. DelVecchio is the passenger. He turns his head once more in the direction of the house. He catches Susan's eyes. Too late to move away, she stands and looks back at him.

He smiles at her, a bigger, toothier smile than Susan has previously seen him reveal, as he makes a little saluting motion with two fingers to his forehead. Seeing no alternative, Susan returns the smile, lifts her left hand, taps two fingers to her own forehead, mirroring his salute. The game is afoot, they signal. The car backs up, turns around, and crunches out to the road, under the picturesque porte-cochère.

Susan pivots, leans against the glass and deflates. Slowly, she slides all the way down to the floor. She rakes her trembling fingers through her hair, dislodging her ponytail. She leans her head forward to her knees and continues the repetitive motion. Cal and Plin bolt from the kitchen and join her there, scrambling for her lap.

8

Susan remains on the floor until her shaking subsides. Consciously, she makes the mental gearshift from panic mode to action mode. She has allowed herself a little collapse, but enough, she determines, is enough. Resolved, she re-ties her ponytail, picks herself up and strides into the kitchen, where she finds Helen at the sink.

"I'm going to New York. I'll stay the night but I'm leaving the dogs here." Susan stoops to pat both dogs who have, naturally, trailed her into the room.

"Oh, but it's Thursday! Mr. Jack will be here soon! Picnic night!" Susan knows that Helen loves helping her get ready every Thursday for the multi-family cookout at the beach club.

"Yes. No. He knows. Well, I'll tell him. I'll be back tomorrow."

"Do you need a ride to the station?"

"No." She hesitates. "No. I prefer to drive."

"Do you want me to pack for you?"

"I'll wear what I have there." Susan returns to the front hall to find her purse sitting on the round table, next to her signature bowl of white hydrangeas. Her bag is orange crocodile, Nancy Gonzalez, chic and summery fun. Fun was what she'd had in mind when she'd bought the bag at Bergdorf—a long way from Winkleman's.

She sets her hands on it and pauses, running a mental checklist. She takes her cell phone from her pocket and puts it into the purse, changes her mind, then puts it back in her pocket. She pulls out her wallet and gives a quick check inside for cash and cards. She rummages for her sunglasses and finds them, as usual, atop her head.

"I'm leaving!" she calls, then remembers her laptop upstairs. Best not to leave such a thing behind. She takes two steps at a time as she bolts to her room to grab it and trots downstairs in a flash. She steps out the front door, closing it carefully behind her so that she doesn't clip Calpurnia or Pliny, both of whom try to follow her.

Susan gets into her car, a brand new Mini Cooper Countryman, the four-door model, in jungle green. Fun was what she was thinking, again, when she had bought this car. Who did she think she was kidding to act like she had ever been entitled to fun?

She places her purse on the passenger seat and hooks her phone into its jack. Before she backs up, looking over her shoulder to avoid the stone walls nearest the house, she punches in a number on her speed dial list.

"Ford Properties," the voice coming through the car speakers cheerily answers. One good thing today—they have trained their receptionists well. Susan's pet peeve is the protracted phone greeting, forcing the caller to wait while the receptionist prattles off an interminable series of unctuous phrases—Good morning! Ford Properties! This is Samantha! How may I direct your call!—all ending in exclamation points.

But not at Ford Properties. A simple, cheery, "Ford Properties," conveys it all by tone alone.

"Hi Samantha, this is Susan calling Jack."

"Good morning, Mrs. Ford. You've had a number of calls since we spoke earlier this morning. Would you like me to run messages with you now?"

"No. Thank you, Samantha. I'll call back later."

"Certainly, Mrs. Ford. Just one moment, please, while I get Mr. Ford." She waits.

"Hi, Mom." Despite the fact that they are roughly the same age, Jack Ford Jr. and Susan Ford, his stepmother, have addressed each other this way ever since Susan married his father. "What's up? Samantha said you tried to reach me earlier?"

"Hi, Son. I've decided to drive down to New York. I'd love to catch you up in person. I could meet you at Harry's for a drink. I'll buy."

"Of course, you'll buy. You're the mother."

"You always make me laugh, Jack."

"That's why I'm the family mascot."

"Five-thirty?"

"Sure."

"Thanks."

"You okay? You sound a little off."

"Of course, I'm okay. I'm always okay."

"That's my girl."

Susan presses the button on the steering wheel to click off the phone. The soft tones of BBC reporter James Robbins can be heard on her satellite radio.

"They're climbing higher and higher into the barren Sinjar Mountains of Northern Iraq. These Yazidis are some of the thousands, from an ancient religious minority, fleeing for their lives from the militant fighters from the self-proclaimed Islamic State, seizing more and more of Iraq. This woman says, 'We and our children ran away to save our lives and left everything behind....'"

She fiddles with the volume.

"...Iraqi Christians, too, are fleeing other areas being overrun by the Islamist fighters. The largest Christian town is Qaraqosh. It is now reported virtually empty. The entire population of around fifty thousand have fled."

Susan reaches down again to channel surf. The Goldberg Variations arrest her, and she settles in for the drive, desperate for the sedative of Bach.

9

Thursday, August 7, 2014
New York

The city is hot and deserted. Heat radiates in waves off the tarmac, distorting light and color and heightening Susan's sense that reality is slipping away from her. She feels her tires stick to the road when she sits too long at a light. Despite the blasting AC, her clothes are glued to her body.

Coming down the east side, she makes it across the snarl of Second Avenue subway construction and decides to take Park Avenue. If she hits the lights right, she can sail without stopping. Today, there are few cars and, mercifully, no school buses, this being August. All it takes is one taxi, however, halting in the middle of the road to pick up a passenger to mess with Susan's algorithm.

She makes it a point never to come to New York in the summer if it can be avoided. She limits her visits to two or three trips, concentrating her errands and appointments. When she needs to, she comes down on a Tuesday, after morning traffic, and heads back up on Thursday, to arrive in time for the cookout.

Damn. The cookout. She was supposed to sit with the Grants and the Thatchers. She'd forgotten to call Cecilia before leaving Watch Hill and she had committed to bringing the meat, which would leave a gaping hole in the menu. She now realizes that was what Helen had been doing in the kitchen, seasoning the marinade for lamb chops.

Should she call Cecilia and risk an explanation? Better to call Helen at Gull Cottage and have her bring the lamb over to Cecilia's house. Susan can talk to Cecilia another day, once this mess is sorted out. She doesn't even want to put the idea into Cecilia's head that something untoward is happening in Susan's life. She won't give her the satisfaction—the chance to remind them both that Cecilia Thatcher is Watch Hill, while Susan only married it.

A red light finally stops her progress down Park. Susan glances at the street sign and notices that she is at 69th. Her heart tugs sharply and her eyes can't help turning to the left. There, right next to her, is the large Delano & Aldrich edifice of the Union Club. Its white limestone is brilliant in the August sun.

She remembers a different day, a day with no sunshine.

Her wedding day.

The snow fell that day the way that it falls in New York—casting a hush over the city and causing all traffic to vanish. Susan and Jack were married at St. Vincent Ferrer, a pretty Catholic church, on Lexington and 65th. For something as important as her wedding, Susan wanted to marry in the church of her Michigan childhood. Jack, an Episcopalian, had graciously obliged her. He signed away their future children, the children they never would have, to be raised in the Catholic faith.

Susan had entered the church that day and paused for an instant at the back. Jack Jr., her best friend, stood next to her. It was he who would give her away. Funny notion, that—to give a person away. But the sweetness of the gesture still warms her. He was her friend and he was with her and she would lean on him, just a little, as they made their way down the aisle.

But first, she had allowed herself a moment to take it all in. Candles filled the sanctuary, small circles of amber light dispersing in the cavernous spaces, never reaching the stone walls or stained-glass windows. Evergreens trailed the pews and great bowers of them flanked the altar.

Friends were there, sitting toward the front. Smiling, they rotated in the pews to look at her.

Jack Sr., her intended, stood close to the altar, waiting for her there—a lean man with pale blue eyes in a dark blue suit. She had to squint to see him. He, too, smiled in her direction.

Jack Jr. gave her arm a reassuring squeeze and smiled at her, as well. Bigger than his father, with eyes more gray than blue, he, too, wore a blue suit. Together, they stepped forward, the son delivering the bride to the father.

Afterwards, their little party walked to the Union Club for dinner, over from Lexington and up a silent and snowy Park Avenue, in the middle of the street. Susan, in her long white dress, a heavy coat and snow boots—Jack, in his crisp blue suit without a coat. That was Jack. He always wore a blue suit and he never wore a coat. He said he was unaffected by weather.

Why did people lay so much blame on the weather, anyway? On that day, so long ago, dark in the blowing snow, Susan's life had seemed to be all beginnings. Here, on a brilliant summer day, her life could be falling apart.

The weather didn't have a damn thing to do with it.

"Welcome back, Mrs. Ford." George, the doorman at the Sherry-Netherland, snaps her out of her daydream as he opens her car door. "Would you like us to park the car?"

"Yes, please, George. I'll stay the night."

"Any luggage that you'd like us to bring up for you?"

"No luggage."

Susan pushes her way through the revolving door of the Sherry and crosses the ornate lobby. Built in 1927, exactly when the Vanderbilt mansion across the street was being demolished, the Sherry-Netherland had absorbed salvage from that grand house. It was far too opulent for Jack's tastes, yet it was he who had chosen this hotel/apartment combination for its proximity to his office—it allowed him to pop home on a whim for a quick half hour nap.

A nap would be just the thing for Susan right about now. She still has four hours in front of her before she meets Jack Jr. Though sleep, she concedes, will be elusive.

"Hi, Kathy," Susan calls out to the pretty receptionist.

"Mrs. Ford! Good afternoon," Kathy answers cheerily. "What a surprise to see you here!"

"Yes," Susan agrees. "I'm more surprised than you are."

10

The Fords' apartment in New York is a striking contrast to their house in Watch Hill. Darkly paneled—its fabrics run to deep, jewel tones in velvets and Fortuny. Collections of rare books, Old Masters, and Boucher drawings, Delftware, and silver objects grace the walls and surfaces. Recessed windows look out on the park, not too far above the tree line. Like Watch Hill, it evokes an earlier time, though it feels more European than American.

Susan dumps her things on the hall table and goes directly to her bedroom closet. In it, she finds a medium-sized safe, not even as big as a dorm refrigerator, and quickly taps in a code. She removes a stack of jewelry boxes and sets it on the floor. Next, she pulls out a pile of papers and realizes she's missing her glasses.

Up off the floor she climbs and goes back down the hall to the entry, where she rummages around in her purse. Her eyeglass case turns out to be empty.

Catching a glimpse of herself in the mirror, Susan frowns at her disheveled appearance. As if in agreement, both her sunglasses and her normal glasses wink back at her from atop her head. Feeling increasingly vertiginous, she yanks them off—ripping out a few hairs in the process— tosses one pair in her handbag and shoves the other one on her face.

She turns to go back to the safe.

Sitting cross-legged, Susan picks up the pile of papers, methodically setting each one aside once she has examined it thoroughly. In the middle of the stack, she finds a small white envelope—old, stained, and tattered—that she turns over in her hands. Front to back and back to front, she rotates it. Its paper feels dry on her summer swollen fingers. Cool and a little dusty. A disintegrating thing. Like herself, she would have to acknowledge.

Susan does not open the envelope. She places it apart, avoiding the pile of papers, and reaches into the safe again. Groping in the dark, she discovers it—there at the back—the object of her attention. A small gun.

Really, a pistol. A .38 caliber Smith & Wesson.

Susan lays her hand on the barrel and slides it down to the grip. It is cold, which is strange on this hot day. She puts the jewelry and papers—all but the dingy envelope—back into the safe. Then she closes and latches the door. She hauls herself up from the floor, retraces her steps to the hallway, and places the gun and the envelope inside her orange purse.

She has done what she came here to do; now the afternoon stretches in front of her.

She sits at the dining table and flips open her laptop. She goes into her office email account and scrolls through the roughly two hundred that have come in already today—deals that are closing, client inquiries, contracts, details, minutiae—each small item requiring one tiny touch, like little birds pecking at her, holding their mouths open to be fed. It would be good to knock these off, to use her time efficiently, answer questions needing answering, and take care of business. It would be smart to call Samantha back, get her messages, and return her calls.

But she is incapable of doing any of those things right now.

Susan snaps her laptop closed. She wanders back to the kitchen, boils water for tea, and checks her watch. Unable to sleep, unable to read, unable to work, she settles on a bath—her cure-all for just about anything that ails her. She runs the water as hot as she can stand it, throws in some Epsom salt, and gets in. The Pavlovian response—her body's purely physical and automatic reaction of calm provoked by the warmth of the water begins to talk to her brain.

Susan closes her eyes and wills her mind to drift. This is a technique she has practiced for years, the reverse of the mindfulness of meditation. She has cultivated her own brand of mindlessness. Mind erasure, she might choose to call it—a prying of the jaws of her terrier brain off tenacious and troubling thoughts, a repositioning of them on more palatable pictures.

She will not go where she does not choose to go. Not to this morning or the past it threatens to bring up. She is not ready to face that just yet. In the heat of the bath, she yokes her imagination and reins it toward more pleasant memories—to the early nineties, a dozen or so years into her life in New York. To the Upper East Side on an afternoon when she wasn't watching where she was going.

She had met Jack Jr. on a subway platform. Literally *upon* the platform because that is where she landed when they collided with each other rushing top speed in opposite directions. Susan had lost her balance and fallen to the ground and Jack Jr. had dropped everything to help her.

"Oh my God! I'm so sorry," he'd said as he jettisoned his briefcase to lift her to her feet. The way he so freely abandoned his bag had won her over instantly. New York could be a rough town where pickpockets abounded. But Jack had put the welfare of a total stranger above his own; he had cast his possessions aside to come to her aid. It was an act of simple chivalry and it made its impression.

"I'm fine," she asserted in a voice that did not come out as authoritatively as she had intended. They both could see that she was badly shaken. Jack was a big man and the force of him had landed her hard on her hip.

"Oh no. I'm taking you to the hospital. We're going to Lenox Hill and you're getting an X-ray and I won't take no for an answer." He flashed a million-dollar smile. "Maybe you'll let me buy you dinner afterwards."

Susan, who had been alone for some years, felt tears spring up in her eyes. Jack Jr. thought she was crying from the pain of the fall. But, really, she was crying from his kindness. It felt so unfamiliar but, in a primal way, recalled a memory of gentler times.

They waited at Lenox Hill Hospital for hours. Susan, with her bruised hip, did not compete with the true emergencies that were walked or wheeled through the doors. Jack popped out, from time to time, to bring them coffee and food.

"If we keep eating this way, I don't think I can face that dinner you mentioned. I think we've consumed about six full meals since we've been here."

"Man up, young lady, I intend to feed you back to wellness today and we've only just begun."

"I'm serious. Muffins, chips, cookies—you haven't left any room for dinner."

But Jack Jr. had prevailed. By the time Susan was called to the back, X-rayed, and seen by a doctor, by the time she was iced, bandaged, and advised to take ibuprofen, she had surprisingly worked up an appetite.

"I think if we spend any more time together I'll get fat!" she said as she tucked into a mound of linguini Carbonara. Jack Jr. had taken her to his favorite little Italian place around the corner.

"Well, that's good, because I like you. That way, there'll just be more of you to like."

"Listen, Jack." Susan put down her fork to look straight at him. "You seem like a great guy—a very charming guy. In fact, you're so charming I'm going to venture a guess that you're dating quite a few women right now. I don't see a ring, so I'm guessing you're not married. But I could be wrong on that one. I've been wrong before."

Jack burst out laughing. "What are you, a shrink?"

"You think it requires a degree in psychiatry to see that you're a world-class flirt?"

"Touché. So, what are you saying? No go?"

"No go. To put it as delicately as possible, I've had my fill of that. I wouldn't mind being your friend, though. In my experience, any foray off that path can get in the way of a good friendship."

"Well. You can't blame a guy for trying."

"No. A guy cannot be blamed."

Jack Jr. raised his glass of Montepulciano and Susan followed suit. He clinked his to hers and said, "All right, then. It's funny that we ran into each other today—funny, strange, not funny, ha-ha. You're right, I do have a fair number of women in my life. And not one of them is a friend. So, if you'll give me a roadmap in this friendship between a man and a woman thing, I'll give it a try. To friendship!"

"I'm not sure I know how to do it, either. But I promise to take the lead. To friendship."

And they touched glasses again to seal it.

11

Henry opens the elevator doors on one.

"Lobby, Mrs. Ford. Stay cool tonight."

"Oh, thank you, Henry. I won't be going out."

"Smart move. It's a scorcher."

"Yes," she says and exits the elevator to the splendor of the lobby before her. Marginally restored from her bath, Susan allows herself a moment to admire the flowers, to really stop and look. They are always here—a changing array of branches and blooms—in a palace-sized urn atop an ormolu table. But tonight—dislodged as she is from her normal awareness of her usual surroundings—Susan's vision feels more acute.

"Beautiful," she says back to Henry, who waits with his elevator door open.

"Yes, ma'am. They sure are."

Susan breaks off to make her way into Cipriani.

From the items in her city closet, she has chosen a pale blue linen dress. The crispness of the linen augments her tentative grasp on composure. The fact that she hasn't left the cocoon of air conditioning for several hours helps as well.

After a good deal of waffling, she has decided to keep the gun and the envelope with her, tucked deeply in her bright orange purse. Before heading downstairs, she has grabbed an orange sweater to throw around her shoulders, hoping it might deflect attention from her bag, glowing—in her mind—like Exhibit A.

At five p.m. on a Thursday in August, Cipriani is sparsely populated. An offshoot of the famous Harry's Bar in Venice, where the Bellini cocktail was invented in 1948, the look is mid-century, glossy wood veneers with highly visible grain, glass sconces, low tables and chairs. The late afternoon sun streams in the westward-facing windows. Sergio comes over and warmly greets her with the requisite *ciaos* and cheek kisses and ushers her toward a table in front, next to the windows looking out on the park.

"Actually, no, Sergio," Susan demurs. "It's such a warm day that I'd love to sit farther in. A little more out of the way."

"*Certo, Signora* Ford," Sergio pulls out her chair. "Your usual Pellegrino with lemon? Or may I bring you one of our Bellinis today?"

"Pellegrino, thank you."

Susan takes her seat and surveys the crowd while she waits. They are neither downtown nor uptown in style. No Brooklyn hipsters and no Upper East Side headband blondes. There is a Euro-element—creased jeans and blazers, and double, triple cheek kisses—and a smattering of Americans in summer suits and ties. All the women are fully made up. The feeling is clubby, though it is unclear to what club they all might belong.

"Hi, Mom." Jack Jr. bends to give Susan a kiss on the cheek. "Sorry I'm late."

"You're not late. I'm early."

As Jack sits, a waiter returns with Susan's Pellegrino and pours from the large bottle into her glass.

"Dewar's on the rocks," Jack orders.

Stockier than he was when she had first met him, like an ex-athlete gone soft, Jack Jr. is still a very handsome man. The ladies in Cipriani take a moment to watch him as he settles into his chair.

"So," says Jack.

"So," Susan parrots back.

"Are you okay? What's going on? Wait—before you begin, I forgot to tell you; I wasn't going to come up to Watch Hill tonight for the cookout.

I'd committed to a dinner tonight with some Brits down at Balthazar; they really like the downtown scene. Why don't you come with me? It's a deal for a row of townhouses in Brooklyn that they want to punch through and do up as offices. We'd need a zoning variance."

The waiter brings Jack's scotch.

"I don't know about dinner, Jack, I'm pretty tired. Who are these people? Do you even know Brooklyn?"

"I'm not sure but my contact is pretty attractive."

"You want to drag me downtown to pick up a girl? What makes you think they're for real?"

"I've been doing this a long time—longer than you. I got you into the real estate profession, if you remember."

"Yes, Jack, I remember. I also remember that other English guy you got involved with—the one who was in the music business with the heavy Cockney accent."

"Oh God, yes! John Zee!" Jack laughs loudly.

"What kind of name was John Zee?"

"Excellent point. Probably made up."

"Remember he kept you going for two or three years? You thought he must work for some really big rock band or something to be able to afford the kind of properties he had you showing him."

"He did test my patience, Mr. John Zee."

"What ratted him out in the end?" Susan asks. "I can't remember that part."

"His shoes."

"That's right."

"When he told me his father always wore John Lobb shoes, I knew he was full of shit. It was pretty damned unlikely, with that accent, that his father, back in the day, would've had his shoes custom made at John Lobb. Mr. Zee had stretched credulity beyond its breaking point."

"Well, like I said, vet these people we're meeting tonight."

"Yes, *Mom*. Now, you want to tell me what's going on with you?"

"Well, I just wanted to talk to you about a strange thing that happened today. It's probably nothing. But you're a lawyer, after all."

"A lawyer? Is it something serious?"

"No! I mean, I don't *officially* need a lawyer. It's just—your legal background might not hurt in this situation."

"What *is* the situation?"

"I don't know where to begin."

Gesturing with both palms, he cedes the floor to her.

12

Saturday, July 14, 1979
Suburban Detroit

Day One at Frankie's Disco began at five p.m.

Despite the heat, Susan wore a light coat over her skimpy outfit to get in and out of her car without notice. Plus, as her mother had always said, what if she were in an accident? What would they think at the hospital? At least she'd have the coat. Although, once the nurses threw her on a gurney and undressed her, all bets were off as to what conclusions they'd draw.

She arrived fifteen minutes before the appointed hour, wanting to get the lay of the land. She was uncertain which entry she was meant to use, where she was supposed to go, or whom she was meant to seek out. Looking around, she opted for the front door. As she opened it, she was hit by a rank aroma of stale cigarettes, rancid beer, cleaning fluid, and musty carpeting. How had she not noticed it yesterday?

Inside, the place was dark and sticky. The lights were on but even at their maximum capacity, the interior couldn't be called bright. The black walls showed scuff marks; the mirrored surfaces looked streaked or—worse—had dried drips running down them. The edges of the black Formica tables were banged up, as were the chairs. The disco ball hung limply over the center of the dance floor.

Susan felt the bottoms of her shoes suctioning slightly as she moved across the charcoal carpet. Squinting down, she could see blobs of stuck gum and stains all over its surface.

What would her father think of this place, that elegant, gentle man from Tennessee? William Elton Bentley always went by Elton. It was the use of his middle name, yes—but also the old-timey quality of the name itself that set him apart—dated and placed him as an American Southerner of an age gone by. Susan's own name, she knew, was no less a road map to the time and location of her birth—Middle America in the middle of the twentieth century—the era of Susies and Debbies. Depressingly middling all the way.

Susan thought about Elton as she took off her coat and looked around the disco, knowing he'd be disappointed to see her here. The daughter he must have known from the outset he would not see grown, married, or launched in life. What was Elton thinking, at fifty-seven, when he'd had a child with his twenty-one-year-old bride? He must have assured himself that Maggie would be there—helping Susan grow up, guiding her through the byways that this disco represented.

He had been asleep when she left today. Susan did not know how to explain to him her transition from sales clerk at the respectable Winkleman's to cocktail waitress here, so she had said nothing. He wouldn't ask, either. Susan's relationship with her father was close, but not intimate. They talked a great deal and he cared about her opinions, but they stuck to safe subjects. Elton was interested in what Susan wanted to do with her life, why she studied French or dance, what books and movies she liked and why. But he never asked her the embarrassing things, the things that might actually lead him to know what moved her at a primal level.

Susan tried, from time to time, to draw stories out of her father about his own life—his two earlier marriages, the son from his first wife who had died before Susan could meet him, his relationship with Susan's mother. Elton would tell one little story, only ever a funny one, then quickly move away from the intimate to the abstract. His firewall would go up.

"Hi! My name's Diane!" A girlish voice sliced into Susan's thoughts. She focused and saw that it belonged to a waitress who was so fresh-faced that she made Susan look overdone. She had dark shoulder-length hair with bangs over big brown eyes and freckles, and she wore not a speck of make-up—not even lip gloss.

"Hi," Susan responded. "I'm Susan. It's my first day."

"I know. That makes me the old pro." This was hard to fathom, since Diane looked and sounded like a child. Yet, despite her breathy voice, her cadence was crisp and polished. "You'll want to hang that coat in a locker in the back."

"Okay, thanks," Susan said. "How about you? Have you worked here long?"

"Just since I graduated high school this spring."

"When do you leave for college?"

"Oh, I'm not doing that. My parents want me to go, but this is it for me," Diane said with finality.

"This place?" Susan could not imagine it.

"Well, maybe not *this* place, but school was not my shining moment. I'm not really a bookish person."

"I'm surprised," Susan said. "You sound like someone who would be going off to college. You sound—I don't know—educated."

"Good! I'm as educated as I want to be."

Susan couldn't help but frown. "Never say never. You might change your mind. I mean, I'm not much older than you, but you're still pretty young. So much can happen."

"That's exactly what I'm looking for—something to happen."

"Are you from Warren?" Susan asked.

Diane did not have the chance to answer because Frankie sidled up to them at that exact moment. "Susan, meet Diane, our twelve-year-old cocktail waitress." Frankie laughed as he said it. "Doesn't she look like she should be wearing saddle shoes?"

"Cute, Frankie," said Diane.

"No, you're the cute one." Frankie winked at Diane. Then he turned an appraising eye on Susan and examined her top to bottom. "Welcome to Frankie's," he finally said. "You meet my brothers? Vito? Carmine?"

"Uh, no. I haven't really met anyone but Diane."

"Well, you will. Okay, enough small talk." Susan felt his dismissal as he abruptly turned his back on both of them. "Get to work, you two," he called over his shoulder. "Suse, you're going to trail Sherry over there."

Susan snapped to attention and walked over to the woman Frankie had indicated with a parting wave of his hand. Sherry was older, thirty maybe, with layered, frosted hair and heavy make-up. Naturally, she, too, was dressed in the Playboy-Bunny-Meets-Wall-Street get up.

"All right," said Sherry. "We're pushin' Wallbangers tonight, 'cause we got Galliano runnin' outta our asses."

"Pushing what?" Susan, wanting to get it right, wished she'd brought a notepad and pen.

"Are you serious? Where'd you waitress before, a boilermaker bar?"

"I, um, I..."

"Fuck. You've never done this before. You don't know anything, do you?" said Sherry looking dead into Susan's eyes. "Frankie!" She turned and stomped off to consult with their boss privately, out of Susan's earshot.

Annie made her entrance right at that moment, airily tossing an apology for her lateness, confident of the world's forgiveness. She tumbled in, wearing her ubiquitous Candies, which scuffed and slid as she walked, her step a bit mincing and forward-leaning as if she might tip over from the weight of her breasts, now tightly swaddled in her shirt and vest. She wore no coat. Her legs were exposed; her hair was in a low bun and—Susan observed with a small pang of envy—somehow this ridiculous outfit actually looked made for her: sexy librarian in a Vegas chorus line.

Frankie and Sherry, huddling close together, drew Susan's attention away from Annie. Frankie held Sherry by one arm in a way that torqued up her shoulder and looked uncomfortable to Susan. After the wink at Diane and his weird stare at Susan, Frankie's familiarity with his female staff was making her feel uneasy. He mumbled something to Sherry that Susan couldn't hear, released her arm, and turned to the various assembly that had gathered to open the bar.

"Good evening, Annie," Frankie said, rotating to survey the crowd, making sure they were all listening. He never looked at Annie. His voice was low, but it silenced the room. It was cold and quiet in a way that made everyone lean in—commanding their attention more than a shout would have done. "Annie, here, is late," he told them, pivoting some more like an orator. "Annie thinks she's special. Special Annie gets to come in late. Do you all think that Annie's special?"

Annie stopped short and Susan could see that she was frantically seeking eye contact with Frankie. He continued to look at everyone but her. Annie cast a glance around the room, as did Susan, only to meet the stares of the various waitresses, bartenders and busboys who'd momentarily suspended their set-ups to focus on the little show that the boss was putting on at the new girl's expense.

No one answered his question. Susan got the feeling that this crew was accustomed to these outbursts; everyone looked simultaneously uncomfortable that this was happening and relieved that it wasn't happening to them. The ensuing silence was long and palpable.

Finally, Annie sputtered into the stillness, "I'm sorry I'm late. I needed gas." She was floundering, looking at Frankie, searching for a pair of kind eyes anywhere in the room. "It won't happen again."

"See that it doesn't or you're out." For the first time, Frankie shot a steely look at Annie. Then, just as quickly, he turned his back on her. "Sherry, baby, you get 'em both." With that, Frankie slapped Sherry on the rear end and walked out of the room. Susan was stunned. He had literally slapped her ass, in front of everyone present, and not a single one of them raised an eyebrow, not even Sherry. The slap served as an auditory period on his sentence—like the clapper signaling the start of film action at the beginning of a scene, only this clap meant that the scene was over. All of the workers in Frankie's Discothèque were released from his spell and returned to their various chores.

"Great, just great! You two get your sorry asses over here. Have *you* ever waitressed before?" Sherry shot accusingly at Annie.

"No." Annie's voice was much smaller than Susan had heard it before.

"Fuck. I don't know why I followed my asshole of a husband to this asshole of a town. Can either of you answer that question?" Sherry leaned in on Annie and Susan. "Huh?"

Neither girl responded.

"I should never have left Boston!" Sherry turned and stomped rapidly toward the kitchen. "C'mon you two know-nothing nitwits! You'll start on salad prep!"

"Toto, I guess we're not in Kansas anymore," Susan whispered to Annie as they scurried after the retreating Sherry. She peeked over at her new friend, this person she had barely known yet had followed into this sordid scene, hoping that, with a little camaraderie, they might get through it together.

Annie did not look back at Susan.

Susan felt a jolt of aloneness, fearing that she might have read more meaning into their budding friendship than Annie had. And then, silently, Annie reached out to grasp Susan's hand. Still without looking at her, Annie gave her hand a little squeeze.

The gesture flooded Susan with relief and, still clutching her coat, she accompanied her friend through the swinging doors of the kitchen.

13

Tuesday, July 17, 1979

With what meager enthusiasm she could muster, Susan turned from the service bar, her tray laden with drinks. Three days in, she was determined to demonstrate that she had mastered the finer points of swinging a tray over her head. She'd watched the wrist twist used by the pros, Sherry chief among them, though Diane had a mean wrist swivel too. It was actually rather elegant to see a woman with a heavy load twirl it effortlessly up and above through a flick of her stick-thin wrist—it forced the posture straight, it allowed the waitress to pass through the crowd and it garnered admiring stares.

It seemed that the trick was to do it fast; grab the tray with two hands, slide it to rest on the flattened palm of your dominant hand—in Susan's case, the left—and then pivot that wrist around to lift the tray over your head. Susan felt ready to give it a try. She was a dancer, after all; how hard could it possibly be?

She moved a few paces away from the bar. Positioning the tray on her left hand, she began the turn of her wrist and the sweeping arc overhead just as Sherry abruptly materialized out of the crowd and bore down on her.

"Susan! Move it!" Sherry barked in her face.

Susan reached her right hand up to steady her load in the wake of Sherry's passing, but it had all occurred at the wrong moment of the operation. Over the throb of the music, Susan could hear the tinkle of wobbling glasses. Or, maybe she just felt its vibration, like a coming seismic shift. Sherry, who had been in such a hurry two seconds before, completely stopped moving to watch her.

Beer, vodka, gin; stickies like Cointreau and grenadine; fruit, olives and onions: all of it poured down on Susan. She felt like human spin art. Glop slopped down her hair, her face, her sharp white shirt; broken glass crunched underfoot. The worst of it was, she couldn't open her eyes, which were stinging badly. She could neither see to put down the tray nor reach a napkin to wipe her eyes. And, Sherry never lifted a finger to help her. She was probably still standing there gloating. For all Susan knew, the whole bar could have turned around to watch her.

Her mortification was complete.

"Oh, honey." Susan recognized Diane's sweet voice as the dangling tray was lifted out of her hands. Diane dabbed at Susan's eyes with what felt like dry napkins, then placed those napkins in Susan's hand.

"Come with me," she said, holding Susan by the shoulders and guiding her across the disco toward the female employees' bathroom.

"Here." Diane handed Susan a clean kitchen towel that she'd run under the hot faucet. It felt so deliciously good on her face that Susan could have cried. She held it there, breathing into the steaming terry cloth, as she heard Diane leave the room.

"That was pretty rough," Diane said as she returned to the bathroom with a milk crate. "Sit down. I have some extra uniform stuff in my locker."

"Oh, Diane, thank you. I don't think I'm your size, though. You're so tiny."

"You're not so big, yourself."

"Hey!" Annie popped her head through the door. "What the hell happened? Frankie just yelled at Sherry and she looks like she's ready to kill someone. Wow, look at you!"

"Oh, God!" Susan sank onto the milk crate. "I wish he hadn't done that."

"Don't worry; he yells at her all the time. She'll get over it," Diane said. She turned to address Annie. "I can look after Susan from here—can you cover our tables?"

"Oh. Okay," Annie said, looking from one girl to the other. "Sure," she added. Then she turned and left the room. Susan was surprised to think that Annie might be a little jealous.

"Here." Diane came back from her locker on the opposite wall and handed Susan a pile of clothes. "Put these on. You can go in the stall. Take that wet towel with you."

"How do you do it?" Susan asked from the cubicle as she wiped herself down. "How do you work here? I mean, this is like one of the nine circles of Hell."

"It's all right, really, once you get used to it. You just have to learn the dos and don'ts."

"Yeah. Don't drop drinks on your head when Sherry's watching."

"Well, sure, but Sherry's not the only one you have to watch out for. You know the brothers who own the place, right?"

"Just Frankie."

"Well, there are three of them. Vito's the oldest and he's the brains of the operation. You'll see him at the corner table every night with his crew. Stay away from that table unless you've been assigned to work it—which you probably won't be. Frankie usually has Sherry do it.

"Carmine, the middle brother, is a recluse; he keeps the books and only comes in during the day. He works in the office back here. You won't ever see him, unless you come in early. And then, Frankie's the baby."

"Some baby."

"He can be sweet. You just don't know him."

"Oh, Diane, you can do better than that," Susan said as she exited the toilet stall.

"I don't know about that. You know who they are, right?"

"What do you mean? Who are they?"

"The Castiglione brothers? They're kind of famous in Detroit. Their grandfather was the guy who started Papa Vito's Pizza."

"Wow. That's a huge chain."

"I guess these three couldn't get the kind of action they wanted at the pizzerias, so they graduated to the disco business."

"I guess," Susan concurred. "But, are you trying to tell me something? I mean, Frankie was really weird that first day with you and Annie. Even with Sherry. What are you saying?"

"I'm not saying anything. Forget it. Look, we better get back to work before Sherry comes looking for us."

Susan regarded Diane for a moment, but Diane did not meet her gaze. So she turned to herself in the mirror. Her hair was still clumped in tufts, a toothpick lodged on one side. "I can't go back out there."

"You'll be fine." Diane started to open the door, then looked back at Susan. "And, watch your friend. She could get into some trouble here. It's not so bad if you know the rules—but, she doesn't seem like someone who plays by the rules."

14

Friday, July 20, 1979

On a perfect afternoon, six days into their odyssey at Frankie's Disco, Susan and Annie arrived at Metro Beach, a thousand-foot sweep of sand twenty miles to the north of Detroit. The girls grabbed burgers, fries, and Cokes as they made their way through the crowd. They squeezed their towels on a small patch of sand at the halfway point, equidistant between Lake St. Clair and the concession stand. Peeling off jean shorts and tank tops, they settled down in their bikinis to enjoy lunch.

"So what do you think?" Annie asked as she slathered on baby oil mixed with iodine, the homegrown recipe for a good dark tan. "Frankie's is kind of fun, isn't it?"

"You're kidding, right?" Susan had brought a tube of Bain de Soleil. She loved the way it smelled and halfway hoped it would give her a better tan. A French Riviera tan.

"All right, I admit I got off to an awkward start with Frankie. And you, spilling drinks on your head! Here, would you do my back?"

Susan took the baby oil concoction and applied it to Annie's back. "Awkward is an understatement. Frankie's creepy. And Sherry's awful."

"Well, who gives a you-know-what is what I say. Want me to do your back?"

"Sure." Susan turned away from Annie. "I like Diane, though."

"She's okay."

"It's funny, she said she doesn't want to go to college. I don't under-stand it. She sounds like a girl who would."

Annie rubbed the suntan lotion vigorously. "Well, you know, it's not for everyone."

"But don't you like it? I love it!"

"That's because you're in some swanky girls' school and you live in a dorm and you're all bonding all the time over your Fair Isles sweaters or kilts or something."

Susan couldn't help but laugh. "Kilts aside, what's it like at Oakland University?"

"It's okay. I mean, I don't live there or anything. I just go for my classes."

"Why don't you transfer?"

"It's probably expensive, and I don't even really know what I want to do. Anyway, tell me more about Diane."

"She's only eighteen, and she's really sweet. I can't figure out what she's doing there," Susan said. "Of course, I could say that about us too. Too late now, though. You realize we've burned our bridges and we're stuck at Frankie's for the rest of this summer?"

"Yes, I realize that, Susan. I fully appreciate the gravity of my sins and I'm ready to make a full confession. Bless me, Father, for I have sinned."

Susan turned around to peer at her. "Geez! What's bothering you all of a sudden?"

"Well that's how you sound half the time—like you're poised on the precipice of tragedy." Annie grabbed her burger from the bag on the towel and commenced eating.

"I don't think I talk about my problems all that much!"

"That's not what I mean. You're just so…I don't know. You're like Mary Poppins! Practically perfect in every way."

"What are you talking about? You're the perfect one. Look at you—every person you meet falls over their own two feet when they see you coming."

"Not everyone. My stepfather hates me. My mother hates me, too. And my half-sister doesn't like me much—although, in her case, I prob-ably like her less than she likes me."

"I'm sure you're exaggerating," Susan said.

"You have no idea what it's like in my family. No idea." Annie grew sulky and silently ate her burger.

"I'm sorry. You're right. I don't know anything about it."

"I mean, c'mon Susan, don't you think I would be more like you if I could? Hey!" She suddenly brightened. "Maybe you could teach me French!"

Susan could not tell if Annie was sincere or teasing. "Okay. Um. I'm not sure how much you could learn in a summer."

"Don't you want to continue our friendship after the summer ends?"

"Well, sure. I do." And she did. She felt like a foolish schoolgirl trying to find out if a boy really liked her, but she could not help herself. Annie had that effect. "Don't you?"

"Of course, I do! I wanna be friends with you forever! Hey!" Annie made another conversational U-turn and practically yelled. "Truth or Dare?"

"Not again! Last time, I made a fool of myself." Susan laughed as she rummaged around the bag for her food.

"And yet I've come to like you in spite of how prissy you are."

"Annie, you're trying to goad me."

"Why, Susan, yes I am."

"I do *not* respond to goading." Susan, still laughing, started eating.

"Okay, I'll go first."

"That's a ridiculously transparent attempt to get me to bare my soul!"

"What? Like wearing that cowl neck sweater is the worst thing you ever did?"

"That is *not* the worst thing I ever did." Susan realized with some irritation that she was, in fact, responding to Annie's goading. "I never suggested it was. I said it was a foolish thing and I don't like feeling foolish."

"So what *is* your worst thing?"

"It's none of your business, okay?" Susan sipped her Coke and looked out to the water. "Geez, Annie, don't you ever give up?"

"Nope. Just ask my stepfather. He'd tell you I'm as persistent as a mosquito." Annie stared out at the lake, as well. "Dontcha love that comparison? That's how they see me in my family—the big, fat mosquito, sucking the life out of everyone else. They clam up when I walk into the room—like they're in the middle of the most engaging conversation they've ever had—then I come in and they all just shut up. They might as well chase me out with a flyswatter!"

Susan looked at her friend with compassion.

"Don't pity me, Susan." Annie snapped at her.

"I don't! I'm sorry. I just…" Susan did not want to tell her new friend that she actually could understand how Annie's megawatt personality might be overwhelming to some. But to her family? In fact, she did feel pity for Annie.

"You want to know the worst thing I ever did?" Susan wedged her Coke in the sand as she sighed. "Fine. I was fifteen. My mother wasn't well, and for about a year, I'd been smoking a little pot with this girl, Christina. She had this big, hunky brother called Dolph."

"Dolph?"

"They were German. Anyway, Dolph was running off the rails, dealing drugs, and who knows what all. One day, we went up to Stratford, Ontario, for the Shakespeare Festival. It was a field trip with our English class to see *Twelfth Night*. Right after we left, Christina showed me these mushrooms that Dolph had given her. They were psilocybins—hallucinogens. He told her we should eat them on the bus."

"That's it? You did drugs?"

"If you don't stop interrupting, I won't tell you at all. Where was I?" Susan took a moment to gather her thoughts. "Right. Well, we ate them. They were disgusting. Then the whole long day was surreal. In a restaurant, I was transfixed by a glass of water for what seemed like a year. I don't know how we got to the theatre. I love *Twelfth Night*, but I have no memory of it.

"When we got back, my neighbor, Mrs. Banks, was waiting for me in the school parking lot, and she drove me straight to the hospital. My mother had taken a turn for the worse and they'd rushed her there while I was gone.

"I arrived to find her dying. Try as I might, I couldn't collect my thoughts. I couldn't talk to her. I couldn't talk to my father, who was sitting in the chair next to her. I looked at my mother and thought I saw the skin melt off of her skull. She was dying, and I was tripping.

"Mrs. Banks took me home because everyone could see there was something wrong with me. They thought I was drunk. My mother died in the middle of the night and I wasn't with her at the end. I was home in bed, trying to come down from those mushrooms.

"So, now you know. That's what I did—my worst thing." Susan turned back to Annie. "How about you?" she asked sharply.

For once in her life, Annie Nelson was speechless.

15

Thursday, August 2, 1979

To make the best of the situation into which she had thrust herself, like Margaret Mead, Susan studied the indigenous peoples of Frankie's.

The regulars were a curious mix: Italian-American men, Chaldean men, odd unaffiliated men, and pretty girls. The girls were not from strict Italian or Chaldean families. They were leggy all-Americans, whose parents neither knew nor cared where they went on hot summer nights.

The alcoholics arrived first, the quiet, working-class drunks. These were tool and die makers, welders, foremen who wouldn't stay once the disco got rolling, but who—for reasons of preference or proximity—chose Frankies' over nearby watering holes like The Barleycorn or The Shamrock. They sat at the bar, ate dinners of meat and potatoes, and drank their drinks of choice: always hard alcohol, usually grain, often in double shots. The hardest of the hardcore would mix these with milk. Scotch and milk, for the guy in some stage of cirrhosis, was seen as a healing tonic. A few enjoyed the boilermakers that Sherry had mentioned on Susan's first day of work—a tall glass of beer with a neat shot of whiskey gulped first.

These drinkers were quietly polite to the girls and the bartender, but they didn't say much. They finished up early, left wads of cash on the bar, and stumbled out into bright summer nights. In Michigan, the western-most edge of the Eastern Time Zone, midsummer daylight lingered after nine p.m. Susan watched them, night after night, inching themselves closer to oblivion by way of the bottle.

There was a lag after they departed before the night got rolling. Then the Italians arrived, the big wheels who were close with the Castiglione brothers and had some importance that would never be clearly defined. At the owners' table of choice—a high top nestled in the front corner, exactly as Diane had described—there was to be found a core group of three, the holy trinity of Frankie's. Vito Castiglione was seated farthest to the right, Johnny Buscemi took the middle, and Danny the Cop sat by the door, protecting the other two from Susan knew not what.

Though Officer Daniel Ravello never wore his uniform to the bar— that wouldn't have been permitted—his cronies made no secret of his status as one of Detroit's finest. "Get the officer a drink," they would say to a waitress. "Officer Danny, here, has just crossed the border from deepest, darkest Detroit! He needs some liquid rescue!"

Detroit's blacks did not frequent Frankie's Disco. Detroit's blacks hardly crossed Eight Mile Road. And—since the riots of sixty-seven— the white citizens of Warren did not traverse that divide in the opposite direction much either.

And, then there was Johnny Buscemi.

Johnny stood out from any crowd on the basis of his movie-star good looks. About thirty-five years old, he dressed in three-piece suits, and, in them, bore a striking resemblance to John Travolta's character, Tony Manero, in *Saturday Night Fever*. Because of this, people sometimes called him Tony, or Tony Fever.

This phenomenon was not unique to Johnny Buscemi and the Italians. Susan had observed that the Chaldeans, who seemed to tread a careful distance from the Italians, also operated with multiple monikers.

Susan knew Italians; she'd grown up in Warren, where Italians were plentiful. But Chaldeans were something with which she was not familiar. She did not know where they came from in the world, and she did not know where they lived in the Detroit metropolitan area. She'd never met any in Warren.

There was one among them who intrigued her. He circulated with the Chaldeans, but Susan wasn't sure he was part of them. She had heard him referred to as Frenchy, and this only heightened her attraction. Could this man possibly be French?

Wherever he was from, everything about him beguiled her—pulled at her from her self-imposed hibernation—for the first time since her high school romance with Todd.

To start with, he had the type of looks that tweaked Susan's heartstrings. He was tall and lean—skinny, really. Everything about him was long—his legs, his arms, his fingers. He never danced, but when he walked into the room he moved his limbs, his body, in a languid way that was graceful and loose. His skin was olive, his nose aquiline, his hair blue-black. Like Frankie's, his hair had a habit of falling over his eyes, which were a limpid brown. Unlike Frankie's hair, his was bone straight. More than handsome, Susan found him beautiful.

She took to watching him. She knew when he was in the room, could feel it when he walked in. She might have been busy—waiting at the service bar, delivering drinks, even picking up food in the kitchen—but she could always sense it when he entered the house. A heated chill rose up her body, starting low and flushing her face and scalp.

She sensed him watching her, too. Their eyes met numerous times in the course of an evening. Every time it happened, the same rush came over her. It was such an intense sensation that she feared it was visible to others. She was pretty sure it was plain to him.

Yet he hadn't approached her. This made her question her own perceptions. Maybe the guy had a wandering eye and looked at every woman the way he looked at her. Maybe it was just dark, and she wasn't seeing what she thought she was seeing. She couldn't be certain.

On this night, he came in earlier than his usual time, before Susan had even looked for him. And he came in alone, which was also not his habit.

In a fit of boldness, Susan asked Diane to switch sections.

Diane regarded her with her big brown eyes. "Is there someone you want to get close to?"

"I don't know." Susan felt herself blushing. "Maybe."

"All right, my friend." Diane made a silly little bow. "All yours."

The place was still relatively quiet. Consciously counting her steps, Susan walked over to his table. She took his order without extraneous conversation, left quickly, and just as quickly returned with his Cuba Libre.

Susan grabbed a cocktail napkin from the carefully fanned stack on her tray, set it on the table, and placed his rum and Coke with lime on top of it. She had learned from Diane the correct way to fan the napkins in a complete circle. A highball glass laid sideways atop the pile of napkins, then gently pressed and rotated clockwise was the way to create the perfect starburst of cocktail napkins, making them easier to grasp one at a time. "Are you French?" she asked before she could stop herself. She fiddled nervously with the napkins.

He looked up at her and smiled. His teeth were very white against his dark skin. She hadn't anticipated his smile, nor the renewed frisson of excitement it would cause her.

"Do you think I'm French?" he said, with the slightest hint of an accent. He reached up to push his hair back from his face. The sensuality of the gesture weakened her.

"I was just wondering. I hear people call you Frenchy." She paused to see if he would save her. He did not.

Susan spoke faster. "I studied in France. Last year. It was my academic term abroad. In Paris?" She concluded on an up note, as though he might not have heard of the place. She blushed at her own idiocy.

"So, you like French men?" He laughed, which embarrassed her further.

"Okay." She could see he wasn't going to answer her. "I've got to get back to work."

"Have you stopped working?"

"Um, no. But I've got to go work somewhere else." Susan started to turn away.

"Why don't you work here a little longer?" He reached out and grabbed her wrist—but, not hard, not hard at all. Susan was electrified by the touch of his hand on her arm. She stood stock still, staring down at it, unable and unwilling to end the interlude.

Sherry, who could always be counted upon to spoil a mood, reliably did so as she passed the table. "On a break there, Susan?" she sniped as she moved off in the direction of the bar.

"Right." Susan disengaged. It wasn't difficult. He really had no hold on her at all. "I've got to go. That'll be a dollar twenty-five."

"Start me a tab," he said. And then, their cat and mouse game suspended for now, he surrendered a little information. "And I'm not French. I've lived there—that's why they call me that—but I'm not French. And I'm not Italian, either. Someday I'll tell you my story." He paused. "You like stories, don't you?"

"Maybe. I think so." Susan's cheeks were burning from the way he spoke to her and the subject was only his nationality. But she could not safely prolong the conversation any further. She turned to go, then halted. "What name shall I use for your tab?"

"Sammy Fakhouri," he said, and smiled his dazzling white smile once again.

16

The dinner at Balthazar is interminable. Susan stifles a yawn and discreetly checks her watch. Time does not seem to be moving forward.

To Susan, this group does not look like serious contenders. At eight, there are too many of them. They drink too much, eat too much, laugh too much. Their jokes aren't even funny.

One woman, Eleanor, the one who Jack has clearly targeted, is too much in every way. Her dress is too short. Her décolletage too exposed. Her lipstick too red. She is like a cartoon version of a woman. Jack Jr. doesn't seem to mind.

For some reason, Eleanor wants Susan's approval. She checks in with Susan repeatedly and has taken it upon herself to call her Sue. If there is one thing Susan despises, it is the nickname, Sue.

"Sue, darling, you don't mind if I sit next to Jack, do you?"

"Sue, sweetie, you don't mind if I flirt with Jack, do you?"

"Sue, dear, you don't mind if I slide my hand up his leg and grab his willy under the table, do you?"

Well, she didn't really say that, Susan has to admit.

"Sue, darling, you don't mind…"

"I'm his mother," Susan says, to shut her up.

"His…"

"Mother."

"Oh. I thought you were his wife."

"Well *that* certainly makes it better."

It works. A chastened Eleanor does not address "Sue" for the remainder of the evening.

And that leaves Susan time to contemplate her stepson, sitting at the opposite end of the table, laughing at a story just told. She works to piece together the sides of this man that she knows and loves like a brother. Or, ironically, given that they are practically the same age, a son.

Despite the stresses of the day, Susan looks at him admiringly. Even in summer, the Ford men have always worn suits in the city. You had to hand it to both of them, father and son. Jack Jr., like his father before him, is a stylish man. Tonight, his suit is seersucker—Paul Smith with a more forward edge than his father's bespoke variety—and it is just the right level of rumpled. His bowtie and pocket square are in matching yellow silk with a tiny pattern of Labrador Retrievers.

Susan smiles as she thinks about her husband's strong preferences. Yellow ties, he would not wear. She never knew why. She won't mention that to his son. Jack Jr. already spends far too much time comparing himself to his father. Susan knows he believes he does not measure up.

And therein, she recognizes, lies the problem.

Jack Ford Jr. is smart. He got into Columbia Law School. Well, maybe his father helped a little there, but he passed the bar in one go. Definitely smart. He is cultured. He is athletic. He is kind. He has almost every attribute that he needs to be successful in life. But he lacks some subtle discernment, some ability to judge character that, from time to time, lands him in settings like this one. Perhaps it is the gentle padding of privilege that allows him to assume the best of everyone.

Of course, Susan concedes, had Jack Jr. had a more astute insight into the human animal, it is possible that he would never have befriended the likes of her in the first place.

Maybe it is his drinking. Has he always drunk this much? Susan drifts back to the early years with Jack Jr., the years when they were the closest. Before she knew his father, before their relationship took on the occasionally awkward complication of step-family dynamics.

In the nineties, Jack Jr. was one of those guys who just glowed. The aura of his youthful triumphs—on the tennis court, the lacrosse field, in sailing races—was not far behind him and remained undimmed.

It was a miracle they'd never dated. Jack Jr., at that time, was one of the all-time great ladies' men. But some instinct had steered Susan toward a different path. And Jack had respectfully followed.

But, when did he start to drink so much? He is a big man—he can metabolize more alcohol than most. But she feels a niggling thread of concern about the way he is currently knocking back the Margaux.

And that leads her directly back to this dinner, which will be incredibly expensive. She knows because she has been counting the wine bottles. Susan watches Jack enjoying himself with this wrecking crew. It is abundantly clear to her that these people are not going to buy any real estate from Jack Jr. It would have been clear to Jack Sr. ages ago that that was the case. What chip is her stepson missing that keeps him blind to these social cues? And how can she, his friend and his stepmother, let him know that she thinks this is a deal he should not waste any more time on?

"Sue, dear…" Eleanor is back.

"Jack, I'm heading out." Susan summarily rises and moves to the exit. "I'll talk to you tomorrow."

She bursts out the door and hails a taxi—a good old-fashioned smelly yellow taxi with not an ounce of suspension or air conditioning.

"Fifty-Ninth and Fifth," she shouts, hoping the driver will know where that is. This is only slightly cynical; she once encountered a driver who did not know how to get to Central Park.

The taxi lurches forward and Susan accepts with relief the hot gust of garbage-scented air in her face.

17

Susan drags herself through the revolving doors of the Sherry, exhausted enough to sleep on the lobby floor. She greets the desk clerk on duty and exchanges weary pleasantries with the elevator operator. He opens the door for her on ten and she makes the short walk to her apartment. The apartment she shared with Jack.

Susan closes the door behind her and kicks off her shoes. She crosses the hall without turning on lights; no apartment is ever truly dark in New York if the curtains are open. Avoiding her bedroom and its big, lonely bed, she moves by the light of the city across the library to one of a pair of chairs by the window.

Jack had insisted on this particular arrangement of furniture—two by two, like Noah's Ark. Always two big armchairs near the window, where they could sit together, Jack and Susan—face to face, feet on a stool between them—talking. Jack was a talker. Remarkably, he was also a listener. A rare combination.

Susan sits in her chair. Five years on, she still cannot sit in Jack's. She looks out at the park. Taxi lights, white in the front, red in the rear, traverse the winding drive and shoot in straight arrows on 59th and on Fifth. From a narrow sliver, it could be Edith Wharton's New York. Well, maybe not at night, with all the lights. At night, it could be Mary McCarthy's New York. Or Dorothy Parker's.

Susan returns to the game she plays; curating her world, selecting what she looks at to control the experience she has. She has seen enough of the seamy side of life and she wishes to see no more of it. She has spent the past decades systematically scissoring unwanted scenes from her field of vision. It is more than a game—it is the crux of her coping skills.

Tonight, though, it may take a while.

Susan gazes across the park and selects a memory from the fan deck of those she keeps on hand. She makes sure it's a good one: the first night Jack took her out to dinner. Right there, across the park, at Café des Artistes.

First, she pictures Jack: his pale blue eyes, laser sharp in focus, crinkly soft when he laughed; his spare frame, his smooth walk, his gentle hand on her back.

Next, she pictures the room. She conjures up images of the frolicking nymphs in the Howard Chandler Christy murals. The candles and their roseate flicker. Jack looking at her as if she were the only woman in the world. He ordered his drink, a Lillet on the rocks. She had to ask him about that. She didn't know what it was.

"You lived in Paris," he tilted his head, "and you've never had a Lillet?"

"I lived in a sixth-floor walk-up and I certainly did not go out for cocktails. And, even if I had, Chablis would have been the outer limits of my sophistication."

Together, they laughed at that.

She continues the memory, teasing it out a little longer.

"You wear a lot of colors together," she playfully said to him.

"I love color," was his simple answer.

Delicately, or so she thought, she had asked him if he might be just a little bit colorblind.

That had made him roar with laughter.

That was the thing about Jack. He was so sure of himself. He was so much his own man that he was virtually un-insultable. Comments that would offend a lesser person just made him laugh.

Susan longs for his laughter tonight.

Unable to hold the mental playback any longer, her focus returns to the window, the room and the chairs. Jack's chair—heavy with the absent weight of its occupant. Her chair—weighed down by the brick of her heart. Losses like a layer cake stack one on top of the other. But the loss of her beloved husband is the only one she has ever been able to own.

She looks toward the park again, but all she can see is her own reflection staring back at her from the glass. When did she get so much older? Bit by bit, she answers herself, as the time unfolded from that horrible day so long ago to this one, when the horror—she fears—is beginning anew.

18

A doorbell rings. Susan blinks her eyes to see that she is still in her chair by the window. She must have dozed off. She checks her watch. It is 2:30 in the morning. Were it not for the wave of fear that is sweeping over her, Susan would find herself highly annoyed. The sound of a doorbell is just about the last thing she expects to hear at this hour and it sets her heart aflutter. She wishes her dogs were here. She jumps from her perch overlooking the park and jams her foot straight into an unruly end table as she moves through the lightless apartment.

"Shit!" she mutters under her breath. The stubbed toe slows her down enough to question the wisdom of answering the door in the dark. Cautiously, she flips on a few lights as she continues. This brings her face to face with her orange purse and its unholy contents. Hesitating only a moment, she decides it is better to have the gun with her than sitting exposed on the table. She hoists the purse over her shoulder.

Like a good New Yorker, Susan looks through the peephole before opening the door. At what she hopes is the close of an endless day of surprises, it could be anybody standing out there.

She sees it is Jack, Jr. and a flood of relief sweeps over her.

"What are you doing here?" She opens the door and motions him in. "Are you just now leaving that dinner?"

"It went on for a bit and then Eleanor and I got to talking."

"Ah, yes. She seemed like a talker."

"What did you say to her? She was rather fascinated with our family tree."

Susan returns to the chairs by the window, still clutching the purse, unsure what to do with it now. She motions for Jack Jr. to sit in her chair. Opposite him, she settles on the arm of Jack's chair, her Jack. Gently, she places her bag on the floor. "Is that really why you're here?"

"I can't sleep. I wanted to ask you a few questions about what you told me over drinks—about your Mr. Fakhouri."

"He's hardly *my* Mr. Fakhouri."

"But he was on his way to see you—all the way from Baghdad. And you *did* lie to the FBI about knowing him. I just don't get it." Jack gets up and goes over to the bar. He pours himself a brandy and takes a sip. "You really have no idea why Fakhouri would look you up after all these years?"

"Not really, no. I mean, I'm imagining he's in some kind of trouble. Maybe he Googled me and knows I have some means. I don't really know."

"Maybe. But your last name is Ford now. And you're pretty reclusive. You don't do social media. It's not like he'd find you splashed all over the Internet."

"I'm just following the example of your dad. What's that line about WASP etiquette? Only let your name appear in the papers twice—when you marry and when you die? But, all kidding aside, I'm sure I'm not so hard to find, if anyone looks hard enough."

"You think he's a resourceful guy?"

"I suppose so."

"How well did you know him?"

"Not very. And it was such a long time ago."

"Let's go back: You say you left Michigan and came to New York and you lost touch with Fakhouri? What about that girl you mentioned—what was her name?"

"Annie."

"You have no idea what happened in the intervening years to either of them? You don't know where Annie is now?"

"Did I say that?" Susan looks up at Jack, her face suddenly flushed. "I'm sorry, Jack, I didn't mean to say it exactly like that. I do know where Annie is. I mean, I do know what happened to her.

"Annie is dead. She died at the end of that summer."

19

Friday, August 8, 2014

Susan opens her eyes in her pretty yellow bedroom in New York. For a moment, all is well. She gazes at the flowers and butterflies climbing up the Pierre Frey fabric on her walls and windows. It is an aesthetic she has cultivated over the years—the same textile covering every surface of the room to create a cocoon—a buffer of civilization.

Then—slam!—memory returns. She flips to her side to control a wave of nausea that overtakes her. It is from Pierre Frey into the fucking fray that she is falling.

Last night, she'd managed to hustle Jack out before the conversation had become too tricky. He was too drunk, and she was far too exhausted to have safely navigated its pitfalls. The subjects of Annie, Sammy, and the FBI had been put to bed for the moment.

But morning has come. She got what she came for and she needs to get back to Watch Hill. She will feel safer in the cloister of that insular community.

Susan picks up the house phone. "Good morning, George. Would you bring my car around? I'll be down in fifteen minutes. Thank you."

She swallows some coffee, splashes water on her face, runs a brush through her hair, and gets dressed. Not bothering to choose something new, she throws on the same white jeans and striped shirt she wore yesterday. A little rank from the heat wave, but she doesn't care. She grabs her bag, feels inside for the gun and the envelope, and heads out the door.

Emerging from the elevator, she makes her way across the lobby.

"Good morning, Mrs. Ford," says Kathy, who looks up from the guest she is helping. "Will you be leaving us already?"

"Yes, short visit, I'm afraid. I want to get on the road to Watch Hill before traffic starts. And that seems to get earlier and earlier these days."

"Safe travels! Hope we see you again soon."

"Yes. Soon."

The man at the desk has lifted the pen from the form he was signing and turned to regard Susan. She is nearing the front door but slackens her stride to look back at him. He is a distinguished-looking man—heavyset, older—probably handsome in youth. There is something familiar about him, but nothing she can fully identify.

He appears to be thinking the same thing, because his eyes are narrowing on her. The two of them pause, heads cocked to the side like dogs who've heard a distant whistle.

"Do we know each other?" he asks. "Mrs. Ford, right?" He motions back in the direction of Kathy, who has just said Susan's name, and takes a step or two in Susan's direction.

"I..." she falters, instinctively stepping backward.

She sees him register her alarm and she can tell that he enjoys the sensation of making a woman uncomfortable. He laughs and disingenuously offers, "I don't mean to make you nervous."

It is those words, but it is also his voice. There is something about his voice.

Susan is on the verge of placing him when Kathy has one more thing to say. "Would you like us to help you with dinner reservations during your stay in New York, Congressman Buscemi?"

The synapses of Susan's brain collide in a train wreck of recognition. As Johnny Buscemi turns around to answer Kathy, Susan spins and bolts toward the revolving doors.

"George!" she cries out, pushing her way through to the outside.

She knew he was a Michigan congressman. Of course, she knew! She'd tracked him over the years, followed his rise from local to national office. She didn't live under a rock, for God's sake! But here? What the hell was he doing here in New York? In her building?

"Good morning, Mrs. Ford." George walks over to open the car door for her.

Susan throws herself inside. And then—she shouldn't, she knows it, but she cannot help herself, when does she ever do what she is supposed to do?—she turns around to take one last peek.

Her eyes meet those of Johnny Buscemi, who has followed her silently to the front of the building.

Fatter, yes. Older, yes. Face puffy and lined. But she sees it now. And he sees it too. They identify their former selves inside these older casings.

She looks at him and he looks at her and, cool and collected in his baritone voice, he says, "Well, well, look at you. I must say, I'm very surprised to see you."

Susan cannot speak to save her life.

"Ford's your new name? You live in Watch Hill now?" He ticks off the information he has only just received. Just to let her know he's received it.

She sits frozen like a rabbit in the cross hairs of a gun.

"You know, I never thought I'd see you again. Never," he repeats icily. "If I'm not mistaken," here he takes a weighty pause, "you still have something that belongs to me."

"Congressman?" Another man appears from the building and approaches Johnny Buscemi. "Your room is ready now. I've had them carry up your bags."

Danny the Cop!

Corralling what is left of her reflexes, Susan stomps on the gas and barely avoids hitting the taxi in front of her. She swerves a lane to the right, horns and brakes screeching their protest around her.

Drive, she thinks. Just drive, drive, drive!

But where on this Earth can she go?

20

Saturday, August 4, 1979
Suburban Detroit

Maybe it was his cruel public scolding that caused Annie to fall for Frankie. Perhaps it was the charm he so easily wore on the day she had first met him. More likely, it was the deadly combination of these two sides of the man that made Annie fall in love with Frankie. Or fall into something that felt like love to her but looked to Susan like thinly masked obsession.

Annie fell hard for Frankie; Frankie fell into bed with Annie.

Around eleven on a record-breaking night, Jimmy, the bartender, asked Diane to get a jar of olives from the storeroom. Martinis were flying, and he'd just run out.

"Where the hell's Sherry?" he barked. "She's supposed to be in charge and I'm not supposed to run outta olives!"

"I haven't seen her," Diane said as she loaded up her tray with the drinks that Jimmy was handing her.

Susan, who was just turning away with her own full tray, offered to go in Diane's place once she'd delivered her orders.

"Are you sure?" asked Diane. "I can go if you're too busy."

"Honestly? I like errands that get me out of here for a few minutes."

"I owe you, then," Diane said as she hoisted her tray.

"I owe *you*!" Susan countered. "Thanks for switching sections the other night."

"Oh yeah. How'd that work out?"

"We'll see. He's cute, though."

"Ladies." Jimmy returned to their end of the bar. "I hate to break up your little tea party, but will one of you go get the damned olives?"

"Sorry! Going!" said Susan, as she and Diane peeled off in different directions.

On her way to the back, Susan passed Annie serving a rowdy bunch of Italians. She looked up at Susan, winked, and blew her a kiss. Since Annie had started dating Frankie, she got to wait on his friends. These were the big tippers—sometimes fifty or a hundred bucks a round. It was also the safest place to be for someone who'd been branded the girl-friend of one of the bosses. All hands were off Annie—literally—which was more than most of the cocktail waitresses at Frankie's could hope for.

Annie had proven a mercurial friend. A strain of coldness, first inti-mated after Frankie's rebuke, had grown. Sometimes, she was the girl Susan had met two months before—funny and playful, connected, and real—like now with the little wink. Often, she was sullen and remote. Their day at the beach was one of the last times that Susan had felt a real intimacy in their friendship. They certainly never went to Sanders any-more. And, French lessons—needless to say—had never begun.

Susan reminded herself continually that she had little more than a month left to her last summer vacation, and no one was hiring seasonal help at this late juncture. She needed the money and she just had to steel herself to get through it.

She arrived at the double swinging doors to the kitchen. The protocol was to enter through the door on the right and come back out through the door on the right again, from the inside, to avoid collisions. Once inside, Susan swung around farther to the right, and was surprised to find the back hall in darkness. She fumbled to find the light switch before she could continue.

Inside the storeroom, she moved quickly to the shelf stacked with industrial sized jars—olives, onions, pickles, cherries—food not requiring refrigeration. She didn't need to turn on the light in here since there was a large window in the door that let in enough illumination to complete her task. The olives were just to the left of the doorway. She would grab the jar and be out in a flash.

Nearing the shelves, Susan bumped her toe into something where nothing should have been. She hadn't hurt herself but was again caught off balance. She leaned down to find a cardboard case of ketchup bottles on the floor. Sloppy, that someone would have left it there. Just the sort of disorder that bothered her. She lifted it to the shelf in front of her.

As she was reaching up to take hold of the olives, she heard voices deeper in the storeroom, which froze her in her place. She now regretted not having turned on the light. The act of flipping that switch would have announced her presence to whoever was lurking in the shadows. Instead, she felt like a spy, sneaking around in the dark. She stood with her arms raised, touching the olive jar, unsure of what to do.

Susan remained that way for the longest time, listening intently, willing the pounding of her heart to settle. She could hear shuffling and maybe muffled voices, but both were indistinct. Someone was definitely in there. Of that, she was now certain.

As slowly as she possibly could, she lowered her arms and turned toward the interior. In the excruciating minutes that had passed since she'd entered, her eyes had adjusted to the dark. She stared, squinting into the half-light, trying to see who might be in there with her.

All at once, as if a mirage, there materialized the image of Frankie and Sherry, facing each other up close. Oddly, Sherry seemed taller than her normal height. Susan's grey cells raced to compute what subject they could be discussing—in the storeroom, in the dark—when, suddenly she grasped the situation. Sherry was propped up on a shelf, pinned there by Frankie's heaving, bare buttocks. The light from the door reflected off of Sherry's hoisted leg, as well as Frankie's ass, as if a spotlight were shining on them.

Comprehension came to Susan so fast that she gasped, which spiked her level of panic. She stood as still as she could—praying that they hadn't heard her, despairing of a way out—when Frankie turned to face her. The ray of light from the door lit up his eyes as he looked in Susan's direction. Surely, he couldn't see *her* eyes, facing away from the light source as she was?

But she feared that was not true. Frankie stared at Susan as he continued to pump into Sherry, knocking her back against the paper towels and toilet paper on the standing racks. Sherry gave out little moans and grunts, but Frankie was utterly silent. Susan was paralyzed in this diorama. Cold sweat trickled down her spine, increasing her sense of dread. And then, Frankie came, there was no mistaking it. He never took his eyes off Susan, but he was clearly at the moment of climax.

Somehow, this broke the spell and released Susan, enabling her to flee. She ran through the kitchen, the wrong side of the swinging doors, and back into the pulsing disco. As she had turned away, Susan saw Sherry see her, too, and her anxiety redoubled. She did not want to be Sherry's adversary, was not trying to antagonize this formidable creature, but it seemed she couldn't help it. Susan burst out the left side of the kitchen door and smack into Annie.

"What the hell's the matter with you?" Annie caught Susan by the shoulders to stop her trajectory.

"Nothing," Susan stammered. "Nothing. I just need to get back to that table in the corner."

"Sheesh! Well, I need to get those stupid olives. Diane said you went to get them, but you never came back. And Jimmy's really pissed. What *is* the matter with you?"

Susan opened her mouth to speak. At that moment, Frankie strode out of the correct side of the swinging doors, laughing. He grabbed Annie and laid a big, wet kiss on her mouth.

He turned his eyes to Susan and said to them both, "Get to work, cuties. Make some money for me. I'm feeling lucky tonight."

Giving Susan a wink, he walked into the crowd, exuding his bounteous charm.

21

Wednesday, August 8, 1979

At high noon, Susan plopped herself in the living room on her mother's old Queen Anne chair, intent on advancing her summer reading. She used to fit into this chair alongside her father when he'd read to her as a little girl. She picked at the frayed cording and leaned her head into one of its wings. Her eyes drifted up to the picture window as she allowed her imagination to lead her.

She'd spent her life in this house, on this block, in this suburb—but she wouldn't raise her children here. She pictured herself in a Norman manor, a governess watching over her brood. Sheep on the lawn, her husband visible on horseback. In a life like that, she would read endlessly—book after book after book.

Of course, with Sammy, that scenario would hardly transpire. Maybe they'd live in a tent, as Bedouins in the desert, their children playing with camels. Though camels were supposed to be mean. Maybe they could have horses, instead.

What was she doing? She needed to reel herself back. They'd barely had one conversation!

Susan leaned forward and narrowed her eyes, surprised to see Annie's rattletrap Corvette pull up to the front of the house. It hit the curb once, corrected itself, and shuddered to a fitful stop.

Susan had never seen a torn car before. Annie just laughed when asked about its deplorable condition, repeating what her stepfather told her: The Corvette Stingray was made of fiberglass, thus had the curious ability to tear, rather than dent like normal cars.

If possible, the disarray of the interior of the car managed to exceed its exterior. Annie kept all manner of items in it: clothing, shoes, makeup, and a large array of drinking glasses. These she carried out of Frankie's at the end of a shift and dropped on the floor when she finished consuming one of her innumerable cranberry juices.

The effect was dizzying. As the car lurched through traffic—Annie drove the same way she walked—the glasses rolled first one way, then the other, pausing as the car halted, then continuing on in their ongoing, tinkling motion. Susan offered to drive whenever the girls went anywhere together.

Today, Annie stumbled out of the car—no easy exit even from a clean Corvette—wearing short shorts, a tube top, and flip-flops. At the front of the Bentleys' ranch house, Annie rang the bell several times in quick succession and rattled the handle on the screen. Because of the heat, Susan had left the wooden door wide open with only the screen door locked.

Susan rounded the corner with her book in hand—Stendhal's, *Le Rouge et Le Noir*. Her outfit wasn't much different from Annie's but managed to cover more flesh.

"All right, I'm here!"

"Wanna go shopping?"

Susan let Annie in. "I need to read this. I have to write about it before classes start."

"Oh God, are you serious? It's such a nice day."

"Don't you have any summer reading?"

"Not really, no. I haven't picked my major," said Annie, evasive, as ever, when the subject of her college career came up. She sat briefly in a kitchen chair, then rose again immediately. "Can I use the bathroom?"

"Use the one down the front hallway. You know where it is." Susan tried to resume her reading, but, sitting in a stiff kitchen chair waiting for Annie's return, she knew she'd lost the thread.

"C'mon." Annie was back. "Go with me. I'm bored, and I need to do something." Annie play-tugged on Susan's arm.

"Maybe. As long as I drive."

"Nope. I've gotta get gas and I can't be late tonight, so I need you to remember."

"You may remind me of *my* mother but I'm starting to feel like yours."

"C'mon, Mama, please?" Annie pulled Susan's arm again.

"You're relentless! Let's go out the back so I can leave the front door locked. My dad's sleeping and his nurse isn't here right now." Susan ushered Annie out of the kitchen and around the side of the house.

"I want to go to Winkleman's, but I don't want to see Nancy, so let's go to Oakland Mall." Annie said as she steered her Corvette into the street.

"Annie, it's awful, what we did to Nancy."

"Oh, come on! She had tons of girls there and she just needed to work out the schedule. Aren't you glad we went to Frankie's? Aren't the tips great?"

"Sure, the tips are good. You've got to admit, though, it's a weird place. I know you're dating Frankie, but don't you feel like Alice going down the rabbit hole?"

"I don't know. I'm having fun. You're too prim, Susan. You're like some old librarian."

"I'm hardly a librarian when I put on my work outfit. I'm practically a Playboy bunny."

"Loosen up," snapped Annie, oddly sharp-edged. The conversation had become strained, as many did these days. Annie shifted so precipitously from one topic to the next that Susan couldn't find stable footing.

"I'll try." Susan gave up trying and concentrated on the scenery passing by. Suburban sprawl—mile after mile of gas stations, medical buildings, and fast food places—was all she had to look at to keep from looking at Annie.

"Aren't you going to get gas?" Susan finally broke her own silence. She imagined them running out and being stuck at the side of the road.

"See! I told you I needed you." Annie reached over and playfully ruffled Susan's hair with one hand as she whipped the car into a nearby gas station with the other.

"Fill 'er up!" Annie smiled at the attendant as she hopped out of the vehicle. "Do you have a bathroom?"

"Yeah, on the left of the building," answered the gangly kid.

Annie retreated around the side of the garage. Susan turned the rearview mirror toward herself and worked to smooth down her hair.

The attendant pumped the gas, washed the windows, and checked the oil. He did not return to the building but stood at attention waiting for Annie. Susan sat waiting as well. They both looked in the direction Annie had disappeared. They did not speak to each other.

After an eternity, Annie returned. She paid the kid and flopped back into the driver's seat, kicking a glass out of her way as she started the car.

Susan searched her mind for a topic of conversation—any topic—about which they could have a pleasant conversation.

"Annie, I have something to tell you. I mean, I don't want to get ahead of myself, but I'm kind of excited about a possibility."

"Yeah? What's that?" Annie leaned forward to fiddle with the radio.

"Well, I think I may have met someone—a guy who might be different. Or special. I don't know. I can't stop thinking about him."

Susan really wished Annie wasn't driving. Each time she turned the radio dial, she synchronized both hands. The car kept making little coordinated lurches to the right.

"Annie, are you listening to me?"

"Huh? Of course, I'm listening to you. I'm just trying to put on some music. So, who do you like? One of Frankie's brothers? We could double date!"

"God, no! They're definitely not my type!"

"Well, you don't have to act so superior!" Annie was still cranking the dial in tandem with the steering wheel and it was making Susan carsick.

"Here," Susan offered. "Let me do that."

Susan bent over to take charge of the radio. As she did so, she noticed a necklace that Annie was wearing, a pendant at the end of a long silver chain, a cheap key-chain style with little metal balls along the length of it. Until then, the pendant had been nestled between Annie's breasts. Somewhere between the bathroom and the car, it had spilled out to dangle down the front of her tube top. Susan squinted at it, not quite sure what it was.

Then it became clear, all at once, like in a magic act, when one thing turns out to be another thing, entirely. The pendant revealed itself to be a coke vial. Amber glass, black plastic screw-on lid with a little spoon attached inside. In the sunlight, Susan could see that the vial was about half full of white power, the spoon hanging down into the middle of it.

Here was the key to the map. Annie's extremes of personality since coming to work at Frankie's were cast in a new light. The highs, the lows, were obviously cocaine induced! Susan didn't know why she hadn't thought of it before. Annie had become erratic. She'd become capricious and even paranoid. She must have been doing a lot of cocaine. Was Frankie her supplier?

But that didn't make any sense. Cocaine was not an asset to Annie's personality. Even Susan, as easy-going as she was, was finding it hard to cope with her unpredictability and intensity. She could guess that this wouldn't be amusing to a man like Frankie, who might like his women unchallenging. Maybe Annie was buying it herself? That was a more likely scenario.

Annie quickly grabbed the vial and dropped it back into its resting place, hidden once again by the striped elasticized fabric stretching across her bust. Cozy little vial, all tucked in. She cut a glance over at Susan and laughed.

"Jesus Christ, Annie!" Susan surprised herself with the anger that welled out of her.

"Oh, fuck you, Susan! You're so high and mighty. You're working at a disco too, babe. And you've got your own little secrets you keep."

Annie hadn't ever spoken to Susan like that. She'd been churlish but had never mounted a direct attack.

"I will *never* tell you another secret!" Susan gasped. "Ever!"

"Who cares?" Annie snapped back at her.

"You know what? I want to go home. Take me home now." Annie kept driving toward the mall, increasing Susan's agitation. "I mean it, Annie. Turn the car around!"

At Annie's lack of response, Susan repeated, "*Now!*"

Precipitously, Annie whipped to the left and made a complete U-turn in the middle of Fourteen Mile Road, across two lanes heading west, the middle turn lane and both lanes going the opposite way. She looked neither to the right nor the left, not in front of her and not in her rearview mirror. Brakes and tire squeals were heard on all sides of the spinning Corvette while inside the car, several glasses vaulted over the transmission tunnel to land on Susan's feet.

"Are you crazy?" Susan didn't know if she should grab the wheel or crouch down on the floorboards. She kicked a glass forward only to have it bounce back, hard, onto her foot. Pain and rage overtook her, and she screamed again, "Are you totally *crazy*?"

Miraculously, within moments, it became apparent that they hadn't been hit. And soon, it also became evident that there were no sirens—ambulance or police. Annie could have killed them both, could have landed them in jail, but they had somehow escaped this stunt unscathed. Susan was livid. She opened her mouth to speak, thought better of it, and shut it again. The girls drove silently back to Susan's house where Annie hit the curb at full force.

Susan fought with the door before she could get out of the worthless Corvette, scattering glasses as she did so. She slammed it hard, stomped up the drive and turned to see Annie peel off—leaving one, lone highball glass spinning, unbroken, on the pavement.

22

Saturday, August 11, 1979

Like a fata morgana, the molecules that were Sammy Fakhouri coalesced in Susan's peripheral vision. As was his custom, he arrived at Frankie's with someone, presumably a Chaldean, and always the same man. Apart from the night of Susan and Sammy's first conversation, Sammy was rarely alone. On this particular night, Susan had just turned from the service bar, tray loaded with drinks, when she saw Sammy and his companion enter. It was clear that he saw her, too, and she reddened. When he smiled, she fumbled her tray.

Susan watched Sammy now, as he moved across the floor. Like most of the men who frequented Frankie's, Sammy wore polyester pants and shirts, and black was his color of choice. That color made him look taller and the fabric gleamed in the lights.

Ironically, it was the advent of all types of synthetics—*Ban-Lon, Dacron, Qiana*—that had ruined Susan's father. Elton had owned several dry cleaners scattered in the northern suburbs. Even the working classes dry-cleaned their clothes until that ended with *Wash-and-Wear*.

Elton had lost his business and his eyesight all in the same year—the year that Susan was twelve. Life in the Bentley family got hard and it got there fast. It was the bleakness of it that had undermined her mother, the unrelieved dreariness of those years that brought her to despair. There was no exit until one day there was. A heavy smoker, her lung cancer was stage four when discovered, treatments were ineffective, and it was soon over. She wasn't even forty.

Then the world grew still.

They coexisted, Susan and Elton, moving wordlessly around the house. It was only when Maggie was gone that it became clear that she had been the voice, the life, the spark of their family. Susan and her father were quiet, introverted people and silence soon engulfed them. Like the castle in Sleeping Beauty in the hundred years when the princess slept and the briars encased it, the Bentley household retreated into itself. Susan felt an invisible wall rise around them, shielding them from the world.

She had her routine, like all teenage girls, and she plodded through it day after day: school and homework, homework and school. She saw a boy, Todd. They went to movies. Films, like books, excited her more than her own life managed to do. She was a dreamy, fanciful girl, living alone with an old man, untouched by her sallies into the outside world. Susan had come to rely upon, to hide behind, that wall.

"Beauty."

"Beauty!"

"*Et alors, ma belle*? Are you alive? Are you awake? Are you here?"

Susan blushed when she realized that Sammy had been trying to get her attention.

"I'm sorry! I was a million miles away."

"I see that. May I introduce you to my cousin, Jacob?"

"Oh!" Susan thrust out her free hand. "Nice to meet you."

"*Enchanté*," Jacob gallantly raised her hand to kiss it. "And might you tell me your name?"

"Susan. I'm sorry, I should have said that."

"Susan," interjected Sammy. "It means 'graceful lily' in Hebrew."

"How did you know that?" Susan asked, amazed.

"Excuse me." Jacob lifted her hand a second time and turned back to Sammy. "*Salut, mon vieux*. Monsieur Frenchy." He grabbed Sammy by the shoulders and kissed him three times: cheek, cheek, and cheek. Sammy shoved him playfully and Jacob moved off.

"How *did* you know that?"

"What?"

"The meaning of my name."

"Ah, *chérie*, I'm from the Middle East. We learn a little of many languages there. Actually, I'm joking. I looked it up."

Susan blinked for a moment then laughed.

"But, Susan," Sammy continued, "is rather a simple name for such a complicated girl."

"What makes you think I'm complicated?"

"You seem to be here but not here."

"I think I'd better take your drink order." Susan knew she'd been standing far too long in one spot solving riddles. Sergeant Sherry could pass by at any moment and give her a demerit.

"Would you like to hear my story?" Sammy asked her straight out.

"I…" she hedged. Was she getting in over her head?

"You've asked me several questions," he went on. "And now I'm ready to answer."

"Well." She hoped she would not come to regret this. "Yes. I think I would."

"Then you may get me a rum and coke now, and I will tell you my story later. What time do you get off?"

"Closing time is always two."

"Then at two, we will go to the beautiful and elegant Denny's Restaurant next door."

"I look forward to it."

"But the price, my beauty, is dear."

"I see."

"It is not what you think."

"I have a pretty good imagination."

"Imagination is a key that unlocks many doors."

Susan laughed. "You speak in parables."

"I want your story, as well."

"That's it?"

"You make it sound easy. I think it might not be so easy for you to tell things about yourself."

"How do you know that?"

"You see more than you say."

At this, Susan laughed again. "You really do sound like some kind of gypsy."

"Maybe that's what I am." Sammy laughed with her. "I'll take that drink now."

For the first time in a very long time, the castle walls were coming down.

23

Sunday, August 12, 1979

At 2:15 on Sunday morning, Susan stepped out of the front door of Frankie's. The night was dark and hazy, the moon waning from its peak on Wednesday, with the first hint of chill in the air. Summer would soon be over.

She had changed from her uniform into jeans, a white V-neck sweater and white tennis shoes. She carried her heels and work clothes in an old Bonwit Teller bag, tattered and taped at the corners. Its sprigs of purple and blue violets were jumbled with green leaves and stems, as though little bouquets had been gathered on a white sheet, tossed up in the air and then painted where they dropped, facing every which way.

Susan held onto this bag, and a hatbox like it, as little talismans connecting her to her mother. Maggie had left Susan her pearls, her Longines watch, and her diamond rings. For Susan, though, the Bonwit Teller bag was her Madeleine, the item that, without fail, conjured the memory of her mother—the look, the feel, the smell of the way things were, before they weren't that way anymore.

It wasn't exactly the shopping that had lodged itself in Susan's sense memory. It wasn't the acquisition of material goods that made her feel temporarily less vulnerable and exposed. Susan and her mother had frequented stores like Bonwit Teller not so much to shop, but as an act of willful shapeshifting. They liked themselves and each other better in the sealed and pristine environment of a luxury department store. It wasn't reality and that was the appeal of it. Reality had lost its charms.

When Maggie fell ill, the otherworldliness of these outings intensified. On their last trip, they had spent three quarters of an hour trying on hats. For those forty-five minutes, nothing else existed. Spring was coming, so many of the hats were pastel colored. Wide brims, narrow, felt, straw, grosgrain ribbons, flowers.

Susan had made her mother buy a hat that day, navy straw with a very wide brim. Really, it was a summer hat—a hat made to block the sun's rays. Maggie shouldn't have bought that hat, as sick as she was. But it meant so much to Susan that she wouldn't leave the store without it. Maggie yielded to her daughter's will, then she died at the end of the month. She didn't make the summer and she didn't wear the hat.

Susan never wore the hat, either. She had no affection for it. It was stuffed in a closet, unloved and unvisited. The box it came in, however, she'd used to store old journals, scraps of poems and stories she had written. Like the bag, it was torn and taped. The seams had come unstuck and Susan had wound masking tape around the inside edges, pushing it in with her fingers, pressing it flat, holding the box together.

In the parking lot, Susan paused with the bag on her arm, slowly scanning for Sammy. Other than a few stragglers, cars that had been parked in the same spots all summer, the lot was empty.

Susan pushed up her sleeves, then tugged them down and glanced around again. She looked at her watch. She had told Sammy she would leave at two and it was now 2:20. Maybe he'd been there and had grown tired of waiting. Maybe he'd only been teasing when he'd made his flirtatious offer. He was gone, that much was certain.

Susan began the deflated walk around the back of the building to where she'd left her car. The parking lot was dark, and the walk was long at this late and lonely hour. Rounding the corner of the building, Susan saw that the night cleaners had left the kitchen door ajar and the narrow slice of light that this provided relieved the jangly nerves that had overtaken her. People were just inside that door, so she wasn't alone. She could hear their scratchy radio; they would be able to hear her.

Without warning, two men stepped out from behind a car. Susan did a little hop in the air and a sound came out of her throat. She stumbled backward into the cinderblock wall of Frankie's and clutched her bag like a paper shield to her chest.

"Are you a nervous girl?" said the man who was closest to her, not more than an arm's length away. This was the guy who sat with Vito Castiglione in the corner, the handsome one. "If you're such a nervous girl, you probably shouldn't creep up on people in the dark."

"I'm sorry, I…" Why was she apologizing? "I'm just heading to my car. Over there." Why was she showing them her car? She wasn't following any of the rules for a woman alone in a deserted parking lot. Not one single rule.

The second man, the cop who sat at that same table, slipped something into the first one's hands—an envelope?—and walked away quickly, around the corner of the disco.

"You want me to walk you to your car?" The handsome one edged a little bit closer. What was his name? She knew it, but her brain right now was a blank.

"No! I mean, I'm fine. It's just over there. I have the light from the kitchen where all the men are cleaning. Right there!" Susan drew his attention to the kitchen door.

"I'm not going to bite you. I see the men in the kitchen." Now he was fully laughing at her. "I'm Johnny Buscemi. You know who I am, right?"

"Yes, of course." Who the hell *was* he? "I mean, I've seen you with Vito. At the corner table."

His melodious voice turned menacing. "Never mind where you see me or who you see me with."

"No! I don't know who you're with. I mean, I don't know who that man was just now…."

"Go. Go to your car." Just like that, he dismissed her as he turned and walked off into the night.

Shaking, Susan slumped against the wall. She saw her car, tantalizingly close, glowing in the beam of light from the open door, like a space ship in a 1950s movie. She hastened her step to get in it and get the hell out of there.

She rummaged in the Bonwit Teller bag for the little clutch where she'd left her keys. Grabbing hold of them, her hands were trembling so badly that she dropped them onto the asphalt. Once again, good judgment had been ignored. She had not followed her mother's cardinal rule to have her keys in hand before leaving a building. She hadn't been sure if she was meant to go with Sammy in his car, or what exactly the plan had been, so now, here she was, on her hands and knees on the ground, groping for her keys.

Susan heard footsteps and sensed a shadow fall over her, casting her deeper into darkness. She froze. Her breath grew shorter and shallower. Johnny Buscemi must have come back. His departure was a trick. She was hardly breathing at all, as if that could make her less noticeable. She mentally reviewed escape routes, while remaining stuck like a stone on all fours.

Then, she heard a soft whistle, followed by, "Beauty!"

Susan lifted her head to look up at Sammy and could barely get the words out. "What are you doing here?"

"We have a date, remember?"

"I thought you'd gone."

"I'm not going anywhere, *ma belle*. I drove my car over to Denny's and have returned to accompany you there in yours. I couldn't let a lady drive by herself at this late hour."

"Geez! You really scared me!"

"You will, I hope, explain this word, 'geez.'"

"I'm serious!" Should she tell Sammy what just happened with Johnny Buscemi? What *had* just happened? "You shouldn't sneak up on people like that."

"My dear, please forgive me." Sammy held out his hands to help her rise. "I should have seen that you were distracted. I was a little distracted, myself, by the sight of you. In your summer sweater and your summer tan, you look like you've spent a long day at the beach with a very good book."

That image made her smile. "Hardly the beach."

"Will you forgive me? Will you allow me to treat you to *les crèpes magnifiques chez* Denny?"

"Well, if you put it that way…"

"Shall I drive?"

"Um…" Susan opened her hand with the keys. "All right."

Sammy took Susan gently by the elbow and led her around her car to the passenger door. He inserted the key in the lock, opened the door, and helped her inside. Then he strolled around the back, let himself in the driver's side and started the engine.

Susan couldn't help noticing as they rounded the front of the building that Johnny Buscemi was still there, talking to the cop.

They both looked up and silently watched her car pass.

24

"So, what exactly is a Chaldean?" Susan asked Sammy over pancakes and coffee, as she tried not to stare at his face. Denny's fluorescents were bright as noontime and he was even more handsome in the light. "I'm kind of embarrassed that I don't know. I've looked it up in our encyclopedia, but there's nothing between Chain Stores and Chalk."

"What year is your encyclopedia from?" Sammy laughed.

"Compton's, 1949. I guess it belonged to my father. So, we're kind of frozen in amber since we've never bought a new one."

"Chain stores are in the encyclopedia?"

"I know! Isn't that funny? It seems that George H. Hartford came up with a line of food stores back in 1858. That became A & P."

"I love that you read the encyclopedia."

Susan blushed at the compliment. She watched Sammy eating with gusto. The earnestness of it made him look younger and she wondered what he was like as a boy.

"Did you know that chewing gum is mixed in a big vat?" She rambled on. "And bubble gum contains rubber latex?"

Sammy laughed again and wiped his mouth with his napkin. "I've never been a fan of the stuff, but you may have put me off of it forever."

"Well, I thought I might be misspelling Chaldean, so I leafed around a bit. Americans spend about a third as much money for chewing gum as they do for books. At least, that was true in 1949."

"You are a font of thirty-year-old information. I think you're ready for a TV game show."

"Yeah." She reddened again. "I kind of get lost in there."

"Well, maybe you should look up Mesopotamia."

"Is that where you're from?"

"It is. From a village in the north of Iraq. Tel Keppe. It means 'hill of stones.'"

"That sounds austere!" She laughed.

"Well, maybe it looks better than it sounds." He laughed too. God, he was beautiful when he laughed. "Anyway, it's pretty small, but not far from a bigger city called Mosul. It's another world from here."

"Is everyone there Chaldean?"

"Definitely not. Iraq is a melting pot, just like the U.S. Our groups have been around a lot longer, but, as a country, we happen to be newer."

"How did that happen?"

"Well, there was the Ottoman Empire, then the First World War, then the French and the English, and et cetera, et cetera, et cetera. You get the picture."

"Always colonized?"

"Actually, no! There once was a Chaldean Empire that ruled from 625 to 539 B.C. in the same Mesopotamian region. Glory days. Nowadays, Chaldeans are Catholic. But most of our countrymen are Muslim."

"So, what are you doing *here*?"

"This is the land of opportunity, or haven't you heard that one?"

"It rings a bell."

"In Detroit, Chaldeans run the grocery business."

"Like George H. Hartford!"

"Not quite. Our stores tend to be small and family-run. Party stores, as you call them in Michigan. That's really why I came—my parents were here. I was living in Paris when my father died, so I came to help my mother. Clan is important to Chaldeans."

"I'm sorry to hear about your father. My mother died too."

"An orphan recognizes his fellow."

"Is that a Chaldean saying?"

Sammy laughed. "No, I just made it up. I'm sorry you lost your mother."

"Thanks, Sammy." Susan took a sip of her coffee, which she cradled in both hands for warmth and to steady her fluttery fingers. "How does Detroit compare to your home?"

"Well, we've traded the Tigris and Euphrates for the Detroit River, sand for snow, and kebabs for Coney Island hot dogs. The food at home is better. And, definitely the weather. But, in the end, I think that people are people."

"I think that too. It's what I experienced in Paris."

"I knew you were a kindred spirit when I first saw you. But, when you said you'd lived in Paris, *oh la la*! I'd love to go back."

"Me too!"

"I felt more like myself there—like I could be whoever I wanted to be, not who my family or anyone else expected me to be."

"You're different, Sammy."

"Not really. I'm a dime a dozen. That's how you say it, right?"

"It is, but you're not."

"Well. I'm not so sure." Sammy grew silent. "Hey, guess what? We have a new president in Iraq. I'm pretty optimistic for the future. His name is Saddam Hussein and he's part of the pan-Arab movement. Have you studied the Middle East at all?"

"Not really. I guess I just don't feel I've finished with European history yet."

"They're pretty intertwined. You like movies, right? Watch *Lawrence of Arabia*."

"I've been meaning to. I love *Dr. Zhivago*, though. I mean, in terms of David Lean."

"You're a romantic."

Susan blushed again, all the way up to her hairline. "I guess I am."

Sammy rescued her by changing the subject. "Anyway, our new deputy prime minister is a fellow Chaldean. Tariq Aziz. My family knows his family. That's the deal with pan-Arabism. A larger Arab identity that's not so factionalized. I hope it happens."

"I do too, Sammy," Susan said, without fully knowing what she meant.

"Who knows? Maybe all the Detroit Chaldeans will go back to become Iraqi Chaldeans again."

"Do you think you'll go?" She hoped he wouldn't.

"I don't think I'm going anywhere. But I think you are."

"Well. I hope to."

"So, then what are you doing here?"

"My father's sick."

"No, I mean at this disco. What's a nice girl like you doing in a place like this?"

"That's the title of a Martin Scorsese short film."

"See what I mean? You really don't belong here. I mean it, why Frankie's?"

"I needed to work. I got a job at a boutique and met Annie, and—I don't know. One thing led to another and I followed her here."

"You don't seem like the following type."

"You don't really know me."

"Perhaps not. But, I've met college girls from Warren who are off working in Chicago or New York. You should be one of them."

"I just wanted to be home this summer. I don't know how much longer my father has."

"That, I understand."

"I probably shouldn't even go back to school, but my father made me promise. Normal wish from a normal father. But in our circumstances, it's hard to leave him."

"You sound like a good daughter."

"Well." Susan looked up at him. "You sound like a pretty good son."

"So, that's us. The dutiful children."

"God, Sammy. I hope we're more than that!" Susan said and took a bite of her now-cold pancakes.

* * *

Afterwards, Sammy gently held her arm again as he walked her back to her car. He helped her into the driver's seat, bent down, with a lock of his dark hair falling down over his dark eyes and kissed her. Not a sexy kiss, but a gentle variety sweet kiss that made her cry. Right there, in her car, in the parking lot of Denny's, as she looked out at a gas station and a blinking traffic light that had switched into its off hours' mode, tears ran down her face.

Sammy took both of his surprisingly soft hands and wiped her cheeks, from nose to ears, like a child. He smiled broadly, and his beautiful white teeth gleamed at her in the dark. The only thing that Susan could think to say was, "Grandmother! What big teeth you have!" And how Sammy knew this fairy tale, she couldn't rightly say, but nevertheless he responded, "The better to eat you with, my dear."

They both laughed that they had originated in such different parts of the world but knew the same stories. And Susan drove off into the night feeling that she had been seen for the first time. Truly seen. Not just as a pretty girl or a smart girl or a nice girl, but in her entirety, for all that she was and all that she could be.

It didn't even matter that a gun had peeked out from Sammy's waistband when he leaned in to kiss her. Perhaps it was the opposite. Perhaps the gun had made the moment feel more real to Susan than anything had in her life, thus far.

25

Susan sits in the dark again, this time in her living room in Watch Hill. Different room. Different chair. Same mental state. She watches the lighthouse turn, focusing her attention on the rhythmic regularity of its revolutions. She is using it as a metronome to calm her mind, to quell her fears.

It is not working.

Five days have passed since the highway of life has taken a novel turn. Susan, who had already traversed a few forks along that road, recognizes that she had grown complacent. The wariness with which she once had armed herself had lost its edge. She'd been asleep at the wheel, had not seen the other vehicle bearing down on her. That the vehicle had arrived in the form of a Ford Crown Victoria would have, at any other time, struck Susan as ironic.

She misses Jack. Her Jack. She had rested under his protective shield for so many years, even beyond his death, that she came to trust it to be there. She is afraid to think that it may have deserted her, that shield. She is afraid of everything right now.

She harnesses her mind toward her husband.

Brilliant. Visionary. Insightful. Generous. Funny. Kind. How many adjectives would Susan need to describe Jack Ford? How many adjectives

108

have you got? She had met him when she'd given up hope of ever meeting anyone, just like the clichés say. She had been in New York for sixteen years. She had made her life alone. She'd had friends, Jack Jr., for one, but she existed apart.

Jack was different from any man she'd known. The common wisdom was that women were the multi-taskers—through millennia of human evolution that fitted each sex for its role in the survival of the species, women had evolved to notice disparate sensory inputs and keep them properly sorted.

Men, on the other hand, were like horses wearing blinders. They charged forward, looking neither right nor left, into battle. This was their evolutionary adaptation and it, too, assured the continuation of the human race. Two sides of the coin, they complemented each other and created a functioning whole.

So the wisdom went.

Uniquely, Jack checked all of the boxes above. And, like so many others who had come under his influence, it would be impossible to quantify what Susan had learned from him. Much of her world-view had been formed at Jack's side, watching and emulating him.

Susan's husband had died five years ago of a massive heart attack. It was really the only way for a man like Jack to go. No lingering illness would have been tolerable to him, though Susan knew diseases weren't distributed based on a person's ability to withstand them. One fell swoop, one day in April, at the office, doing what he loved, and it was over. No defibrillator, no resuscitation. All in all, it was a good death for a man such as Jack. Charmed, just like his life. Susan and Jack Jr. were left to fend for themselves. Together, they ran the company. And, together, they were just about able to perform half as well as Jack Sr. had done, alone.

Susan stares at the water: at the alternating red and white glow from the lighthouse sweeping in a methodical loop, highlighting whitecaps and waves. She remembers the first time Jack took her out there at night.

Jack's captain had been at the helm. Venus was the name of his boat and she was as beautiful as that name would imply. Built in 1937 as a commuter yacht for a famous financier, Jack and his captain, Eric, had lovingly restored her to perfection.

They had gone out that night, cloudy as it was, because Jack said he had a surprise for her. They motored slowly through the long channel that leads out of the harbor of Watch Hill. Jack asked her to sit at the bow, on the recessed open deck seats at front.

The clouds dropped lower and morphed into fog. Thank God for sonar. The air was chilly and wet, but Jack had tucked them both in with blankets. Maybe it was raining or maybe it was the effect of moving through clouds. Like a carnival boat that floats on a track through a cardboard sky. A champagne bucket lay at their feet. Jack popped the cork and poured for them both.

He recounted some history of the illustrious Venus. "Shirley Temple celebrated her twelfth birthday aboard this boat. During World War II, she was commandeered by the coast guard, painted grey, and used to ferry FDR up and down the Hudson, to and from Hyde Park. After the war, the man who built her kept her for a while but eventually lost interest. She was down in Stuart, Florida when I bought her. The worms were this long."

Jack held his hands about two feet apart to indicate the length of the worms that were crawling in Venus's wood.

"Stop!" Susan laughed. "I think you told me that story before and the worms were only six inches long!"

"Oh. They were?" Jack laughed. Venus moved seamlessly, her enormous engines roaring behind them, thrumming a steady vibration all through the boat. From where they were sitting, they could not see Captain Eric at the helm. Susan wondered if he could see the two of them.

"Darling. Do you know why I brought you out here tonight?"

"Not really, no. But I'm not complaining."

Jack reached down to retrieve a small, shiny navy bag, tied with a white ribbon. "Do you recognize this?"

"No. Am I failing a quiz?"

Jack laughed and handed it to her. "This is a Betteridge bag—from one of my favorite stores in Greenwich. Why don't you open it?"

"All right." Susan took the bag into her hands and untied the ribbon. Inside, was a box, also wrapped in glossy navy paper with another white ribbon. "Is it like Russian nesting dolls? A box within a box within a box?"

"Why don't you find out?" He laughed again.

God, she misses laughing with him.

Inside the box Susan found the most exquisite pair of earrings she had ever seen. Each earring had three stones—graduating in size from slightly smaller than a pea to a little bigger than two peas—arranged in an off-balance way. The stones, from what she could see in the dim light, were pale blue. Tiny dark stones were scattered among the larger ones. "These are so beautiful. What are they?"

"Seaman Schepps—another favorite of mine. The stones are moon-stones. I was hoping for a moonlit night to give them to you, but I don't always get my wish."

"You don't? From the looks of your life, I'd say you usually get what you wish for, Jack."

"Well, darling, going forward, much of that will depend on you."

Grief, like a low, slow moan, permeates Susan.

She longs for Jack. She misses him in a visceral way, like a toxin that moves through her muscles. She remembers that when he died, she lay in bed shaking for days. Just shaking. It was that physical sensation that had nearly unhinged her. She had steeled herself for the heartache. The pain was ferocious, yet she had expected it. But she had not anticipated the tremors. Her doctor had prescribed potassium and magnesium. He said she was dehydrated. He said this was grief. He said to be patient—there was nothing for it but time.

Tonight, she is back in that place as if not a day had elapsed.

Susan rises and walks to the bar off of the sunroom. She drops to her knees, opens the liquor cabinet and stares at the bottles. She thinks back to the summer of 1979, the summer she has run from all these years—the summer that has reared its gruesome head this week. She slams the cabinet closed.

Jack Jr. is upstairs, asleep in his room. Tomorrow is D-Day. Together, they will drive to Boston to see the FBI. He will be with her to answer their questions about Sammy. He will support her when she repeats the story to the agents. Provenzano—the good cop, DelVecchio—the inquisitor. Jack Jr. has always been there for her. She does not know what she would do without him now.

Susan opens the cabinet again and places her hand on the cool side of a bottle of bourbon. She extracts the bottle quietly, as though Jack, both Jacks, the ghost and the man, might hear her, and touches the same cool side to her cheek, first one, then the other.

She again tells herself she has nothing to fear. It will all be smooth sailing tomorrow because Jack Jr. will be with her. He will help her make it clear to the FBI that she does not know Sammy Fakhouri anymore. She meant to say precisely that when she said she didn't know him. She meant not *anymore*. When they understand that, she will be able to return to the life that she made with Jack.

And the subject of Johnny need never come up.

The shaking is spreading to her arms now and traveling down her legs.

Susan opens the top of the bottle; she smells the bourbon inside. She sets it down on the floor beside her, then she picks it up again. She brings the bottle to her lips. She tells herself that these are extraordinary circumstances that call for extraordinary measures. She remembers the phrase: These are the times that try men's souls. Was it from typing class? History? She doesn't remember. It doesn't matter.

She has kept hold of herself all this time, through her lonely years, her married years, her widowhood, she has remained in control. Even when Jack died and she lay in bed, trembling. She heaves herself up and moves to the window, taking the long way around, avoiding the open bottle she has left on the floor.

The lighthouse is there, always there, turning. It never stops. What normally anchors her only serves to unmoor her now.

She grasps at her memory trick. She works to drag her mind from the present moment into a past event, one that will recalibrate her equilibrium. She struggles for a good one, the best one really, the one she uses sparingly. She trots out the recollection of the night she met her husband.

The night her life changed. The night she turned the final corner away from the ugly "before" and toward the beautiful "after."

Susan mentally wrenches herself back to that hot July evening in New York. She places herself in the setting: French restaurant, Meat Packing district, cobblestone streets, steam rising up from the manholes. She turns her imaginary self to face the façade of the restaurant. She can see the wall of glass, the name, Florent, in neon. She walks herself through the door, past the other tables, all the way to the back to find their group.

She had been friends—close friends—with Jack Jr. for a few years by that point, but she had never met his father. No reason, really. It just hadn't happened.

She seats herself at the table, on the banquette side in back. It was Bastille Day. The room was singing *la Marseillaise*. Jack Jr. told everyone that someone was coming. He asked Susan to make room. She does that in her mind, now, slides to the right on the bench.

Jack Jr. was always her hero. His chivalry, yet again, shone through. He had once picked her up from the subway floor. That night in New York, he picked her up from her own, lonely life by placing his father right next to her.

Had Jack Jr. known they would fall in love? Had he hoped for it? Had he regretted it at all? Susan has asked him this many times over the years, but he has remained coy.

Anyway, it does not matter his intent. That night, Jack and Susan met. That night, silly as it sounds for people their age—she, thirty-eight, he, fifty-seven—they both experienced that thunderbolt, that crazy *coup de foudre*. Jack Sr. had walked into the room and he and Susan had locked eyes and all her years of solitude and sadness had floated up through the ceiling of the restaurant.

Susan searches for the magic of that moment. She scans her mental movie to find the image of Jack approaching. The length of his stride. The color of his clothes. The blue of his eyes. Something specific like that will root her, ground her, start the film rolling and get her the hell out of where she is right now.

Her thoughts become increasingly jumbled and frantic. Her game is not working. Even this, the practiced reminiscence of her first meeting with Jack, the ace in her deck of card tricks is failing her tonight.

She cannot escape where she is right now—here in the room by the window facing the lighthouse alone. Jack Jr. is upstairs. Jack Sr. is dead. Sammy Fakhouri is being held somewhere by the FBI. Johnny Buscemi is wandering around New York.

No trick of memory can save her.

26

Thursday, August 16, 1979
Suburban Detroit

Susan turned away from the service bar, where she was waiting for drinks, in order to watch a particularly graceful couple at the center of the dance floor. The girl moved so effortlessly that Susan recognized a fellow ballerina.

Tonight, the mood at Frankie's was electric. France Joli pulsed over the speakers; an orchestra of violins lifting her sultry *Come to Me* into every dark and dingy corner of the bar. On the floor, couples danced elegantly. Dancing at Frankie's was a thing of beauty. The grace exuded by couples doing the Hustle under the disco ball elevated the place out of its surroundings, and looked, from a certain angle, ethereal.

The girls wore colorful leotards and matching Qiana skirts that wrapped around and tied at the waist. When the men spun the girls, and they did this often, the skirts lifted and revealed legs and leotards underneath. They always danced in heels. Some of them opted for Candies, Annie's shoe of choice. But many of them wore Capezio character shoes—high heels with straps favored by Broadway dancers.

The DJ seamlessly switched to Thelma Houston's *Don't Leave Me This Way*, another anthem of love and longing. The couple that Susan was watching twirled effervescently, heads held high, smiling radiantly.

"Get your head outta the clouds!" barked Sherry, Susan's self-appointed watchdog. She was standing far too close for Susan's comfort and Susan backed up as much as she could in the small area at the side of the bar.

"Excuse me?"

"Jesus, Mary, and Joseph, get me out of this backwater," Sherry spoke to the ceiling like a Christian martyr before turning her gaze to Susan. "Have you seen Diane?"

"No. I haven't seen her at all this week. Was she on the schedule?"

"Listen, missy, don't you worry about the schedule. You're just here to do your job. Can you manage that?"

"I'm sorry. I was just wondering."

"Well, wonder about this—there's some bimbo barfing in the bathroom. Get the bucket and clean it up!"

What was Susan going to say? *No? Do it yourself?* At least it was a good excuse to get away from Sherry.

"Sure," Susan said, "but I have this order to deliver."

"I'll do that. You go get the bucket."

Susan surrendered her tray to Sherry. "This goes to table ten."

Susan made her way through the tightly packed crowd, talking, laughing, sloshing drinks all over the floor and themselves, and elbowed herself toward the kitchen. She expected to find the bucket in a small broom closet down the back hall, past the large food storage room and close to where the Castiglione brothers had their office.

Pushing her way through the swinging doors, Susan noticed her watch was missing. What a stupid girl she was! She should not be wearing her mother's Longines watch when she came to work at Frankie's. She knew that, of course, yet it had not stopped her from doing it. Wearing that watch felt like armoring herself with a shield from her own very different—and, superior, to use Annie's word—life.

Clearly, the shield had not worked. She'd checked the clasp as she always did; it must have loosened anyway. It would be impossible to find during work hours; she would need to tell the cleaning crew to keep an eye out for it later. Disgusted with her own imprudence, Susan held her naked wrist with her opposite hand as she turned to head down the back hall toward the broom closet.

Frankie's Disco had only one office that the three brothers shared. Carmine, rarely present at night, used it during the day. Vito began his evenings there, reviewing the books that Carmine kept, before settling into his perch at the corner table with Johnny Buscemi, Officer Danny, and the rest of his crew. Frankie wasn't really the office type, so Susan was surprised to see the light on and Frankie standing facing someone she couldn't see from the way the door was positioned, half closed. She truly, deeply wished that she wouldn't keep running into Frankie, back of house.

Annie's voice rose above the disco music, still audible but less throbbing at this distance. Annie's voice, in fact, could be heard above quite a lot of noise right now, ringing strident and sharp as it moved from entreaty to threat.

"Frankie, just tell me!" she shrieked. "I know you're sleeping with Sherry. Tell me, Frankie! Why don't you just *tell* me?" Annie was talking rapidly. Far too rapidly to Susan's ear. She must be high on cocaine tonight. She was probably high every night now. Susan clutched her watchless wrist even tighter.

"C'mon, baby, c'mere."

Susan had to hand it to Frankie for trying the charm route. It really was one of his best tools.

"Frankie, don't touch me! Just tell me! I need you to *tell* me." The door was creaking slowly backward, exposing Annie in her florid state.

"Aw, Annie, c'mon, I love you, baby." Susan could tell he was nearing his limit. She prayed that Annie had the sense God gave her to notice the same thing, but knew it wasn't likely.

"Frankie, Goddamn it! I said don't touch me! I'll scream, Frankie! Honest to God, I'll scream!"

"Who gives a shit if you scream?" Susan could practically hear Frankie's tether snapping. "What the fuck is that supposed to mean? We're in the goddamn back of a goddamn disco, for Christ's sake. Scream, baby, scream!" Frankie started laughing maniacally. Maybe he was on coke, too.

Susan was coming to see herself as the Olivia de Havilland character in the movie, *Snakepit*, descending ever deeper into the levels of madness surrounding her. Here she was again, an audience of one in a theatre from which she wished she could exit. Standing still was really the only option. The doorknob to the broom closet was near, but any move toward it might have caught Frankie's eye. Maybe she'd died and gone to hell and was doomed to repeat these voyeuristic scenes with Frankie and the various women in his life for all eternity.

"Tell me, Frankie! Tell me! Tell me! Tell me!" Annie resumed her refrain. Susan thought she might scream herself, her nerves were frayed to breaking. She saw Frankie look at the unhinged Annie, squint into her face, and then she watched him lift his left arm and, almost in slow motion, haul off and backhand her, hard, across the face.

The relief Susan felt at seeing her friend get hit in the face surprised and shamed her. A woman seeing another woman slapped should feel nothing but revulsion. Susan was appalled but she was also grateful that Annie had finally shut up. The benefit of the doubt that Susan had granted Annie from the first moment she'd met her had ebbed since their ugly fight in the car. And she'd never seen anyone in the state that Annie had been in just now. Some outside force *had* to be employed to stop her. And that force was Frankie. *Deus ex machina* in a disco.

His left hand had struck her on the left cheek. Susan saw the blood before she noticed that Frankie was wearing a diamond pinkie ring. The blood popped from Annie's perfect cheekbone and ran in a straight line down the side of her face and onto her neck. There it bloomed in a red starburst, like a Rorschach test, on her white shirt collar, creeping toward the knot of her tie.

The force of the slap had rotated Annie's face toward Susan. Her eyes were huge and round as she turned them speechlessly to her friend. And that, in turn, drew Frankie's regard in the same direction. Once more, Susan was staring eye to eye with Frankie and a woman with whom he was having an intimate moment.

It was Annie who broke the stare down with three words, delivered staccato-like, each word punctuated by a full stop. "Fuck. You. Susan," she said, then she turned to Frankie, crying like a little girl. Frankie, sensing his opportunity, took Annie into his arms and gently closed the office door with his foot.

Susan was alone in the hall near the broom closet. She felt a surge of repugnance and rage, which compelled her to bolt in the direction of the employee's bathroom where, she too—like the inebriated patron in the front hall ladies' room—threw up into the toilet.

She threw up until she dry-heaved. And when she was finished, she laid her cheek on the seat of the filthy toilet and stared at the names scratched on the stall wall. She had no intention of cleaning up the vomit of the patron in front. She had no intention of getting up. She had no intention of any kind at this moment, other than to rest her head on the toilet seat and read the graffiti—the names and initials of those who had loved and lived, for a time, in this God-forsaken bar.

27

Wednesday, August 13, 2014
Watch Hill

Susan awakens to the sound of birds. Seagulls are swooping overhead, calling out ownership of gable perches and fighting over oysters. The noise is harsh and provokes a pain in her head that matches the stiffness in her body. A wave of sick remorse overtakes her when she opens her eyes to discover that she is lying on the floor of the bar, her cheek pressed into the bottle cap. She is falling apart, when she can least afford it. She drags herself up, closes the wretched bottle, cleans up the scene and hurries to her room before Jack Jr. wakes.

An hour later, Jack navigates his black on black Mercedes SL northward, from Watch Hill to Boston. Susan sits back and rests her eyes behind her black-on-black sunglasses. She hopes, this way, to avoid conversation. Jack Jr. tends to be talkative.

They have left early to allow time for the unforeseen. Which pretty much sums up events of late. Susan wouldn't be surprised to see Santa Claus and the Easter Bunny driving the opposite way down the highway.

Jack locates the large, midcentury brick building at One Center Plaza with no difficulty and parks in the garage. They have more than an hour's wait until Susan's scheduled interview.

They are faced with two time-killing choices: to the left is the Kinsale Irish Pub, which, at this early hour, is closed. That narrows the field to the deli on their right, which goes by the name of Finagle A Bagel.

"That's funny," Jack says, without laughing, as he holds the door for Susan. Jack enjoys an everything bagel with everything on it. Susan orders coffee and lets it grow cold.

"Look, this is just a courtesy." Jack reads her wariness. A blindfolded man could perceive Susan's anxiety right now. "You're here to be polite."

"Thanks, Son."

"Of course, Mom. It *will* be all right."

"You're the best."

"I know." Jack consults his watch. It is half an hour before Susan's appointment time. "Shall we? Early in, early out. Maybe we can get in nine holes this afternoon?"

"Yes." Susan's voice is barely above a whisper. "No point sitting here."

"C'mere." Jack embraces her in a big bear hug when they are out on the sidewalk. "I know you're upset. But it *is* all going to be all right."

"Oh, Jack. Thank you." She allows herself to touch the cheek of this man who is, in many ways, still a child. Yet, will never be *her* child. "Thank you for everything."

The building is nondescript. There is no sign in the lobby to indicate the presence of the FBI. It could be a building filled with dentists, but this is the address they were given.

They cross the lobby to the elevator and enter with a small group, asking someone to hit the button for the sixth floor. As they rise, fellow riders slowly vacate the car. When they are the last ones on the elevator, one floor to go, Jack turns to Susan, "You okay? You look a little wrecked. If I didn't know better, I'd say you tied one on last night."

"Good thing you know me better than that."

The elevator stops at six, pings softly, and the doors sigh open. Susan and Jack emerge and are confronted by two very large men, police officers in uniform, in front of an enormous wall sign announcing the Federal Bureau of Investigation. One officer sits at a desk to the left and the other mans the metal detector. They are cordial, smiling. Jack and Susan are told to proceed through the security apparatus.

Susan summarily opens her gun-free purse for a bag check, places it on the conveyor belt, and walks through the arched device. Jack Jr. follows.

It is only steps to the reception desk where they announce themselves to the young woman seated there. She checks their IDs, asks them to sign in, and waves her arm to indicate the general direction of the chairs.

Jack is, of course, wearing a suit: navy Prince of Wales check, white spread collar shirt, red silk knot cufflinks, and a pale blue tie. Brown shoes. As always, he looks good, very much in the mold of his father.

Susan has chosen a dress of tan linen, a nondescript color, one that she thinks sets the right tone. She wears her gold shrimp earrings—Seaman Schepps, in honor of Jack Sr.—her wedding rings, and her Longines watch. No other jewelry. Brown ostrich pumps and a brown ostrich bag complete her discreet look—a little brown mouse. Albeit a well-dressed mouse.

There is a large wall clock hanging over the receptionist's head. Nine forty a.m.—twenty minutes to go. Jack alternates between checking his iPhone and rifling through papers that he has brought along in his briefcase. Susan merely sits. From time to time, Jack casts a glance at her, motionless, beside him. Once or twice, he squeezes her hand.

At ten minutes to ten, Special Agent Provenzano, the tall one, the good cop, opens the door to the right of the receptionist and warmly greets Susan and Jack. He thanks them for their punctuality and ushers them down a short hall and into a small room.

Save for a large mirror, which probably indicates a viewing room on the other side of the wall, this room has no décor—no photos or prints, no rug, no lamp. A plain metal table and chairs are the final cue to visitors that this is not a social call. There is a window in the door, so passersby and the room's inhabitants can see each other clearly. Jack sits next to Susan on one side of the table and Special Agent Provenzano takes the opposite seat. One chair remains empty.

"Good morning, Mrs. Ford," Provenzano, ever amiable, repeats what he'd said in the hall. "Mr. Ford. Thank you both for coming in today."

"Of course," Susan answers.

Jack Jr. adds, "Just reminding everyone that I am here as Mrs. Ford's stepson. This is unofficial. Everyone understands that?"

"Certainly, Mr. Ford. This is a friendly visit." Agent Provenzano smiles in a friendly way.

"Will your partner be joining us this morning?" Susan looks at the empty chair.

"Oh, Agent DelVecchio?" Provenzano appears not to have considered this possibility. "Well, he may. Or he may not."

"I see," she says, though she really doesn't.

"But let's talk about you, Mrs. Ford. Have you given any thought to Mr. Fakhouri?"

"Yes, in fact, I have. I do remember him now. He was a patron of a restaurant where I worked as a college student."

"A restaurant?"

"Yes, it was a restaurant. Dinner was served. There was music, as well."

"Like a supper club?" Provenzano asks.

"Like that," Susan answers.

"And you knew Mr. Fakhouri in a professional capacity only?"

"He was a patron. He was friendly. We chatted."

"I see. Do you have any idea why we might be interested in Mr. Fakhouri now, Mrs. Ford?"

"None whatsoever. I can assure you of that."

"Do you have any idea why he might have been on his way to your house last week?"

"No."

"Look." Jack had been quiet to this point. "Why don't you give us a little help here? In view of efficiency."

Provenzano turns to him. "Well. With efficiency in mind, I'll give you a little recap on why we're here today. Mr. Fakhouri was picked up on his way to see Mrs. Ford directly after he returned to the U.S. from Iraq.

"To get right to it, Samuel Fakhouri has been spending some time in recent months in the north of Iraq. He's from there, after all. From the north, near Mosul. Did you know that? Mosul, the place that's in the papers every day now?"

Susan hesitates. Then she lies. "Not really. I don't think so."

Jack is slowly turning his neck to look at the face of his stepmother.

"A village called Tel Keppe." Agent Provenzano continues. "That's where ISIS is on a rampage this summer. And the people they've been killing in that region are the Chaldeans. Yazidis and others too. But the Chaldean people are Samuel Fakhouri's people. So, Fakhouri traveled from Baghdad to Mosul to Mehran. Mehran is about three hundred miles from Mosul but it happens to be in the country of Iran. We believe Fakhouri crossed that border, and then navigated back again into Iraq. As you can imagine, this is of note to the United States."

Jack Jr. speaks. "I can certainly appreciate our government's interest in Mr. Fakhouri's movements, but I don't really see what that has to do with my stepmother."

"Exactly what we're wondering, as well." Provenzano pauses here. He stands up and wanders around the room, before turning back to Susan and Jack. "We've taken the liberty to learn some things about you, Mrs. Ford. You studied at Lake Erie College, in Painesville, Ohio, isn't that right?"

"Yes. That's right."

"Class of nineteen eighty. Is that correct?"

"Yes."

"Our research hits a bit of an impasse somewhere along about when you were working at the, um, supper club. You worked there in the summer of nineteen seventy-nine. Is that correct?"

"Yes. I worked at Frankie's Discothèque that summer."

"Yes. Yes. A discothèque. That's what it was. Not so much a supper club as a discothèque?"

"Where are you going with this?" Jack asks.

"We're just trying to understand why Mr. Fakhouri would fly all the way back from his little sojourn in Iran and Iraq this summer and we find ourselves thinking about the events of the summer of nineteen seventy-nine."

"If you have a specific question, please ask it," says Jack.

"Of course, I don't mean to stretch your patience, Mr. Ford." Agent Provenzano returns to his chair. "Just a little question, first, not the big question, probably nothing to do with anything. We've looked into your school records and seem to come to a little hole. We can't find any mention of you going back to school after the summer of nineteen seventy-nine. We can't find any records of you having graduated from Lake Erie College in nineteen eighty. So, we find ourselves wondering, and I have to ask you, did you go back to college, Mrs. Ford?"

In all their years of friendship, Susan knows that she has never told Jack that she dropped out of college. Why hadn't she ever mentioned it? Told in a different context, it wouldn't seem to be such a big deal. But now, here, with everything else, a fact like that would appear to carry weight on the scale of significant life events. It is something you would mention to a good friend—your best friend, to be precise.

Jack turns, full body, in his chair, to study her.

"No." Susan says it flat out, just like that. She casts a quick glance at Jack Jr. and sees it all over his face. She is losing his trust. "Jack, I..." She, too, turns, and speaks directly to him, ignoring the FBI agent across the table. "I'm sorry I never mentioned this. It's true. I didn't return to college. My friend died. And then my father died. I did not return to college. I just didn't. And I didn't ever know how to talk about it."

Jack cuts a quick glance at Provenzano and tersely says to Susan, "Let's talk about this later."

"Well," Provenzano says. "I didn't mean to upset you, Mrs. Ford. I like to look at a case like a jigsaw puzzle, see what all the pieces are before I can understand how they fit together. Let me ask you another question about that time. Would this friend who died, happen to have been Annie Nelson, who also worked at Frankie's Discothèque during that same summer?"

"Yes. My friend, Annie Nelson, died at the end of the summer. And I did not return to college. I meant to. I wanted to. Annie died. Then my father died later that year. And then time passed. I never went back. I'm not proud of that. I don't normally tell people." She looks back at Jack when she says this.

"I'm sorry, Mrs. Ford, to probe into subjects that are unpleasant for you. But I'm trying to understand the connection to Mr. Fakhouri."

"Of course." Susan's voice is barely audible.

"We're doing some research into that period of Fakhouri's life, the time when your life intersected with his. Newspaper articles on microfiche, that sort of thing."

"Can we come to a point here?" Jack is flustered, off balance, talking a little too loudly.

"The point is: did Samuel Fakhouri have anything to do with Miss Nelson's death? Could her death have been a homicide? And I must be honest here, Mrs. Ford, we are wondering just what you might know about that."

"You know what? I think we need a recess. I'd like some time to confer with my stepmother." Jack says this in a rush, casting a cool eye on Susan, his stepmother and longtime friend, who is—she is vividly aware—showing herself to be more and more of a liar as the days roll by.

28

Tuesday, August 28, 1979
Suburban Detroit

Susan was going on a date! An official date with Sammy. He'd called her at home the day before and they'd arranged it for her night off. He would not say where they were going but suggested she dress casually. That, in and of itself, was a minefield. What did he mean by casual? Jeans? Corduroys? A dress? She rifled through her closet, from one end to the next, then back again to repeat. He'd also encouraged her to bring a sweater.

Susan had even told her father. She didn't tell him everything—Chaldean might be too much to explain right now. But, she had told him the important things. 1. Sammy's first name. 2. The fact that he was nice. 3. The fact that he was smart. 4. Well, no, she didn't mention how handsome he was. Her father was suspicious of a good-looking man.

Her father had asked where Sammy had gone to college and she could honestly say she didn't know. But she assured him that she would find out. Her father had soon tired, she'd kissed him goodnight, and promised to pop in when she got home.

She moved over to her dresser to look at her sweaters. The infamous black cowl neck appeared at the back of a drawer. Susan yanked it out and laughed, imagining herself with Sammy, in this sweater upside down. "Nope," she said to herself. "Not tonight."

Finally, she landed on a dress. A wrap dress like Annie had worn the first day she had met her, what felt like a lifetime ago. The shape was flattering, the color was good on her—a swirly emerald and white—and, with flats, it would look more casual. Some lipstick, blush, and mascara, and a little shake of her hair. She liked it short, no matter what her father said. She *did* think it made her look European.

The doorbell rang.

Susan took one last look in the full-length mirror on the back of her bedroom door and saw that she'd been wrong. The dress looked stupid with flats. She kicked them off as quickly as she could and dropped down to search through her shoes.

The doorbell rang again.

She grabbed a pair of Candies and went back to the full-length mirror. How did Annie walk in these stupid things all the time? Deciding she looked good, she grabbed her sweater and purse and headed down the hall.

"Hi," she said as she opened the door to Sammy, in his usual black pants and shirt.

"You look beautiful," he said, smiling. His smile always got her. "Really beautiful, Susan."

"Thank you, Sammy. Um…" she began. "Do you want to come in?"

"No. I mean, we need to get going."

"Okay." She stepped out the door. "Is there a start time to whatever we're doing?"

"There is, in fact." Sammy leaned in to kiss her. He was always leaning since he was so tall. "Come on!"

He led her to his shiny, black car. Of course, his car would be black.

"Nice car!" Susan said. "I don't think I've really seen it before."

"This is my baby. Nineteen sixty-nine Mustang. I take very good care of her. Shall I put the top down?"

"Sure! I mean, if we have time."

"I'll be fast." Sammy got to work and moved forward and back, lowering the hood and tucking it into its place. In no time, he helped Susan in the passenger door and hopped inside his own. Then he roared the engine to life.

"Wow! That's quite a motor." Susan laughed.

"Well, maybe I've doctored it a bit," Sammy said proudly. "Would you like some heat? There's nothing like an open car on a summer night with the heat on."

"That sounds wonderful!"

They drove for a long while, west into neighborhoods she did not know.

"Where are we going?"

"Ah, *ma belle*, it's a surprise, remember?"

Susan wished she could prolong this forever—this ride in the car with the heat from below and the cool above as the sun was starting to set. She really did not need to get anywhere. She knew, once they arrived, the clock would start ticking and this evening would come to an end. She imagined them driving forever and time not moving at all.

Just as the sun dipped beyond the horizon, Sammy turned into a driveway. There, looming in front of them, was an enormous art deco slab. At the top, in neon, were the words, "Ford-Wyoming."

"What's this?" She asked him. "Where are we?"

"This, *ma belle*, is a drive-in!" Sammy announced with a flourish of his hand. "We're in Dearborn and we're going to the movies. But, we're going to sit in my car!"

Susan craned her neck around to find a marquee. To the right she saw it. There, in big black letters:

DAVID LEAN
DOUBLE FEATURE
DR. HIVAGO
LAWRENCE OF ARABIA
1 SHOWING ONLY
TONIGHT
9 PM

"Oh, Sammy! This is the best!"

It was the first time she'd seen him blush. "Do you like it?" he asked shyly.

"I do! It's really perfect."

He looked back at the marquee. "I guess they didn't have a 'Z' for Zhivago."

"It doesn't matter." And it didn't. Sammy had created this evening specifically and perfectly for her.

"Shall we go in?"

As much as she didn't want their car ride to end, she did want to see these movies with Sammy. "Yes. Let's go in."

Sammy turned the wheel of his Mustang and drove them into the theatre, out under the open sky.

They found a spot and pulled up to the stand with speakers.

"Want to get some popcorn?" He asked.

"That sounds great." They walked across the lot—holding hands like sweethearts—to the little concession building. Cars were trickling in, but the place was sparsely filled. "I guess not a lot of people are interested in these old films."

"Wouldn't it be fun to have the place to ourselves?" Sammy asked as he opened the door. He ushered Susan to the popcorn line and handed her a twenty-dollar bill. "Listen, I need to go find a pay phone."

That was a startling departure from the flow of the evening for Susan.

"Just get some popcorn and I'll be right back. All right?" He smiled at her. "Don't worry. I just need to check in with my cousin. Remember Jacob? The hand kisser?"

Susan laughed but still, she felt uneasy. "Sure. How could I forget?"

"Can you move up?" a man behind her asked. "The line is moving."

"Oh, sorry." Susan edged forward.

"I'll be back in under two minutes," Sammy said, as he gave her a peck and turned to leave the building.

Susan waited in line. She could not help wondering what she would do if Sammy never returned. She was very far from home, an hour away at least. She had the twenty and some change in her purse. Would she have enough for a taxi? There was no one at home she could call. Not her dad. Not Annie, who was on the schedule at Frankie's tonight and, anyway, had become increasingly distant. Her mind drifted back to her old boyfriend, Todd, and her long-lost friend, Christina. She certainly couldn't call them.

"Lady." The man behind tapped her shoulder. "Can you move up?"

"Sure." She stepped forward again.

"Listen." Sammy appeared next to her, but his smile had disappeared. "I don't even know how to tell you this. We've got to go."

"What?"

"I'm sorry. Come on." He grabbed her elbow and walked her to the door, through it and toward the car. She felt like a zombie. None of it made any sense.

Inside the Mustang, he detached the drive-in speaker and started the car with the same roar. It rang hollow to Susan now. How could the evening have gone so badly, when it had started out so well? She sat, staring forward, and Sammy was stonily silent.

"Susan, listen," he finally said. "I have a crazy, complicated life. There's a problem at one of our stores and I need to go help my cousin."

"Sure." Her voice came out as a squeak. "It's fine. No problem."

"Susan, I know it's not fine. I'm sorry. I hate when this happens, but I can't leave Jacob alone here. I've got to go help him out."

"What's happening?"

"I…Look. I can't really talk about work stuff. Okay? I'm sorry."

"You're sorry a lot tonight." She knew she sounded petulant.

"I am. I'm truly sorry. Please let me make it up to you. Please?" Sammy reached over and placed his hand on her leg. This was all so strange. Dream dates begun and suspended in minutes. "Susan?"

"What?" Her mother would have chastised her for answering so snappishly.

"Please forgive me. I know you're disappointed. I am too. I'm sorry. I really have to do this."

"It's fine."

"It's not fine. But, it's the best I can do right now."

They drove the rest of the way to her house in silence. Sammy walked her to the door and kissed her. But, she could tell that he was distracted.

"Goodnight, my beauty. I promise you, I'll make it up to you." He touched a little piece of her hair and felt it between his fingers. "I love your hair."

"You do?" In the middle of this ruined date, it made her feel better that he liked her hair. He was probably the only one who did.

"I do." And he kissed her again with more feeling.

"Goodnight, Sammy." She broke away and turned to let herself in.

Sammy waited until she'd unlocked the door, opened it and shut it behind her. Then, he sprinted to his car. He actually ran. She watched him from the window in the door.

29

Wednesday, September 5, 1979

The moon, in its nearly twenty-eight-day orbit, had almost returned to its fullest since the day when the girls had set off for the mall. Tomorrow, the moon would be full. Tomorrow, Susan would drive back to college. Tomorrow, summer would officially be over.

She had given her notice at Frankie's and worked her last night on Sunday, the eve of Labor Day. There had been no cake, no farewell party, no acknowledgment that she would soon be gone. There had been no pool of interns, also returning to college, with whom she could go out for a celebratory drink. Sherry did not say goodbye. Neither did Annie and Frankie. She hadn't seen Diane for weeks.

Susan had cleaned up her station alone, slid her tray into the tray rack alone, and, alone, she had prepared to leave Frankie's for the last time.

She had changed out of her uniform and folded it into the ragged Bonwit Teller bag, tossing both into the industrial waste bin outside the kitchen door. Arcing high, up and over the side of the dumpster, she watched them disappear.

Annie had shown no signs of returning to her own studies, whatever those might have been. Susan felt a cringing embarrassment at having been witness to the raw passion of Frankie and Annie's romance. She did not know what Annie felt. Their friendship appeared to be over.

And Sammy. Where *were* things going with Sammy? He had been the bright spot of Susan's summer. His beautiful eyes, his beautiful smile, his beautiful mind. But he cast a few shadows as well. He had waited in the parking lot for Susan that night. She saw him leaning against her car, head tossed back, looking up. Her gaze followed his to the starry sky above them.

"It's beautiful," she said.

"Ah, *ma belle*. It's not like at home. There, from the desert, you can see the whole bowl of the sky filled with stars. Here, there's too much ambient light from the city."

"I'd like to see that."

"Someday, I'll show it to you."

"That would be nice." She waited for Sammy to say something. Something concrete and tangible regarding their future. Something resembling a commitment. She wondered what had happened to him on their date last week and found it strange that they hadn't discussed it since. But, she would not be the one to bring it up.

"All right, *mademoiselle*." Sammy walked Susan around to the passenger side of her car. "*On y va?*"

"*Oui.*" Susan was glad to vacate the premises of Frankie's Disco. "*On y va.*"

Sammy got into the driver's seat and started the car. The radio was playing Donna Summers's *Last Dance*.

"This is too good to be true," he said.

"What?"

"You know, all this summer in a discothèque, and you and I have never danced?"

"Is that what you're proposing now?"

"It is."

Sammy cranked up the sound and hopped out of the car. He went around to open Susan's door and extended his hand to her. "Last dance. Last chance for love. Yes, it's my last chance for romance tonight," Sammy sang along with Donna Summers. He was off-key, but that only made the effect more touching.

Susan reached up and took his hand. "I never knew you could sing."

"Like I said," Sammy studiously placed his hands on her in a formal, old-fashioned dance pose—one on her waist and the other holding her right hand aloft. "It's good to retain a little mystery."

"I think you've retained more than a little."

Sammy moved closer to her, pressing his body against hers as he sang very softly, "I need you. By me. Beside me. To guide me." Susan relaxed her hold on herself and rested her head on his shoulder. As moments go, this one was near perfect. It went pretty far in helping her forget their broken date.

Then the tempo picked up—the thump-thumps vibrating out of Susan's little car. Sammy shifted effortlessly to lead her into the hustle. Susan followed without missing a beat.

"And I didn't know *you* could dance," Sammy said, spinning her.

"You never asked."

"I'm glad to discover your secret here in the parking lot." Sammy spun her around and then did it again and again, until Susan was breathless from laughter.

Sammy slowed to a stop. He took Susan's face in his hands. "Susan of many secrets," he softly said to her.

"You're pretty secretive yourself," she responded.

Sammy brushed his hands down the sides of her face, along her neck, across her shoulders, to rest on her arms. Gently, ever so gently, he pulled her closer.

"Last dance. Last chance for love," Sammy whispered. "Susan. May I ask you something now?"

Susan felt her stomach flip. "All right."

"I haven't told you everything about my life. You can see that, I know. There are parts of it that I just need to sort out and, now that I've met you, I'm going to try to do that. You don't know what I'm talking about."

"No."

"No matter. You only need to know that since I met you, I feel like I can see a future that I haven't been able to see in a very long time."

"I've felt that way too."

"So, I'm going to ask you to promise me something. Like your father asked you."

"To go back to college?"

"Not that!" Sammy laughed. "It sounds crazy, but if things don't go the way I plan—if anything gets messed up—I want you to meet me, Susan. In one year. In Paris."

The brutality of it made her sick. "I don't understand. Don't you want to see me anymore?"

"I do! I haven't felt this way about anyone. *Ever*. I just…I don't know…there are things going on and…I know it's a lot to ask."

"Sammy, what are you saying? I thought we felt the same way. I…are you ending it?"

"I'm not! I promise you, I'm not! I love you, Susan."

So, there it was, exactly what she'd been waiting for—his little gift—but all wrapped up in a package of loss. Why was there always loss? "I don't understand why you're saying it like this. One year? What is that supposed to mean?"

"I can't really tell you. Maybe it's stupid. I fully intend to see you but—I just—if we lose each other somehow, I just want to know that there's some date in the future when I know we'll reconnect."

Susan started to cry. She tried not to—turned her face away, looked up at the sky, blinked back her tears—but, the flood came anyway.

"I'm sorry," Sammy said as he kissed her face, her cheeks, her forehead, her nose. "I'm sorry. I shouldn't have said it. I thought it might come out romantic or, I don't know. I'm sorry."

"No. No. It's okay. I just feel like I never, *ever* get anything whole. Everything in halves or parts or temporaries. I just want something *whole*."

"I love you, Susan. All of me loves all of you. My life is just a mess. I can't tell you any more than that."

Susan looked at him in the moonlight and she had no doubt that she loved him. "What if I say I'll meet you in a year in Paris? Does that mean we won't see each other in the meantime?"

"No! We'll see each other all the time. I just… Hey, how far is your college?"

"It's a four-hour drive."

"Well, that sounds just right, in my little Mustang."

"It's really not far. Please come see me, Sammy."

"I'll come. I promise I'll come."

"Everything is so strange!" She suddenly said as she pushed away from Sammy. She faced up to the stars and shouted, "Everyone here is strange!"

"Well, I hope I'm strange in a good way." Sammy laughed. "So, what's today's date?"

"Um." She thought about it as she wiped her eyes. "It's very early morning on Monday, September third."

"Then, September third, nineteen eighty it is. Call it an insurance policy. A little safety marker."

Susan stared at him—this beautiful man from another universe— and she engaged her ability to spin reality into fantasy. "I guess it could be kind of like a movie," she conceded.

"Well, if we were in a movie," Sammy pulled her back to him. "We would meet under a clock, wouldn't we?"

"I guess so."

"How about the clock at the Gare d'Orsay?" he asked.

"Didn't that just close? Aren't they're turning it into a museum?"

"Surely, they'll keep the clock."

Susan shook her head in dismay. "All right, then. The Gare d'Orsay in nineteen eighty. Under the clock."

"Don't forget September the third."

"I won't forget if you won't forget."

"Consider me an elephant," Sammy said. He touched her face once more and then he leaned in to kiss her. Really kiss her finally—a whole kiss, not a half.

She felt herself fall, as they dropped backward into the tiny back seat of her car.

* * *

Susan had spent the following days packing and preparing for her departure. Seeking a degree of normalcy, she had grilled hamburgers on Labor Day and eaten them on a tray in her father's bedroom. Elton hadn't had an appetite that day, so Susan ate two, his and hers, which made it feel, illogically, she knew, like they had shared a celebration.

She ate them both as she sat with William Elton, the television on, playing a holiday back-to-back run of the Doris Day/Rock Hudson *oeuvre*. She stayed in his room for hours, watching all three movies: *Pillow Talk, Lover Come Back, Send Me No Flowers*. The phone in the kitchen never rang.

When the films were finished, when Elton was asleep, and Susan could no longer prolong the day, she clicked off the TV, washed the dishes, brushed her teeth, and went to bed.

"Goodnight, Daddy," she had said. But she knew he hadn't heard her.

By Wednesday, she had packed her bags, cleaned the house and conferred with Elton's nurse. He was failing, and it was with trepidation that Susan would leave him. But it was her way out of this dead-end town, this crazy summer, this loneliness. Susan knew that, but she also knew that her father would likely be among the ballast jettisoned to the side of the road. Elton, who had been Susan's rock for the past twenty-one years, might not live to Susan's graduation. Alive or not, he certainly would not be in attendance.

On Wednesday night, just like Tuesday and Monday before it, Susan went to bed early. She read for a while, finishing up *Le Rouge et Le Noir* just in the nick of time. Not her style at all. She set the book on her bedside table, the small wooden stand with her grandmother's *Famille Rose* lamp.

She looked around her childhood room before turning off the light. She saw her twin bed, the grass cloth wallpaper she had put up herself three years before—having refused Todd's offer of help—the dresser that had been there since she was a toddler and no longer fit her adult clothes, the skirted dressing table with its mirror surrounded by round,

Hollywood-style light bulbs. Her mother had given her that mirror. A movie star mirror. Maggie's touch of glamour.

Susan turned off the light and laid her head on the pillow.

She slept fitfully, as she often did before a trip. Travel anxiety kept her turning in bed, as did the fan, which soon made the room feel cold. She got up to switch it off and climbed back into bed, where more hours dragged by. After two, Susan was just beginning to dream when the sound of the fan woke her again, the repetitive little whack that her old fan made as the blades turned around. Susan was slow to consciousness and a bit slower in remembering that she had already turned the fan off.

That got her attention.

She opened her ears before opening her eyes. She lay in bed listening hard. There was distinctly a sound that was not the normal sound of a house creaking late at night. Susan strained, trying to understand if it was coming from her father's room or somewhere else in the house. It was a clicking, like the fan made, but she soon observed that it was not occurring as regularly as the fan sound normally would.

Susan's eyes popped wide. The sound was coming from her window.

She sat up, looked at the curtains softly blowing into the room, and mentally confirmed that this was the source of the sound. Susan sat frozen in place. She could not imagine walking over and parting the curtains and was equally incapable of executing a run to her father's room. What could he do to help, anyway? There was one phone in the entire house, on the wall of the kitchen.

It was then that she heard her own name. Someone outside the window distinctly said, "Susan?"

"*Annie*?" This was really beyond the pale. Susan had not had a conversation with Annie for nearly a month. Annie hadn't even spoken to her on her last night at Frankie's. What on Earth was she doing outside Susan's window now, at this late hour?

Susan rose from the bed and parted the curtains. Indeed, there stood Annie on the lawn under the plum tree, chucking stones at her window.

"Stop it!" Susan hissed. "What are you doing here?"

"Susan, I need your help."

"Annie, we haven't even talked for weeks. What do you want from me?"

"I really need you. Please come to the front door. Please."

"Damn it. Damn it. Damn it. Damn it," Susan exhaled in a loud, rhythmic stage whisper as she made her way down the hall to the front door.

"Damn it!" she said again, a little more full-voiced, as she stepped out onto the small porch. "What do you want, Annie? What do you need?"

"Is that what you wear to sleep in?" Annie giggled as she looked over Susan's Lanz nightgown, long and frilly in delicate white cotton.

"No, Annie, I'm going out on a date right now and this is my outfit. Honestly, what *do* you want from me in the middle of the night?"

At this, Annie changed on a dime from laughter to tears, "It's Frankie. He's with another woman tonight. I know it. He's on his boat. He takes girls there and he screws them, and he knows I know but he doesn't care. I need to go there and tell him I can't take it anymore and I need you to go with me." All this was delivered in one single breath, no pause for air.

"Wait a minute. How do you know he's there? How do you know any of this?"

"Jesus Christ!" Annie made another rapid mood switch. "That's hardly the point, dontcha think?"

"You know what I think?" Susan had had enough. "I think you're a really selfish person. You do *whatever* you want, *whenever* you want, and you drag anybody you feel like dragging along for the ride. For companionship or…or…I don't even know what use you have for the people you drag along. Maybe you need a fan club. Well, that was me you were dragging around all summer and I won't be dragged anymore!"

"But you're my best friend!"

"Your *what*? That's ridiculous! You've been a complete bitch practically since we started that job and I'm done with it. I leave for college in the morning; my car is already packed up in the garage. You *knew* I was going and you didn't even say goodbye!"

"Well, I'm here now, to say goodbye to you."

"Oh bull*shit*, Annie. You did not come to say goodbye to me!"

Annie tried another tack. "I'm going to that boat and I'm going to confront him tonight, with or without you."

"Is that supposed to entice me?"

"Susan, if you don't go with me, you'll regret this the way you regret not being there for your mother on her deathbed!"

Susan was stunned. She could not believe that Annie had trotted out her most private shame to get her to go chase after some guy—some idiot guy—who Susan could have told her long ago was not worthy of any woman's affections. "That's a low blow, Annie. A really low blow."

"I'm sorry, but I'm really upset!"

"That, I would say, is an understatement." Susan paused, spent of her emotional load, and took a minute to collect herself. Annie was on drugs. That was the only explanation for her reprehensible words and actions. And, as Annie had just pointed out, who was Susan to cast the first stone? Look at the grief her own drug use had caused.

Susan softened. "Listen, why don't you come into the house and let me make you some tea or hot milk, something to calm you down?"

"Susan, please. Please." Annie was folding over, bent at the waist, and Susan couldn't tell what she would do next. "Please, I'm begging you. Please help me."

With that, Annie wrapped both arms around Susan, in her white Lanz nightgown, and crumpled until she was sitting on the porch, crying onto Susan's legs.

"Annie, get up." Susan tried to move, to dislodge her legs, but Annie had her pinioned. "Come on. It's going to be all right. You don't need Frankie or his disco. You can go back to college."

She couldn't adequately bend down to comfort Annie, the way she was holding onto her legs and sobbing, so loudly she was in danger of waking the neighbors. Her father would hear nothing, but the neighbors might call the police.

"Come on, now. Get up. Stop crying."

"I'll stop."

"Good."

"I'll do anything, if you'll help me. If you'll come with me, I'll stop doing drugs."

Susan was skeptical. At the same time, what if this was the scare that Annie needed to turn her life around. "Really?"

"I promise, Susan. I promise. Please. Please. Please."

"Okay, I'll go!" Susan said. "Just let me go back into the house and change."

"No!" Annie was too smart for that. "I know you won't come back! Just get in the car with me. Please, please, please, please, please." She was like a four-year-old, Susan thought helplessly.

"Fiiiiine! Fine! I'll go on another fool's errand with you. I must be out of my fucking mind, but fine!"

"Susan, when did you start swearing so much?" Just like that, Annie was up and trotting to the car.

With no good response to that question, Susan walked silently, head held high, like the dancer she was, her hair blowing and her long white gown flapping in the breeze. She looked every bit like Mr. Rochester's mad bride escaped from the attic, crossing the lawn to Annie's Corvette.

30

Annie sped east on Ten Mile Road toward Lake St. Clair.

"Where are we going?" Susan asked.

"Jefferson Beach Marina. You don't think the Castigliones got into the Grosse Pointe Yacht Club, do you?"

Susan looked around at St. Clair Shores, a working-class town, comparable to Warren, but improved by a waterfront. "I hadn't really given it much thought," she answered, then silently leaned back in the Corvette's deep seat. She wistfully pictured her own car, resting and ready to go. That was what she should be doing, too, since she planned to leave in a few hours. She had already said goodbye to her father. She did not want to disturb him when she tiptoed down the path to the garage at the back of their yard the next morning. He would not hear her start the car. The garage was too far from the house.

Annie pulled the Corvette into a parking lot and slammed the gearshift into park. She swiveled her head around scanning for Frankie's car.

"Party on the boat. That's what he always calls it," Annie said. "Do you know what that means?"

"I can imagine."

"That's right, you're so smart." Annie was becoming snarly again. "Frankie always tells me how smart you are."

"Annie…"

"Well, I didn't know what it meant because I'm not as smart as you. It means he's fucking someone."

"Look, I think we should go home."

"Did you know he was fucking Sherry?"

Now, this was a tricky question. Susan had never told Annie about her encounter with Sherry and Frankie in the storeroom. She had considered telling her, but, each time she'd thought to do so, Annie was unapproachable or churlish or wired to the rafters on cocaine. Shoot the messenger was what people were supposed to do when they received such news and Susan had come to the chilling conclusion that Annie was capable of shooting her at point blank range.

"No," Susan lied through her teeth. "I didn't know that."

"Well, he is," Annie turned to look more closely at Susan. "Maybe he's fucking you!"

"Annie!" Susan could no longer remember why she had gotten into the car with Annie tonight.

A woman with a mission, Annie flung open her door and slid out of the Corvette, glasses rolling beneath her feet as she did so. "Are you coming?"

"I'm not dressed. Maybe I should wait in the car."

"God, Susan, you are such a coward!" Annie bestowed a withering glance upon Susan then abruptly turned on her heel to march down the dock toward Frankie's boat and the fate that awaited her there.

As Annie's footfall faded, the marina became very quiet. Water lapped against pilings, boats and bumpers rubbed, making soft, sad groans, but no other sounds were heard.

Large boats surrounded Susan. Some of them were Chris Craft Constellations—"Connies" to their owners. Most of those were fifty to sixty feet and gave the impression of great mass, to a girl sitting in a Corvette at the edge of the dock. They did, in fact, look like party boats to Susan.

An eternity passed as Susan waited for Annie. Without her watch, she noticed that Annie's dashboard clock was broken. It figured.

At one point, Susan exited the Corvette and walked haltingly in the direction she'd seen her friend disappear. But she quickly reminded herself that she didn't actually know which boat was Frankie's and lost her nerve. Afraid of getting splinters from walking barefooted on a dock in the dark, Susan returned to the car and waited.

She may have dozed off—she couldn't be sure. Suddenly, Annie was next to her, starting the engine.

"What happened? Are you all right?"

"That asshole wasn't there."

"Isn't that good?" Susan was newly hopeful of a merciful end to this escapade. "Doesn't that mean he's not having a party on the boat?"

"Don't be naïve."

"You know, I have to admit I'm in uncharted territory here. Let's go home now so you and Frankie can laugh about this tomorrow."

"I really don't see what's funny here! I don't!" And with that, Annie made one of her signature U-turns in the middle of the road and headed down Jefferson Avenue toward Grosse Pointe.

The distance Annie drove was short—about four miles—from Jefferson Beach Marina to Sunningdale Drive in Grosse Pointe Shores. Jefferson Avenue turned into Lake Shore Drive. The water opened up to the left and was brilliantly illuminated by the moon, which was still visible, albeit low, on the opposite end of the sky. She took a few turns—right, left, right—Vernier, Morningside, Sunningdale. But Susan barely paid attention to the route. She sat stock still, in her nightgown, staring straight ahead. Annie did the same, looking forward with fierce intensity.

"Where are we going now?" Susan broke her own silence.

"Here," Annie answered. "Frankie's." She swung wide to the right into the driveway of a white brick Colonial of 1960s vintage—two stories, black shutters, attached garage, which opened to the right side of the house. Annie continued around to the garage to stop alongside Frankie's Cadillac. No other cars were in the driveway.

Annie jumped out of the Corvette and darted around her car to slap her hands on the hood of the Cadillac.

"I knew it!" she cried. "Hot! This hood is hot! He just got here. He said he was having dinner with his mother. He's with someone for sure."

"Oh my God, Annie, this is out of control. He probably did have dinner with his mother and fell asleep on her sofa or something. Then he drove home."

"You're a cool liar, Susan."

"I'm not lying! I'm guessing! I'm with you, remember? You plucked me out of bed! I have no idea where he was or what he did with whom."

Annie, not deigning to answer, turned her back on Susan and strode around the front of the house, out of Susan's eyesight. Once again, Susan was sitting alone in a car in the night. Once again, the night grew exceedingly quiet. And dark. And cold. As the minutes passed, Susan became uncomfortably aware that her nightgown was insufficient cover for a September night in Michigan. As her adrenalin settled, a chill came over her. She crossed her arms, closed her eyes and drifted. Back to a night, three years before, with Todd, before she'd left him for college.

That evening had been cold too—unseasonably so. They were in the basement of Susan's house; in front of the yellow brick fireplace that Susan's father had installed when she was a little girl. This was their private spot, the place where they could be alone, where Elton wouldn't surprise them as he shuffled around the house. He never came downstairs anymore to the pretty room he had built for his family—a rec room with paneling, the large gas fireplace, built-in bookshelves and benches. And filled with the 1940s maple furniture that reminded Susan of an *I Love Lucy* episode; furniture from an earlier life of Elton's, before Maggie and before Susan.

That night, Susan and Todd had gazed at the fire and tried not to think about their future. They had seventeen days before she went away. Seventeen days to count before life shifted a few degrees in another direction. They did not know what that direction would be, but they knew that a change was coming.

Why had that moment stood out? Why did she only remember that night, not any others, in the lead-up to her departure? She had no recollection of the twenty-day mark, or the fifteen or the two. Just seventeen. That moment was crystallized in her mind and conjured with ease, even now, three years later.

Did we only remember the moments when we truly paid attention? Would she remember this night, sitting in this driveway, years from now? She certainly felt she was focused, excessively so, but perhaps that was illusory. What happened in the mind to shine a spotlight on a particular moment, often the least consequential, to allow us to remember it, years later, with such clarity?

Such were the thoughts that occupied Susan Bentley in the night, in the car, in Grosse Pointe. She thought about Todd and she thought about Sammy; she thought about memory and she tried to keep warm. She glanced at the cars parked on the street, but she did not connect them to Frankie's.

She was not paying attention at all.

31

Special Agent Provenzano nods his head, granting permission for Susan and Jack Jr. to go. He adds a postscript and asks her to remain available for further questioning.

"We're meeting some others on this case. We'll want to talk with you again." He walks Susan and Jack back down the short corridor to the door to the reception area.

Jack follows Susan into the waiting room where they see Special Agent DelVecchio, crisply suited as ever, talking to a middle-aged woman, both of them standing.

The woman's attire might have come from a donation bin. She wears stretch pants that are purple and an oversized T-shirt announcing her affinity for the Red Sox. The background color of that shirt was probably white at some point but currently falls into the general category of gray. Her hair color has grown out at the roots and flip-flops complete her ensemble.

In simple curiosity, Susan finds herself staring.

DelVecchio and the woman are talking, chuckling about something that Jack and Susan haven't heard. The woman's laugh is a smoker's chortle, with a phlegm-y cough to punctuate it. DelVecchio takes the woman by the arm and starts to lead her in Susan and Jack's direction, presumably to guide her in through the door they just exited.

As the woman turns, she looks at Susan and Jack with coolness and a little contempt. She wears an expression of defiance in the face of two strangers who indisputably have had more advantages in life than she has. She makes eye contact with Jack first, gives him a little once-over. Then she allows her eyes to travel to Susan.

All of this happens quickly, but the point is made: "I won't be cowed by you rich folks." As the woman looks at Susan, Susan cannot help looking back. The two of them hold each other's gaze for a moment—and then a moment longer. The woman's smile has frozen and is drooping a bit at the sides. She is no longer actually smiling, but she hasn't quite released all of the muscles yet, so her expression is an odd, blank grimace. Like a Halloween pumpkin.

"Jesus H. Christ," she blurts, to no one in particular, but staring directly at Susan. "I don't fucking believe my eyes."

Everyone is looking at everyone else at this moment, when Susan says, almost inaudibly, even to Jack who is standing right next to her, "Sherry?"

No one else, least of all Sherry, hears her say it.

32

Time isn't fixed. No matter that sixty seconds make a minute, sixty minutes make an hour and twenty-four of those make a day; time is malleable. Like putty, it stretches and contracts in the hand. For Susan, standing in the waiting room of the FBI office in Boston, time begins to telescope. Looking at Sherry, standing so near, looking so old and worn, Susan leaps back to Frankie's Disco in the summer of 1979.

The telescope morphs into a kaleidoscope in the hands of a small child, turning it this way and that, as Susan sees Sherry moving toward her and away from her at the same time. The room alters. The chairs and tables, the receptionist's desk, the clock on the wall, all shift in her peripheral vision.

Sherry says something, which causes everyone else to look at Susan. Susan cannot quite make out what Sherry is saying as she keeps walking toward her. The room appears to grow longer, and Sherry does not seem to advance.

At the end of a tunnel she hears what Sherry says next, "Annie? Jesus Christ, Annie? You're supposed to be dead!"

Through spots and shadows, she sees the blanched alarm on Jack's face. "Look!" he says. "Who are you? This is my stepmother, Susan Ford."

She is unable to respond to what Sherry says next.

"I don't know who you are, but you sure as hell don't know who this is! And, she's not fit to be anybody's mother! This is Annie Nelson! I'd stake my life on it! Hey, I was interviewed for the newspaper when Annie died! When they all died! I was part of it all!"

A creeping fog encroaches, obscuring light and sound. It takes the ground out from under her and she crumples to the floor. Neither Jack Jr., who is closest to her, nor Agent DelVecchio, farther away, and certainly not Agent Provenzano, farther still, is able to mitigate her fall.

Distantly, she hears Sherry feigning, "I think I'm gonna faint too!"

She hears the three men scurry around the room to cope with the two inert women. She wonders where the receptionist is. That nice girl, who may have been able to add some order, had she been present, is missing. Maybe she is in the ladies' room, maybe getting coffee. Her mind starts to travel with the receptionist.

Finally, blackness comes. For this moment, she is granted a reprieve, mercifully allowed a brief respite from the vise that is closing in on her.

33

Thursday, September 6, 1979
Suburban Detroit

"Susan!" Sammy leaned into Annie's Corvette parked in the drive-way of Frankie's house where Susan sat with her eyes closed. She hadn't seen him approach and gave a squeal at the close proximity of his voice. "What are you doing here?"

"Sammy? What are *you* doing here?"

"I asked you the same question."

"I'm with Annie! She's crazy. She came to my house hysterical. We went to Frankie's boat and now we're here. She thinks he's with a woman in there." Susan paused. "But why are you here? Are you and Frankie friends?"

"She *is* crazy. Crazy and stupid. Why would you follow Annie here on a night like tonight?"

"I don't know what a night like tonight means and I don't really know why I came. She was so wound up, carrying on like a madwoman. I thought my neighbors would call the police." Susan eyed him. "But you're not answering me. Why are you in Frankie's driveway?"

"Susan, it would have been so much better if the police had come and kept you home."

"You're kind of freaking me out, Sammy. What's going *on* here?"

"Susan, get in the driver's seat. Turn the car around and get ready to drive out of here. I was leaving but I will go back in and get your foolish friend out of the house. Just do what I say. I'll explain later."

"Geez," Susan said as she exited the car to follow Sammy's instructions.

"What are you wearing?" Sammy asked.

"I wish everyone would stop asking me that! I'm wearing a night-gown! It's the middle of the night!"

"All right, I'm sorry." Sammy took her arm to move her a bit faster around the car and into the starting position of what was clearly going to be some sort of race. "It just seems unusual, is all."

"Really, Sammy?" Susan stopped walking and spun to face him. "You think my nightgown is unusual? I can't even begin to tell you how unusual I find this night. I just don't even know where to start."

"Susan, please hurry. There is no time for sarcasm now." Unceremoniously, he hustled her toward the driver's seat.

"Oh God, Sammy! What do you mean, now? What's happening?"

"Now is the time to go. Get behind the wheel. Turn the car around. Wait for Annie. Be a good girl."

Susan looked at Sammy, moonlight hitting his shiny black hair, and, good girl that she was, obeyed him. Sammy saw her settled into the driver's seat and hesitated. For a second, Susan thought—hoped—he would bend and kiss her. Just one kiss more—here, now, on this night that she should not be here and did not know why. But he just looked at her, took his long finger, touched it to his own lips and then touched it to hers. Then he turned and walked back around the garage to the rear of the house.

Susan was alone again.

Slowly, as quietly as possible, with hands shaking, she started the car, and did the drive/reverse dance required to position it, facing down the driveway. The cranberry juice glasses rolled in time to her shifts and made the tinkling noises that were now so familiar to her as to almost go unnoticed. She fumbled around for a seatbelt and found it wedged between the cracks of the seat. She adjusted the rearview mirror to better see the house behind her. She shifted into drive and kept her foot on the brake. She placed her hands at ten and two on the steering wheel.

And then she waited.

She heard the pops first, a quick and irregular succession of loud cracking sounds. Then she saw the front door fly open. Incongruously, she could see through the open door that the interior of the house was brilliantly lit. It looked like every light in the place was on.

Annie suddenly emerged from the door at a dead run. She was screaming and heading for where the car had been. This caused Susan to scream back, "Over here, Annie! I'm over here!" giving the horn a series of little taps.

Annie stopped short and stumbled forward from the suddenness of it. Her head spun wildly to find Susan and the Corvette in a different place than where she'd left them, at which point she started running again, down the length of the driveway.

"I'm driving!" Susan yelled. "Get in the other side! I'm driving!"

Annie bolted to the passenger side of the car, grabbed the door and made a leap into the seat, as Susan was already screeching out of the driveway and turning onto the street, past the parked cars that neither girl had noticed on arrival.

Annie was crying full tilt and was, as Susan could now see, covered with blood. There was blood all over her, her face, her hair, her clothes—everywhere.

"Oh my God, Annie, what happened? Have you been shot?" Susan was driving wildly down the roads, making turns as she came to intersections, right and left, left and right. There was no rhyme or reason to it. "Annie, answer me! Have you been hurt? Have you been shot?"

"I don't know. I don't know. I don't think so. It was Frankie!" At this Annie started to wail. "It was Frankie!"

"Frankie *shot* you?"

"They shot him!" She was hyperventilating and sobbing loudly.

"*Who* shot him?" Susan was driving in increasingly meaningless patterns.

"There were all these men. They all shot each other!"

"Oh my God!"

"Where are you going?" Annie was beginning to focus. "Where the hell are you going?"

"I have no idea!" Susan joined Annie's train of thought and scanned the scenery around her. It would have been impossible for her to say how far they had gone from Frankie's house or in which direction. It also felt impossible for her to alter her style of driving. Despite her mental chaos, Susan slowly became aware that a car was following them.

"Annie!"

Annie was not listening. She was whimpering in a world of her own.

"Annie!" Susan needed her now. She practically screamed in her ear, "*Annie*! Someone's behind us! I think they're following us!"

Annie looked at Susan, then swiveled her body fully around to peer out the small back window of the Corvette. Naturally, she wasn't wearing a seatbelt. "Holy shit," was all she said.

"What should I do? I'm really lost! What's the street name? Look, please! Can you see it?"

"It says Alter Road!" shouted Annie. "We're going into Detroit."

Alter Road, to the denizens of the East Side of Detroit and to Grosse Pointers, was well known as the dividing line between suburb and city. It was not as famous around the world as its big sister, Eight Mile Road, but it functioned in much the same way. Two different worlds faced each other from opposite sides of Alter Road.

Susan tore across it.

"Turn! Turn! Turn! Susan, you have to turn!"

"Okay!" Susan whipped the car around in a series of turns. The car behind them kept pace.

"Oh God! I think it's someone from Frankie's. I think they're coming to kill us!"

All of a sudden, their car lifted up on some sort of road bump on steroids and came crashing, nose down, on the far side. Sparks rose from the front of the Corvette and both girls screamed. Susan managed to regain control of the vehicle, the back end of which had skidded perilously to the right when they landed. She kept driving.

Instinctively, Annie grabbed for Susan's hand.

"What is that?" Susan screamed.

"What?" Annie twisted to look behind them again.

"On your wrist! What the fuck do you have on your wrist?"

"Are you nuts?"

"Goddamn it, Annie! Where did you get that watch! That's my mother's watch!"

"I found it on the floor at Frankie's. Jesus Christ, Susan! Is this the time for this now?"

"This is not my life!" Susan wailed, to no one in particular. Not to Annie, who was only two feet away from her, but hailed from a different planet. Not to herself, whom she couldn't locate if she tried. To the cosmos, to the gods, to the heavens above, she howled it again with full voice, "THIS IS NOT MY LIFE!!!"

"Susan!" Annie screamed. "Watch the road!"

ANNIE

"One alters the past to form the future."

—*A Sport and a Pastime,* James Salter

34

Monday, July 9, 1979
Suburban Detroit

Annie exhaled with a snort of derision as she spun her Corvette onto Leisure Drive. The only designation more ridiculous for the street on which she'd grown up would have been to call it Easy Street. She would not come back here anymore.

She was returning today only to retrieve some clothes she'd forgotten the last time she'd gone to her grandmother's. Moving in and out of her grandmother's house was something she'd done with frequency as a teenager, but she was determined that this was to be her last foray to Leisure Drive. If her mother wanted to see her, she could just drive herself over to Hazel Park.

Fat chance of that.

The screen door banged open and Angela bolted out in Annie's sweater. "Hi, sis!" she bellowed, about three octaves too loudly. Angela always called her sis, whereas half sis would have suited Annie better. "Babysitting for the Harris kids! All six of them!"

"Ange, take off my sweater."

"I'm already late."

"I'm here for my stuff so just give it back."

"Fine!" Angela ripped off the sweater and thrust it at Annie. She hopped on her bike and tore down the road. "You are *not* a nice sister!" she shouted over her shoulder.

Not bothering to respond, Annie leapt up the porch steps and yelled for her mother as she opened the door. She moved down the hall to the room she shared with Angela. Wanting to get out before her stepfather, Joe, came home from work, she began stuffing clothes into the paper grocery bags she'd brought with her.

"Annie." Her mother appeared in the doorway. The years since Laura had married Joe Nelson had not treated her kindly—drudgery had dimmed her youthful vigor. "Why were you yelling at your sister?"

"She took my sweater and I wanted it back."

"Why can't you be more sharing?"

"Because she's fat and stretches it out."

"Annie, that's cruel."

"How can it be cruel if it's true?"

"It's not right to say those things about people. And she's not fat, she's just going through puberty."

"I went through puberty and I wasn't fat."

"Well, Annie, we can't all be perfect like you."

"Mom, I was thinking—I want to talk to my father."

"Please don't start that again. He's never tried to find you. Never given a dime to support you. I don't know why you return to this subject over and over."

"Now who's cruel?"

"Well, it's true."

"Do you even hear yourself? Contradicting yourself all over the place?" Annie continued to cram articles of clothing into bags. "You said his name was Bo. Is that Bo as in B-O? Or is it B-E-A-U?"

"You've asked me that a million times. I don't know."

"See, I don't really understand that, Mother. How could you possibly not know how to spell your lover's name?"

"Annie, don't be crude!"

"You slept with him and you weren't married to him or anything. Who's the crude one here?"

Laura stared at her daughter with a sad-puppy look. No wonder she drove her husband crazy. No wonder Annie's father had left her. No wonder to any of it at all, when Laura played the victim all the time.

"I can't keep having this same conversation with you. I need to cook dinner for Joe." Laura sighed and walked down the hall.

"Mom, come back." Annie followed, forgetting her urgency to get out. "Please tell me his last name. You said his family left Hazel Park, but I really want to find them."

"Oh, Annie. I just don't want you to be disappointed."

"Well, it's a little late for that!"

Annie had hit her mark and watched her mother's face crumple. "You are ruthless. Get out."

Annie did not move.

"Get out of my house! Go ask your grandmother to tell you all this ancient history! *Go!*"

Livid, Annie strode to the bedroom, grabbed the bags, and launched a syncopated march toward the door. She lifted each knee high, stomped her foot to the floor, and slammed the bunch of bags into the walls, shouting, "I hate you!" as she went. Down the hall she trudged—stomp, slam, "I hate you!" to the left, stomp, slam, "I hate you!" to the right-until she looked up and saw Joe bearing down on her.

She braced herself. The first blow was always the worst.

* * *

Annie slumped on the floor of her childhood room—the point of her haste dissipated. Joe was no longer a threat to her. She knew what he would be doing—what he always did after he beat her. Joe Nelson, specimen of Warren's finest, Police Officer of the Year for three years running—1973, 1974, and 1975—would right now be screwing his wife. And her mother lay down for all of it. She did not intervene when her husband raised his fist to her daughter; she did not complain when he made his demands of her.

Annie rose to look at herself in the ratty old mirror above the dresser. Angela had colonized the edges of the glass with smiley-face stickers and magazine cut-outs of her favorite TV shows—*Mork and Mindy, Three's Company, The Love Boat*. In the middle of that jumble, Annie's face gazed back at her, perfect as it always had been. She had to hand it to Joe. It must be his cop training—he never left marks above the neck.

Annie had always relied on her face. Miraculously, puberty had given her a body that was her face's equal. She hadn't done anything to deserve it, but she was conscious of her favored status. Even when she was small, people had stared at her. As she grew older, the looks became bolder. Women gawked openly in her direction. Men found a way to approach her.

Annie defined herself by her desirability. She observed it, tested it, and eventually came to control it. When she entered a room, she paused slightly, imperceptibly to others, to gauge the attention of the group. It didn't take long to command it. Her stepfather was the glaring exception to the sway of Annie's charms. She suspected it was because she was the living embodiment of her mother's amorous past.

Laura had married Joe when Annie was six, breaking up the tiny, happy household of Annie, her mother and grandmother in two little bedrooms in Hazel Park—the house that Annie had called home from the day that she was born.

One of Annie's strongest memories of her grandmother, also named Annie, was of their weekly outings to church. On Sunday mornings, while Laura slept late, they would walk the few blocks to Saint Mary Magdalen, her grandmother holding her hand.

Church was Annie's special place where she dropped the performance she put on for the world. No one looked at Annie in church. All eyes were trained forward, on the crucified Christ, the liturgy, the priest. Her grandmother sat, stood and knelt beside her, as the timeless ritual dictated, crossing herself, thumping her fist to her heart, touching her thumb to her forehead, her lips, her chest. *Dominus vobiscum et cum spiritu tuo*—the words drifted in and out of Annie's head, like incense in a thurible. She did not need to understand them with her mind.

The sounds of the Mass—the incantations, the organ, the bells—vibrated deep in Annie's chest cavity. Tone within, tone without, immanent and transcendent. She floated on the notes as she leafed through the tissue-thin pages of the missal. They filled her as she played with her grandmother's hands, as papery as those pages, gently pinching the old skin into a ridge that took its time to settle back to the bones. Her grandmother never stopped her, never pulled her hand away, never made Annie feel self-conscious in any way. In church and with her grandmother, Annie lost herself. She found herself. In church, Annie was the seer and not the seen. She forgot about her face.

That life ended when Laura married Joe Nelson.

Annie knew that Laura and her mother had never gotten along, and it was something of a miracle that Grandma Annie had not rejected her daughter when she turned up pregnant at seventeen. Annie's mother had told her the story more than once.

It was a cold January day in 1958. Laura was talking to the boy on the street—trying to sort out their future—and felt it within her grasp. Just a little more time and it would have been resolved.

Yet there had appeared her mother, calling to her from the porch. Laura spun and tried to hold her off, then she turned back to the boy. But she could see that he was drifting, their tether disconnected. He walked away before she did. As the boy moved in one direction, Laura had moved in the other. Her mother uttered her name again, sharply. Laura knew then that her mother could see it—could identify the bulk under her pea coat. She was amazed that her mother hadn't noticed it before. She mounted the path flanked by overgrown red bayberry bushes. And, as she turned her head to look at the retreating boy, her mother's hand cuffed her hard in the ear. She saw stars, she told Annie. She said that every time she repeated the story.

Then there was the happy part—the tale that her grandmother spun.

The child—a girl—was born in May. On Mother's Day, to be precise. A scant month later, Laura had marched into St. Mary Magdalen, christened the child Annie, after her grandmother, and more or less, handed her over to the older woman.

That is where God had the last laugh because Annie Johnston loved that child, in all the ways she could not love the child's mother and for the very same qualities that she bristled at in Laura. For little Annie was very much like her mother: loud, lively, and exuberant.

But there was a subtle distinction to be made between Laura and her daughter. While Laura's awkwardness held a tentative thread, a palpable fear of the world's disapprobation—which she perversely invited with her own behavior—Annie, instead, exuded confidence. Her grandmother loved her devotedly and the only cloud that marred the girl's horizon was an inchoate awareness that it wasn't quite fair that she was loved so much more than her own mother had been. The child that is born on the Sabbath Day is bonnie and blithe and good and gay.

Joe Nelson changed the world for the three Johnston women. For Laura, he meant escape and respectability. Her child's father hadn't bothered to marry her and liberate her from her mother's house six years earlier. He had simply walked away. For Grandma Annie and little Annie, the beginning of Joe Nelson meant the end of an idyll.

Joe married Laura in November of 1964, at City Hall, on a frigid, blustery day. Chocolate cake and Cold Duck commemorated the occasion. Laura got a trip to Niagara Falls and Annie got one more week with her grandmother.

That Sunday, just like every Sunday before it, Annie and her grandmother went to church. To Annie's astonishment, not being old enough to follow the Second Vatican Council, the Mass was in English. It was disorienting to hear those lofty chants brought down to earth and rendered in every day speech. The magic was gone. The lifetime she had spent with her grandmother was finished, two thousand years of Catholic ritual upended, and as a little girl she conflated the two, blaming Joe Nelson for all of it.

The next day, Joe and Laura came back from Niagara Falls, picked up Annie, and moved her from Battelle Street in Hazel Park to Leisure Drive in Warren.

Eight miles and light years away.

35

Monday, July 23, 1979

Mondays in the bar business were dead, but the Castigliones kept Frankie's open seven days a week, in deference to the regulars. Diane, Annie, and Susan were new hires, at the bottom of the pecking order for shift preference, so Mondays belonged to them. Susan and Diane were uncomplaining, but the tedium grated on Annie, who hated boredom above all else.

This Monday was particularly slow, so one girl would be permitted to leave early. It was left to the three of them to determine which girl it would be.

Diane and Susan had launched a politeness contest. "You go," Diane had said to Susan. "You have all that reading to do."

"No, *you* go," Susan had responded. "I'm sure they won't keep any of us much longer."

"Are you sure? There *is* a party I'm invited to."

"Oh my God!" Annie couldn't stand it. "I'm gonna scream if you keep this up. One of you, please go!"

Diane and Susan looked at her. "Would you like to go?" Diane asked.

"Nope. I'm sticking it out," said Annie. "I want Frankie to take me out later."

"Well, then, if you both don't mind." Diane gathered her things and walked out the door.

By ten p.m., the bar had been empty for an hour. Frankie sat at the corner table with Vito, Johnny Buscemi, and Danny the Cop, too deep in conversation to notice they were alone in the place.

For anyone unlucky enough to pull a shift on a Monday night, there was always a list of catch-up chores to perform. Annie's technique was to procrastinate until an early closing time was called, thus sparing her anything even resembling completion. Susan's method was to buckle down and get the job done. Tonight, Annie and Susan were sent to the cloakroom to do a little cleaning. The idea was to sort out the unclaimed items worth keeping from those ready for the trash bin.

"Oh my God, Susan!" Annie spun around, holding a black bra up to her chest. "What do you think went on in here?"

"Maybe it just fell out of somebody's bag."

"Or maybe someone was fooling around in the cloakroom?"

"I can't imagine that anyone would be doing that right here."

"Well, I can."

"You, my friend"—Susan took the bra from Annie and deposited it in the garbage—"have a very active imagination."

"What's going on in that little imagination of yours?" A deep and velvety male voice came from the doorway. Annie and Susan pivoted in unison to face the large shadow that was blocking light from the lobby. There stood Johnny Buscemi, in all his majesty, backlit and glowing around the edges. "What can you imagine, little girl?"

Susan was frozen mute by such a question but not Annie. "I can imagine a lot of things," she replied.

"Imagination can be a dangerous thing," Johnny said, not budging one centimeter from the doorway, leaving no escape for either of them. Though escape was not on Annie's mind. She studied him. In her assessment of him right now, Annie recognized a man who was her equal—in physical beauty, in carnal attraction, in his ability to bend others to his will. She was hard pressed to resist that.

"Curiosity killed the cat," Johnny continued. "Or haven't you heard that one?"

"I've heard plenty." Annie laughed at her own retort and looked to Susan for backup. Susan's silence irritated her and emboldened her to continue. "Maybe you can tell me something I haven't heard?"

Susan's head snapped back in Annie's direction on that one. Annie knew she was playing with fire, being Frankie's girlfriend, but she certainly didn't want Susan to judge her. Who did Susan think she was, after all? Annie knew a thing or two about her friend's defects.

"Annie, we need to go back to the storeroom to do some work there." Susan offered her a way out.

Annie did not want her rescue and shot back tersely, "I think I'm supposed to stay here and you're supposed to go back there, Susan."

Susan gaped open-mouthed. This made her resemble a fish, which made Annie, in turn, strike out more aggressively.

Annie was not proud of this aspect of her own character. Or she would not have been proud of it, had she actually taken any time for self-analysis. Maybe it was all of the years that she had lived under the thumb of Joe Nelson. Maybe she just had a more reactive nature than most people. But she was always one to rise to the bait, whatever that bait might be. Her grandmother could gentle her out of being so easily provoked, but she was the only person alive who could do so. And, at this moment, in the cloakroom, Annie was being baited on two fronts—one, by Johnny Buscemi, with his silky voice and raw sexuality and, two, by Susan, with her damned prudishness.

"Susan, did you hear me?" Annie repeated. "You're supposed to go back to the storeroom and I'm supposed to stay here."

Susan hesitated, as though she did not quite understand. She continued to stare at Annie. Then she turned to look at Johnny Buscemi in the doorway. Her regard served as the cue for Johnny to move. Slowly, he removed his arms from the doorjamb. He folded them over his chest and stepped aside, opening a narrow path for Susan's exit.

He then turned his full attention to Annie, whose focus was riveted on him. "You think you know a lot," he said, in his most mellifluous voice, as he slowly walked in her direction.

What Annie certainly knew was that she had gone too far and was now entering into perilous terrain. "Maybe. I don't know. Maybe I don't know so much."

He moved closer, backing her up until she stood with her head between the coat hangers, which jingled in her ears, creating an otherworldly soundtrack to the proceedings.

"Listen. I think Susan was right. I made a mistake. I need to go back to the storeroom." She sidestepped quickly to the left to dart around Johnny Buscemi's approaching form.

Not quickly enough. Johnny grabbed both of Annie's arms in a firm grip and held her up close to his face.

"You think you're something, don't you? You're Frankie's girlfriend and you think you can flirt with me? Little girl," he used that phrase again. "You don't know shit from Shinola. I can't tell if you're really stupid or smart like a fox."

"You're hurting me." Annie lowered the register of her voice to add authority. "Let me go."

This was probably the right move because it made Johnny laugh. "Smart like a fox, I think," he said as he released her arms.

It was then that Annie made her big mistake, seducing herself into thinking that she was in charge of the situation. She did not follow through on her original impulse to flee. She stood there, in front of Johnny Buscemi, holding his gaze, gloating in what she perceived to be her own triumph.

Johnny remained uncowed. "Close your eyes," he commanded.

Annie hesitated and then she did so—though she kept them open just the tiniest bit beneath her eyelashes. She was no fool.

"Open your mouth." He gave his second order and, once again, she complied.

Johnny took a small vial from his pocket, unscrewed the lid, licked the tip of his index finger, held it to the top and tipped it over. He took that finger, with white powder sticking to it, and he inserted it into Annie's mouth. He rubbed his finger around her mouth and gums, side to side and up and down and Annie stood still while he did it. He touched her in no other way. When he stopped, he told her to close her mouth. Again, she followed instructions.

"Do you like that, little girl?"

"I don't know." Annie felt the bitter taste all the way in the back of her throat, sliding down to her stomach. Then, an indiscernible second later, she felt a rush moving up to her head. The two sensations passed each other, top speed, inside of Annie.

"Try it like this." He used a little spoon to scoop up the drug. "Hold one nostril closed and breathe it up the other side." Again, Annie obeyed. This time, a sense of elation overtook her as she glimpsed her broken-ness repaired.

"I've got more of this. All you want."

And that was really all it took—nothing more than a little snort in the dark with a tall, dark stranger.

36

Thursday, August 9, 1979

As in a fairy tale, a single gift was bestowed upon Annie and she remained forever uncertain that she had been its intended recipient. It was an enigmatic gift, given in an offhand way, and it didn't even come in a box.

By the night of Thursday, August ninth, Annie's grasp on time was loosening. It had been a month since Frankie had chastised her in front of the staff, two weeks since her encounter with Johnny Buscemi in the cloakroom, only twenty-four hours since her fight with Susan in the car—but it felt like she had been here forever. She could not call to mind her life before Frankie's Disco. This place and who she had become in it were unspooling in a continual now.

Despite the brevity of her life at Frankie's, Annie occasionally succumbed to the illusion that she sat in a seat of importance. She was the boss's girlfriend, after all. Tonight, she looked with benevolence on the usual suspects doing their usual things. The dancers were dancing; the drinkers were drinking. Johnny Buscemi sat in the corner with Vito and Danny, the three of them radiating tanned and smiling self-confidence. Vito, as always, surveyed his empire from the sidelines and Frankie, in turn, moved hither and yon, conferring with his brother and doing his bidding. The roles of Johnny Buscemi and Danny the Cop were, as ever, unclear.

This table and a few others near it were now Annie's exclusive domain. The fact that Sherry had been displaced to wait on a lesser section had not increased her affection for Annie.

A little after two, the last of the patrons were dispersing. Annie was bending over Vito's vacated table, wiping up the sticky spots. Frankie, unable to control his enthusiasm for his new girlfriend's fanny, bumped up into her and held onto her hips. It was a brief moment, but a glowering Sherry watched them. Annie paused, looked straight at Sherry, and held the position a beat or two longer than the actual task required.

"Baby, let's go," Frankie whispered, pushing against Annie's behind another second before he noticed Sherry's sour countenance. At this, he playfully stuck out his tongue at her, which heightened Sherry's outrage. She dropped her tray of dirty glasses onto the table and stomped off toward the kitchen.

"Frankie," Annie giggled. "I'm not finished. I don't want to get in trouble with the boss." She turned to face him and towered over him in her heels.

"I'll give you trouble," he said as he slapped her on the ass. This seemed to be a go-to gesture for Frankie, the right response in a myriad of settings: anger, titillation, jolly good will.

"Frankie!" Annie laughed. Her boyfriend was a mercurial figure and she never quite knew if she was in favor or out of it with him. Cocaine did not aid her powers of perception, but clearly Frankie wanted her, and he wanted her now. "I told my Grandma that I'd be home right after work. She gets worried that I drive all the way home in the middle of the night."

"Oh, Little Red Riding Hood," Frankie breathed in her ear. "Take a walk with me in the woods."

Annie could play that game if he wanted. She slid her hand up Frankie's leg, ignoring the rest of the staff and the few remaining clients. "What a big, bad wolf you are," she cooed.

"Annie!" Sherry was back and standing right next to the two of them, beaming hostility their way. "Move your car. You're blocking me in."

Annie rotated slowly to face the older waitress. "Sure, Sherry." She could easily grant this pittance to a peon and she spoke with what she hoped was the right tone of magnanimity.

"Sherry, don't be a pain in the ass," snapped Frankie, his fun and games interrupted.

"I need to go home to my kid, Frankie, and your girlfriend is in my way."

"Fine. Annie, move your car. Meet me at the boat." And off he strode, leaving Annie to drive herself, alone, to the marina in the middle of the night. Sir Galahad, he was not.

Annie managed to restrain herself from snorting any more cocaine on her way to St. Clair Shores. Well, she had a little bump, to keep herself from freefalling, but that was just basic maintenance. Strangely enough, she reflected, Frankie demonstrated no curiosity as to the identity of her supplier. Similarly, he did not seem to wonder how she paid for her drugs, cocaine being notoriously expensive, even for a girl with the best tables at the disco.

Annie alternated steering the wheel with applying makeup. Wanting to look her best for Frankie, she had changed from her work outfit into a wrap dress and had decided to wear nothing at all underneath. He would like that little surprise.

Parking haphazardly, Annie hopped out and tottered down the dark dock in her Candies. A soft wind lifted the front flap of her dress and excited her. As she climbed the ladder, she felt the breeze rise all the way up between her legs. Frankie always asked her to take off her shoes when she came aboard, but she had no intention of doing that tonight. When she removed her dress, she wanted Frankie to gasp at the length of her legs.

Frankie sat in the saloon, drinking Courvoisier and fiddling with something in his hands. Annie knew he prided himself on his self-control. One brandy after work was his sole indulgence of the day. She paused until he looked up. Then, with all the lights blazing, she slowly took off her dress until she stood naked, but for her shoes. Frankie sat, fully clothed, watching. He said nothing.

Annie waited.

Frankie continued to sit, unstirred. Perhaps she had miscalculated.

Finally, he spoke. "Do you know who I am?" he asked.

"Uh…" She searched for the direction of this conversation. "Frankie?"

"Do you know who my family is?"

"What do you mean?" Annie reached down for her dress and put the damned thing back on. She had definitely misplayed her hand. "Papa Vito's?"

"That is not who we are. We are not a pizzeria, Annie. We're Sicilian! We may even be descended of kings." Frankie stared in the direction of the boat's windows, though Annie figured he couldn't really see out of them in the dark. She waited for some sort of signal of what was supposed to happen next. At last, he continued. "Do you know that, for one day, our town—Salemi—was the capital of Italy? The very first capital! Did you know that?"

"No, Frankie, I didn't. I'm sorry."

"And here I am, in this shitty place and I get no respect. People think I'm just a gofer for my brother and Johnny! Just little Frankie, the baby, he cleans up everybody's mess. Nobody gives a shit how dirty that mess might be! Well, that'll change one day, you mark my word!"

Annie knew better than to respond. Frankie pursed his lips as he studied her.

"Come here," he said, and Annie obeyed.

When she got to him, he did not touch her. Annie felt him retaking control. As if remembering, he looked down at his hands, where he held something shiny. He studied it for a while, then he scrutinized Annie's face.

"Bend over," he said. She started to turn around to face away from him, to lean over the nearby table.

"No, this way," he said, turning her manually back to face him. Annie awkwardly inclined toward Frankie as he reached up to clasp something around her neck. She excitedly touched it and looked down to see that it was a gold necklace, a long, thick chain with a pendant. She moved closer to the light to examine it. It was a question mark—a chunky gold question mark with a ruby as its point.

"What's this, Frankie?" Annie couldn't really believe her eyes, never having owned anything made of real gold before. At least, she hoped it was real gold.

"Don't say I never gave you anything. Now take that dress off again," he said as he pushed her over the chair and took what he wanted in return.

37

Wednesday, August 13, 2014
Boston

It takes the receptionist's return to the waiting room to break the spell that has come over everyone. She enters upon a *tableau vivant* composed of the five key players, frozen as though they had been staged. The scene stops her short at the doorway. "Hello?" she queries.

Provenzano and DelVecchio are bent over Sherry. Jack Jr. sits next to his inert stepmother, who has been lifted to a chair. The receptionist's voice causes four of the five to look up at her. Mrs. Ford keeps her eyes tightly shut, working to maintain her oblivion for a few minutes more. Not one of them responds.

Jack returns to his texting, his thumbs moving furiously on his mobile device. She opens her eyes to watch him.

"Jack?" Her voice comes out hoarse.

"Just listen to me," he says. "You have fainted. Please refrain from speaking for the moment. Do not say a word."

Turning to Sherry, he adds, "Madam, I must ask you to remain silent, as well."

"How dare you ask me any such thing?" Sherry gears up for battle, which spurs DelVecchio and Provenzano into action.

"Ms. Hopkins." Provenzano is ever the gentleman. "Are you able to accompany me into my office? I can offer you a glass of water in there."

176

"There's nothing wrong with me." Sherry stands and explodes in a cough, which momentarily gets the better of her. "I can accompany you wherever you want to go."

"Fine then. Agent DelVecchio will help you down the hall and get you whatever you'd like to drink."

"A scotch is what I'd like to drink right about now," Sherry says as she departs on the arm of DelVecchio.

Provenzano turns to face Mrs. Ford. She stares at her hands in her lap and does not meet his gaze. Her legs are uncrossed, and she is not sitting up with her normal, erect posture. She is half slumped, as she was in her faint, a ragdoll tossed aside.

"Mrs. Ford." His tone is sharper than usual. "Don't leave the building. We need to speak with you again today. We'll call you in shortly. In fact, don't leave our offices at all."

He turns to follow his partner and Sherry. She and Jack are left alone.

Jack gets up and walks over to the receptionist. "Is there someplace we might talk more privately? I'm sorry, what's your name?"

"Melinda." She rises and opens the door to the hallway. "Sure. Follow me."

Jack turns back to his stepmother and gruffly says, "Let's go."

She gets to her feet and tries to smooth her rumpled dress. Linen had been a poor choice for the day this has turned out to be.

Mutely, they traipse down the hall. Melinda ushers them into a carbon copy of the room they so recently left. They both watch her form retreat through its little window.

Jack turns to her and erupts. "Why don't you start by telling me exactly what is going on here?"

"I…"

"Is there any merit to the preposterous accusation that woman just made?"

"I…it's just…I'll tell you everything. I've actually wanted to tell you. I've always cared so much for you."

"Let's really not go there."

"Do you mind if I sit?"

"You can lie down on the floor for all I care! I just want to know what's going on here. I feel like a two-year-old at the circus and I can't follow a fucking thing." Jack drops into a chair opposite her and rubs his forehead with one hand. "Look, I'm still hanging onto the thread that you're going to inject some sense into all this and reel us back off of the ledge."

"Yes, I will try to do that."

At that moment, Melinda knocks on the door, making them both jump. "Agents Provenzano and DelVecchio will see you in half an hour. Would you like some water? Coffee?"

"Water would be fine," says Jack. "Thank you, Melinda."

"Of course." Melinda departs, closing the door softly behind her.

"Well, what the hell is going on?" Jack leans toward her, as far as he possibly can over the table. "And you'd better hold the cue cards pretty high for me because I just don't come across this kind of situation every day, you know, dead people and accusations of impersonating dead people! None of this looks good."

Before she can speak, Melinda knocks again, enters with the water and sets two bottles upon the table between them. Finally, she leaves.

"And that Iraqi man who was coming to see you? Who is he, *really*? What is your relationship to him? And that woman in the other room who looks like she's been run through the fucking dishwasher! Who is she and what is she telling them in there that I should know? What the hell is going on here?"

38

Friday, August 10, 1979
Suburban Detroit

Horses calmed Annie, the twitch of their ears and tails, the steam from their nostrils, their velvety noses, their long, slanting eyelashes. On mild mornings when she was a girl, her grandmother had brought her to Hazel Park Raceway to watch the horses exercise. They came here often, with apple cores and carrot ends, whatever was left over from their own meals. Grandma Annie had shown little Annie how to hold her palm as flat as a plate, stacking fingers tightly together to leave no nibbly bits for horse teeth.

Large or small, any animal was an animal that Annie could love. Her grandmother had had a schnauzer called Mona—a little soldier, erect at attention and bossy. She marched around the house and led the parade when Grandma Annie and little Annie took her out for a walk. Mona was never invited on their outings to the racetrack, though, because Grandma Annie said she might frighten the horses.

After Annie moved away, Mona lived a few years more. Early on, she would hop on Annie's bed when she slept at her grandmother's house. In time, she lost her agility. Annie carried her around until her grandmother made her set the dog down. "You'll make her queasy if you hold her too much," she had said. Annie would then lie on the kitchen floor next to Mona's bed, and try to synchronize her breathing with the dog's.

Her grandmother didn't force her to get up in the way that her mother would have.

Grandma Annie couldn't see her way clear to have another dog after Mona. Too much work for an old lady, she had said. Annie had offered to do all of the work but, of course, Annie wasn't always around.

So here Annie was, on a summer morning, back at the track, visiting the horses. Looking for peace in all the wrong places. As she stood at the rail, watching the exercises, a slick black 1969 Mustang pulled up behind her. It continued a slow roll in her direction, before it stopped and a familiar-looking man with olive skin and floppy black hair emerged.

"Hi," he said, offering his right hand for shaking. "Sammy Fakhouri. I've seen you at Frankie's."

"Did Frankie send you here?" Annie did not take his hand.

"What? I'm sorry, I don't quite know what you mean."

"Did Frankie send you looking for me?" She fluttered a hand to her face, conscious of her smudged mascara and drawn features. She saw him size her up, recognizing that this was the end of her night, instead of the start of a new day.

"Uh, no, Frankie didn't send me. I don't really know Frankie all that well. I just come here sometimes in the mornings. I live nearby, and I like it here."

With this, Annie relaxed. "I like it here too," she said as she turned away from him to face the horses. "My grandmother used to bring me here when I was little."

"It's Annie, right? Like I said, my name is Sammy."

"Look at this." She couldn't concentrate and skittered around subjects. "Frankie gave me this last night. It's a gold question mark. With a ruby! Well, I think it's gold. Do you think it's gold?" Annie fished the chain from between her breasts and thrust it his way.

Electing not to take the item into his hands, Sammy stood looking down at it with his arms firmly folded across his chest.

"Well." He seemed to be thinking deeply. "It does appear to be gold. And the stone does seem to be a ruby. Not that I'm an expert or anything. But I'm sure if Frankie Castiglione gave it to you, it must be real."

Annie's relief was palpable. "I knew that. Frankie wouldn't give me anything that wasn't real."

On that, Sammy made no comment. So, they stood side by side watching the horses.

"What's your name?" She couldn't remember if he'd said it already.

"Like I said, Sammy Fakhouri."

"What kind of name is that?"

"I'm from the Middle East. Iraq. I'm a Chaldean."

"A what?"

"A Chaldean. We're Catholics from Iraq. Well, actually, there are a lot of us here in Detroit, now."

"Hmm." She was having trouble following the train of this conversation. She needed to get some sleep. "I don't know why you'd want to come here."

"It's a long story."

"Hmm," she said again, then lost interest. "I've seen you talking to Susan."

"Yes. I like talking to Susan. She's a nice girl."

"Really? That's the word you'd use? God, I'd hate for a man to describe me as nice!"

He laughed. "I guess you're right. 'Damned by faint praise.' Who said that?"

"Who said what?"

"That expression, 'Damned by faint praise'? Do you know who said that?"

"I have no idea."

They lapsed into silence again. Annie reached into her purse and pulled out a vial of cocaine. She scooped some of it with the underside of her pinkie nail and quickly sucked it up her nose. Then she ran her finger over her gums.

"Wow. Breakfast of champions."

At this, she actually startled and swung around to face him. "What the fuck are you doing here? Did Frankie send you?"

"Mademoiselle, I beg your leave. The hour of departure is upon me," Sammy delivered with his most flowery flourish. "I need to get to work," he concluded, but she was hardly listening. "Have a lovely day," he offered to the air.

Sammy started up his Mustang, which roared to life, and rolled it away from Annie. Annie, in turn, went back to watching the horses.

She almost forgot about him, but her mind had seized on a pesky grain of paranoia. What if Frankie *had* sent him? What if there was some greater meaning to this early morning exchange? What if she just couldn't catch hold of the thread? Sammy's appearance had dislodged any toehold she had established in equanimity.

Annie slowly sank on the grass. Something was radically wrong. Frankie must have sent him to find her. It did not add up that he would just waltz into this racetrack by coincidence. And she *had* seen him talking with Susan. She wasn't sure what Frankie and Susan were up to, but this guy was obviously in on it.

Annie knew she needed rest, but it eluded her. She hadn't been able to sleep last night or the night before. Had she slept the night before that? She couldn't recall. She had to get back to her grandmother's house a few short blocks away.

That was the place she should go—the only place she felt safe. She could close the blinds and crawl into bed and stare at the unchanging ceiling in the way that she had as a little girl. She had memorized the map of its cracks and bumps, the slope of the frosted glass lamp, the faintness of the light bulbs shining through it. She had fallen asleep, mentally wandering that ceiling so many times in her childhood that she knew now, if she were to lie down and look at it for long enough, all would be well.

She remembered what her grandmother said when she was small, quoting Saint Julian of Norwich, "All shall be well and all shall be well and all manner of things shall be well."

If she could just sleep, all would be well.

39

Nothing lasted, she knew. But, less than a week seemed grossly unfair. A week ago, Frankie had given her the necklace. Tonight, he had given her a smack. He had never hit her before. But she knew from living with Joe that once it happened for the first time, it became easier. Easier to justify. Easier to do. Easier for a man to forgive himself.

When she was little, she perceived that Joe felt bad afterward. He would buy her little toys: coloring books, Silly Putty, a Slinky. "I'm sorry," he would say, "but you just don't *listen*, Annie. You just go off and do what you want, and you never consider the consequences. You need to learn to control yourself." An apology peppered with blame: If she could only straightjacket her own vitality, he wouldn't be forced to strike her. Over the years, his apologies lessened but the blame and shame remained.

Annie sat in her silent Corvette in front of Johnny Buscemi's building. She squinted to see her face in the rearview mirror. It was so dark on Johnny's street that her image was a mass of shifting shadows, geometric shapes—a triangle, a circle, a square—overlapping in shades of grey, moving apart, coming together, fusing into a single black blob. And that about summed up Annie's state of mind.

Tonight, when she had asked Frankie a simple question—one question to get at the truth of his philandering—what did she get? A slug on the face that would surely leave a scar.

Damn him for slapping her—and in front of sanctimonious Susan. Damn Johnny, that Pied Piper of illegal drugs, who had seduced her into her current state of obsession. Damn Joe, the man who was supposed to be like a father to her, who never showed a speck of tenderness in her entire life. Damn them all.

Annie reached up to the spot where Frankie had hit her and felt a bump. The cut on the surface of it stung to her touch. She pressed harder and felt the bruise underneath. Well, if she could feel, she was alive. The bastards hadn't killed her yet.

She could have turned around right then, gone home to her grandmother's, crawled into bed, and stayed there until the desire for cocaine went away. She had read about it. She was not an idiot, despite what some people thought. Cocaine was not supposed to be physically addictive. Psychologically? Well, she wouldn't examine that too closely. Freud had thought it was a wonder drug.

"How about that, Miss Susan?" Annie asked of the mirror. "I bet you didn't think I even knew who Freud was, did you?"

In fact, she abruptly decided, she *would* leave. She had a handle on this whole cocaine thing. She would get out of this mess and go to her grandma's right after she put Johnny Buscemi in his place. She would march up those steps, tell him off and turn right around. Piece of cake.

Annie opened the car door and put out a foot. Then she stopped herself from exiting. She turned back and unlatched the gold question mark from around her neck, dropping it into the ashtray. As low as she had admittedly sunk, she couldn't quite bring herself to wear her boyfriend's gift while visiting another man.

Annie walked up the path to Johnny's townhouse and rapped two times on the door, just as he had instructed her.

"Hello, little girl." He swung the door wide and beckoned her in.

"Hi, Johnny," she said as she strode into the middle of his living room right next to his black leather sectional. She turned to face him head on. "So actually, I just came to tell you that this is over. I don't want to see you anymore."

"Then why are you here?"

"Look. I'm just here to be polite. I'm finished with drugs—no more cocaine for me. I don't need to continue in this transactional relationship."

"*This transactional relationship*? Has someone been consulting a dictionary?"

"That's just mean, Johnny."

"Come here, little girl."

"I'm serious. I don't need drugs. I don't need you. I don't need anyone." Annie punctuated this declaration by stalking back in the direction of the door.

The trouble was, this move required her to pass right by Johnny Buscemi.

Just as she did so, he grabbed her by the hair—her long, swinging, dark ponytail. He didn't hurt her. It was a gentle grab, if such a thing existed. And maybe, if she were to be honest, it was ever so slightly erotic.

"Johnny, let go of me."

"You're nervous, little girl. I have something different for you tonight. Something that'll make you feel soft and warm all over."

Annie paused in Johnny's apartment with her hair in the grip of his fist. He loosened his grasp on her pony tail and ran his hand down the length of it, slipping it around her neck. Then, with his other hand, he pulled her face up by the chin and forced it around to face him. "Aren't you tired, little girl? Wouldn't you like a rest?"

Annie felt the seduction of it—the voluptuary lure of sleep.

"I'm fine," she claimed without conviction.

Johnny held up a small silver box, engraved with his initials. He gave it a little shake. She shouldn't react. She wouldn't. She would continue on her way and seal up this chapter behind her. Johnny pried the box open to reveal a Pandora's chest of white pills.

"What are those?" she asked, and she could see that he knew that he had her.

He poured two glasses of champagne.

"Bottoms up," Johnny said, and Annie did not disappoint.

He filled her glass again as he rummaged around in the box.

"What *are* they?" Annie was feeling better already.

"These, little girl, are tranquility and bliss. Take one. I promise you'll feel better."

How could she go wrong with bliss? She'd been looking for it all her life. She reached into the box and took two for good measure.

* * *

Annie came to in Johnny's bed, naked and uncovered. He was standing at the foot of it, in what looked like a silk dressing gown, tied at the waist with a tasseled belt, like an actor in a black and white movie.

"I'm cold," she said. Her throat felt dry and itchy.

"Just a minute," he responded.

"What are you doing?" she asked him.

"Don't move," he said, without moving himself. She did not know why he just stood there.

"Johnny?" she said more forcefully. She was beginning to feel alarmed.

"This is gorgeous, little girl. Really gorgeous."

It was then that she saw the Polaroid. He was actually taking her picture!

"Johnny, don't!" Annie tried to move, to cover herself, but she discovered she was tied to the bed. "Untie me now, Johnny. I mean it." She wrestled some more until a wooziness scrambled her head. "Shit. What did you give me?"

"What did I *give* you? You mean, what did you *take*? Because, as I recall it, you took them pretty willingly. Quaaludes, little girl. Rorers. Seven fourteens."

Click.

The noise of it startled her as Johnny took another photo. The print slid out the front of the camera and he stood for a second shaking it.

"I mean it, Johnny. That's enough."

"Hang on, baby. You look so nice. Just a couple more and you can go."

Click. He did it again.

"Johnny, stop it! I don't want to do this."

Click.

"Come on, Johnny. What about Frankie?"

"You want to talk to me about Frankie? Go ahead. I'd like to hear what you have to say on that subject."

"Okay. I hear you. I've behaved badly. Just untie me. C'mon, Johnny. Come on!"

Click.

"Johnny, let me go!"

Click.

A sickening clarity dawned on her that she had gotten in over her head. She had seen him as a kindred spirit, but he wasn't like her at all. There was a cruelty to him that only now she recognized. "Please, Johnny. I'm saying please."

"Oh, I like that, little girl. I like a girl who begs."

Click. He did it again.

Annie thrashed around in the bed until her nausea got the best of her.

"Imagine you're a butterfly," he said chillingly. "And I've pinned you to the board. You'd best settle down or you might rip your wings."

Awareness of her own impotence grew. She had never had any real power at all. Not now, not then, not ever. What was the point in fighting it? There was nothing to do but surrender.

Johnny took her picture over and over again. Ten in all, until the Polaroid ran out of film. She watched him as he studied the photos under the lamp on the desk.

"You're photogenic, little girl."

"Fuck you, Johnny."

"No more tonight, baby. I'm tired."

Johnny collected the pictures and placed them into a clean white envelope. He sealed it and opened the drawer of his desk. He placed the envelope inside and shut it firmly, with a little snap.

"Now, come on, little girl," he said as he untied her. "Go home. I need some sleep."

Annie reached up and slapped Johnny as hard as she possibly could. He laughed a little, touched his cheek, then he hauled off and slapped her back. "Get out of my house," he said. "The sight of you makes me sick."

She squeezed her eyes tightly to stop any semblance of tears. She would not cry in front of him. Tentatively, she rose from the bed. But, she was at a loss for how to proceed. She scanned the room for her clothes. Surely, she would not need to ask for Johnny's help.

Finally, she saw her pile of clothing discarded on the floor. She grabbed what she could and ran, the front door slamming behind her.

She stood naked in the early dawn on Johnny's front porch, scrambling to get into her dress. She hadn't even collected her shoes.

A bilious rage rose up Annie's legs, then saturated her middle, seeping from her abdomen to suffuse her chest, and blew out the top of her head. She was so mad right now that she could do anything. Truly anything.

She hated Johnny Buscemi more than she hated anyone she had ever met.

With the exception of herself.

40

"Mrs. Ford. Mr. Ford." DelVecchio is at the door of the little room. "Follow me, please."

Down the hall they all troop to the original room in which they had met earlier. Provenzano sits waiting, but Sherry has disappeared.

"Take a seat, please." DelVecchio gestures to the side of the table opposite Provenzano, as though they would consider splitting up to share sides with the FBI agents—like two couples out for dinner.

"Mrs. Ford, I am going to make this very plain." DelVecchio does not sit but stands behind his chair. "You might be in a great deal of trouble. Exactly how much trouble you are in will depend entirely on facts as they unfold and your compliance from this day forward. You are not yet charged with a crime. But, you do understand that you have the right to remain silent, the right to an attorney? If you cannot afford an attorney," he adds with a small smile, "one will be provided for you. Do you understand these rights, and do you wish to speak to me?"

"Yes, I—" she begins.

"Good." DelVecchio cuts her off. "I repeat. You are not yet charged with a crime. However, pursuant to investigation of the accusations that are now being leveled by Mrs. Hopkins, there are numerous state and federal laws that may have been broken." DelVecchio uses the fingers of both

189

hands to tick off his points. "If you are not, in fact, Susan Bentley Ford—if you are, in fact, another woman who has been posing as Susan Bentley Ford—if the real Mrs. Ford is dead or was killed—if you have had any involvement in, or knowledge of, her death or disappearance and have withheld that information from legal authorities—if you, at some point in time, assumed her identity and her property—if you moved that property from one state to another—well, to name a few criminal charges that would be considered—and I stop myself here to assure you that this list is nowhere near comprehensive—we have identity theft, larceny, forgery, illegal transport of stolen goods over state lines, accessory to murder and, make no mistake about this, murder. Is that clear, Mrs. Ford?"

"Yes."

"Good. Now, I have some questions for you. To begin with, do you recognize this object?"

DelVecchio slides his chair to the side, making a slight whine along the floor as he does so. He steps forward to the edge of the table, leaning his legs on the rim. He reaches down to pick up a manila envelope, which she had not noticed earlier. He lifts up the envelope, pinches the little brass clasp, and runs his hand under the flap to loosen it. He tips the envelope to allow its contents to slide out onto his cupped left palm. All eyes are focused on DelVecchio's sleight of hand.

DelVecchio then grasps the object with the thumb and index finger of his right hand, holds it up in the air and lets the length of it fall down and dangle.

Like a man just dropped from the gallows, a pendant shaped like a question mark swings back and forth on a long gold chain in front of all of their faces.

"Do you know what this is, Mrs. Ford?"

"It, uh, it's a necklace," she says.

"Sus..." Jack catches himself. "You don't have to answer this, you know."

She sees DelVecchio register Jack's slip, tally it in his mental file folder.

"Mr. Ford, as I am sure you are well aware," Provenzano says, "under certain conditions, Mrs. Ford's cooperation with an ongoing investigation—an investigation that may involve other parties and other crimes—might ameliorate the effects of any charges brought against her."

"Are you making some sort of offer?" Jack asks.

"I don't mind answering the question," she says. "I have nothing to hide." At that comment, she notices, everyone in the room maintains a studied poker face—Jack Jr. included.

"Have you seen this necklace before?" Provenzano asks.

"Yes, I have."

"Look, I mean it," Jack blurts. "You do not have to answer these questions. Gentlemen, I suggest that we stop these proceedings now. As a family member, I cannot properly act as counsel for this interview."

"Mr. Ford, as I said earlier," DelVecchio explains, "Mrs. Ford has not been charged with any crimes. We are asking for her help in another matter. A case that's been cold for thirty-five years. It would be beneficial to Mrs. Ford to be of assistance to us."

"It's all right, Jack." She reaches out to touch Jack's arm and feels him flinch. She turns back to Provenzano and DelVecchio. "Where did you get that necklace?"

"Why don't you tell us what you know about it," says DelVecchio.

"Look," Jack interjects, leaning toward her across the table to better claim her attention. "I really do not like where this is going. I advise you to stop talking immediately."

"Mrs. Ford, do you remember meeting a young woman by the name of Diane Englund? She may have been a patron at Frankie's Disco. She may have worked there as a waitress. She may not have used her real name."

And with that, Agent Provenzano opens a second manila envelope, larger than the first, and slips out a photo. It looks like a yearbook photo, glossy black and white. In it, Diane, the sweet, young waitress from Frankie's, is smiling. Her hair is curled in a flip, her bangs are combed straight down over her forehead. Her freckles shine out, her eyes are bright, and her smile is wide.

Diane is wearing a dark crewneck sweater—maybe black, maybe blue, maybe even red. Staring at the photo, she remembers the odd fact that red looks like black in a black-and-white image.

Around her neck hangs the gold question mark necklace. It is distinctive. There is no mistaking it; she has never seen another one like it. Not before and not since.

She breathes in sharply.

"I—that's all I have to say right now. I need to go." She rises abruptly, which tips over her chair behind her. It lands with a loud thud.

Jack rises, as well.

"Mrs. Ford, we'll be in touch. We suggest you think seriously about what we said."

Without a word to the agents or each other, Mrs. Jack Ford and Mr. Jack Ford Jr. depart.

41

Friday, August 15, 2014

Two days later, Mrs. Ford strides back into the reception room of the FBI office in Boston. This time, she is alone. She knows now what she must do to right mistakes of the past and contain any further damage. She wears neither heels nor a dress but is less formal in dark pants, a sweater, and loafers.

"Good morning, Melinda," she says.

"Good morning, Mrs. Ford. Please have a seat. I'll let them know you're here."

She sits and waits. Distractedly, she reaches into her bag and pulls out the old white envelope, dingy and yellowed with age.

DelVecchio opens the door. "Mrs. Ford," he says.

"Agent DelVecchio," she answers, stuffing the envelope back in.

She follows him through the reception area, past Melinda at her post, through the door, down the hall and into the interrogation room that is now familiar to her.

"Mrs. Ford," Provenzano greets her. "Please take a seat."

She sits on her usual side of the table and DelVecchio joins Provenzano on theirs.

The room has more objects in it than it had on her visit two days before. A white board is mounted on an easel next to the table. The high school graduation photo of Diane Englund, smiling, freckled, and wearing the gold question mark necklace, is tacked to it. Several other iterations of that picture, each blown up and featuring the necklace in grainy black-and-white closeups, are alongside of it. Hanging below them are some large-scale images of the necklace in full color. New pictures taken from the necklace they now have in their possession.

"Just to establish the facts, you have chosen to return here today unaccompanied by an attorney?" Provenzano asks.

"Yes, I have," she responds.

"And you are willing to cooperate with this investigation?"

"Yes, I am."

"Have you brought the photographs you mentioned on the phone?" DelVecchio cuts to the chase.

"Yes." Again, she extracts the shabby envelope from her purse. "Here they are."

She sets the envelope on the table and slides it across to the agents.

Provenzano takes it and opens it. It is not sealed. He shakes out a stack of Polaroid pictures, ten in all, and, one by one, examines them. He grabs a jeweler's loupe from the table to get a closer look. Once he has gone through the stack three full times, while she and DelVecchio remain silent, he passes the stack and the loupe to his partner.

DelVecchio repeats the process.

"Why didn't you turn in the photos to the police earlier?" asks Provenzano.

"I was frightened."

"Do you understand the ramifications of these pictures? Do you also understand the consequences for you for withholding this information all these years?"

"These pictures scared me." She sinks back onto her chair. "It was a dark time. My life was…well, you don't care about that."

"Why don't you let us decide what we care about and what we don't?" Provenzano says gently.

"What happened to her?" She looks at the smiling Diane on the white board.

"We'll ask the questions, Mrs. Ford," says DelVecchio, not gently at all.

Provenzano steps in. "We don't know what happened to her. Here's what we do know. Diane Englund was a runaway. From a prominent family in Bloomfield Hills. Her father was an executive in the auto industry. With Chrysler.

"Her parents brought that yearbook photo to the police in the summer of nineteen seventy-nine, shortly after she disappeared. The FBI became involved. But nothing of her was ever found. No information about her whereabouts. No body. No calls. No tips. Nothing. Those were different times. This was before computers. There was no internet.

"Eventually, the case went cold. The information was placed in her file, along with the school photo. It was all kept in the property room in Detroit, down in the basement. Another face on a milk box.

"When Samuel Fakhouri turned up in our hands ten days ago, that necklace was in his possession. We had not been looking for it, but it caught our attention. We reviewed everything we had with our office in Detroit and someone there remembered it. They dug around and came up with this case. We ran some dimensions and the necklace is an exact match. We suspect Fakhouri might be our guy."

42

Annie hadn't intended to go to Susan's that night. They were not even on speaking terms. She hadn't meant to go looking for Frankie, either. He had told her he was busy with his mother and had asked her to leave him alone. She hadn't planned out one single aspect of the debacle that unfolded.

The evening had begun at her grandmother's house. She'd promised Grandma Annie a girls' night in, complete with Jiffy Pop, and she had attempted to make it work. She sat on the sofa next to her grandmother, struggled to follow the TV show, tried to choke down popcorn, and endeavored to limit her runs to the bathroom for little maintenance sniffs. Grandma Annie had noticed her agitation.

In the bathroom, Annie calculated her remaining cocaine supply. And that is how she ended up at Johnny's, doing something else she hadn't intended to do that night. She knew she was courting disaster by showing up at his place once again, but she was desperate. Desperate to get those pictures that Johnny had taken of her. And desperate for more cocaine.

It was not so much that Annie enjoyed the feeling of being on cocaine, but that she couldn't bear to come off of it. What happened when the coke wore off was a ripping open of the chasm inside of her, exposing the hole she pretended was not there. To face it was unendurable.

Annie had experienced her first taste of cocaine not quite two months before. How could the drug have become the centerpiece of her waking life in such a short time? It had not happened with a bang but with a sweet slide. Cocaine had inserted itself ever so gently into the empty space that was already primed, ready, and waiting inside Annie. It slipped in neatly, a perfect fit, like a hand in a custom-made glove. The problem now was that, when that glove was removed, the hand it exposed was a slab of raw meat with every nerve exposed.

Annie had backed herself into a tight and airless corner.

The fact that Johnny behaved with impunity filled her with awe and envy. She recognized the boys' club to which he belonged and knew that she stood outside of any benefits it might confer. If Frankie ever figured out that she'd been trading sex for drugs, she would be judged harshly and tossed aside.

On whatever pecking order those men existed, Johnny was above Frankie. Frankie would throw Annie to the curb, but he would forgive Johnny. Maybe not at first—maybe Vito would have to step in and talk sense to him—but, eventually, Johnny's sins would be absolved. He and Frankie would move on together, in their little fraternity, and, over the years, Annie would become a shared anecdote, a reminiscence of the summer of '79.

Perhaps she would not even achieve that status. Maybe she'd simply be forgotten, joining the anonymous masses of girls they had screwed. In any case, they would close ranks and shut her out.

She perceived this, but she could not help herself. She had heard it said that a mugger doesn't mug everyone he sees—he picks his mark. Johnny had chosen her because she had been available to be chosen. Annie could have walked away, could have taken Susan's offer of an exit strategy, but she did not. She had made her bed, as her grandmother would say, and she was lying in it.

So the night that had begun at Grandma Annie's quickly devolved into a whispered call to Johnny from the wall phone in the kitchen. Could he meet her? No. Could he help her out? *Please,* she found herself begging. *Fine,* he acquiesced. He sounded annoyed, not at all happy to hear from her. He said he was going somewhere important and did not have much time. She could come by his place, but she'd better make it quick.

Annie slammed down the phone and dashed out the door, calling a hasty goodbye to Grandma Annie. Had she known that she would never see her grandmother again, she would have said a more respectful farewell to the woman who had loved her beyond all others.

But she didn't.

43

Thursday, September 6, 1979

In the early morning hours, Annie spun her Corvette in the direction of Susan's. Susan would know what to do. She always did. Annie recognized her own peevishness toward Susan and couldn't explain it. She liked Susan. She wasn't even joking when she'd said she wanted to be more like Susan. She also knew Susan was leaving imminently to go back to college and she risked never seeing her again. So, why hadn't she spoken to her in weeks?

That thought skittered toward another, darker truth and Annie bumped up against the question of her own college career. Classes had started already, and she had neither bothered to show up nor to officially resign. Best not to think too deeply on that subject and circle back to Susan. She hoped she hadn't already missed her.

This endless game of mental ping-pong was exhausting and only ratcheted up the bleakness that was creeping like a fog over Annie's cocaine-induced good spirits. She freshened her dosage, which helped, and drove a little faster to Susan's.

Her loveless encounter with Johnny that night had gutted her and left her longing for a friend. Though it had been a victory of sorts. She had gone to Johnny's and done what she needed to do to get what she needed to have. When he left the room to dress, she had rummaged in his drawer and succeeded in retrieving the photos.

It did not take long. The white envelope was sitting right on top of a mess of papers. It practically had a spotlight shining on it. She had grabbed it, stuffed it down the front of her jeans and slammed the drawer shut.

She was gone before he came out of the bathroom.

At two a.m. on that September night, standing on the front lawn at Susan's, Annie's thoughts turned to Frankie. He knew she'd had the night off. She had expected him to take her out for the evening. Maybe not for dinner, she couldn't stomach dinner, but at least for drinks. The bar at the Renaissance Center downtown would have struck the right note of celebration.

Celebration of what? Well, getting ahold of that envelope would certainly qualify as grounds for celebration, but it was not as though she could talk to Frankie about that. She couldn't really talk to Frankie about much, she would have to admit, if she were honest with herself.

And what was that business about dinner with his mother? Had Frankie really thought she'd believe such a transparent lie?

Annie tossed a pebble with a little too much backspin and cringed for a moment as it arced high in the air toward the window. To her relief, it did no damage and was probably the hit that succeeded in waking Susan.

It wasn't really until Susan came out to the porch that Annie hatched her plan to find Frankie. Once born, like a weed in her mental garden, the idea flourished and shadowed all others. In that way, it served to calm her. One obsession was easier to manage than dozens of thoughts ricocheting around in Annie's brain, fighting each other for dominance. She would search for Frankie, Susan would accompany her, and any concept of what might transpire once Frankie was uncovered remained unexplored.

Annie had expected to discover Frankie, in full flagrante, on the boat. She knew that he'd been with Sherry more than once this summer and she had a hard time believing that Susan hadn't noticed anything. It was so damned obvious to her that she suspected Susan must have known. But Susan maintained her ignorance, which reminded Annie that Susan was secretive and perhaps untrustworthy.

The boat had turned out to be a bust. Annie had had the hardest time climbing aboard, with the ladder pulled, but her own sense of moral righteousness catapulted her onto the deck. She'd made so much noise in the process that she paused a moment to catch her breath and listen for Frankie.

As Annie prowled the pitch-dark boat, she cursed Susan sitting comfortably in the car, probably sleeping by now. She had really wanted Susan to serve as her backup on this mission.

Just then, a flashlight clicked on and blinded her. She screamed and stumbled backward toward the stairs.

"Who's there?" she asked shrilly.

"No! It's *me* who wants to know who's *there!*" demanded a booming male voice.

Annie peered through the beam of the flashlight and realized that it was Frankie's boat captain, emerging from the aft stateroom, or somewhere thereabouts.

"It's me. Annie."

"Annie? What are you doing here?"

"Freddie, I'm looking for Frankie. Is he here?"

"What the hell kind of stupid are you?" He wasn't being very nice, and Annie thought he might be hiding Frankie. "Go home."

"I need to talk to Frankie. Is he here?" her voice was gaining strength.

"Listen, get outta here. I mean it. Go home. Frankie's not here and you shouldn't be here, either, in the middle of the night. What the hell's wrong with you?"

"Freddie! You're being rude!"

At that, Captain Freddie grabbed Annie by the arm in a not-too-gentle manner and hustled her along, through the galley to the forward cabin, flipping on lights as he went. "Look. He's not here. Now go home. You don't know what you're getting into."

"Okay, okay! I'm going!" Annie shook herself loose and made a semblance of walking back toward the deck, when she suddenly lunged in the direction of the aft stateroom from which Freddie had just emerged.

"Jesus Christ!" Freddie was right behind her. "You are one fuck-ing nut!"

Annie made sure to get a good look into the room before Freddie unceremoniously hauled her upstairs and across the deck—maintaining his firm grip on her arm as she scrambled back down to the dock. She could see that she was not going to be able to investigate further with this Neanderthal watching her every move.

"Well, goodnight, Freddie." She tried to salvage the relationship. "Thanks."

Freddie stood there in his boxers, glowering at Annie and blurted a final, "Go home!" before she turned and sauntered back toward the car.

She meant to follow his advice at that point. She really did.

44

But Annie did not heed Freddie's counsel. She did not listen to Susan, whose wisdom she had been seeking. She followed nothing but her own dogged determination to confront Frankie. She turned the car in the direction of his house and barreled south along the lake.

Arriving, Annie saw his car in the driveway and believed with the conviction of an evangelist that she had been right all along. She had found her man and would catch him in the act. On feeling the hood and finding it hot, she knew she was right and that she had been wronged.

What did she imagine would happen? Did she think that if she caught Frankie in bed with a babe, he would weep and beg her forgiveness? Drop to one knee and ask her to marry him? Had she even thought that far? There was not much in Annie's mind that night, except that, like a greyhound chasing a decoy around the track, she needed to catch it. And, like the greyhound, she did not understand, could not see the game, stacked as it was by forces larger than she was.

When she practically fell through the front door—it opened so easily—certainty yielded to confusion. Every light in the room was blazing. Men, some of whom she recognized, were standing and sitting everywhere. Still, this did not stop her. Like a rubber band leaving a slingshot, her body moved forward toward Frankie standing on the left of the room near his brothers, Danny, and Johnny.

Annie was so intent on her goal that she did not, at first, register that some of the men, those on the far side of the room, were Chaldeans. All heads turned in Annie's direction when she burst through the door. Hands moved to pockets and waistbands, but Annie did not grasp the meaning. Her mission propelled her closer to Frankie and the showdown that she had imagined.

Vito spoke first, asking his little brother to get his girlfriend the hell out of there. Johnny Buscemi and the cop said nothing, but stood next to Vito, frowning in solidarity. Frankie caught Annie by both arms to stop her forward propulsion. The other men shuffled around and broke the silence with sotto voce mumbling.

Annie, unconcerned about the zeitgeist of the room, theatrically demanded that Frankie account for his whereabouts in the preceding hours of the evening. Vito again commanded Frankie to get the girl out. Frankie, caught between the rock of his brother and the pain-in-the-ass hard place of his girlfriend, shook her a little as he, too, told her she had to go. Annie, tired of men telling her to go home all night long, flatly refused.

No one—not Annie, not any of the Italians and maybe not even the Chaldeans—had focused on Sammy slipping out the back door. It was Sammy's return, what felt like hours into the tense scene, that unleashed the bedlam that followed.

All eyes had been riveted on the domestic drama unfolding between the warring couple. Because of that—the flash in the corner of the eye that was Sammy reappearing, startled someone—tipped that person off balance. One shot rang out, its source unknown. For the briefest moment, it might have been a lone shot and composure may have been regained. The delicate negotiation that had been interrupted by the girlfriend might have transpired, after all.

But that was not to be the case.

For Annie could not stop herself from screaming. The infinitesimal second of silence after the initial gunshot was followed first by Annie's scream and, subsequently, by a barrage of gunfire, ricocheting in all directions.

Annie's first thought, on seeing herself covered in blood, was that she had been hit. It was only when Frankie's steely grip on her arms relaxed and his body began its slow descent down her torso that she realized that it was Frankie who had been shot.

Adrenalin, fueled by cocaine, enabled Annie to shake Frankie's crumpled body off of her feet and run. That same super-human energy kept her sprinting for where she thought she'd left her car and allowed her to nimbly pivot and lurch into it, in its new position, as Susan was already pulling away.

Coming down from coke was always bad. But there was no equal to the black hole that opened to swallow Annie as she sat in the car, her own Corvette, driven blindly by Susan through the sleeping streets of Grosse Pointe, just before dawn that morning.

Even in her addled state, Annie recognized that she had been an actor in this tragedy. Even she could perceive that she had played a starring role. She sat and whimpered, turning over in her mind the rudimentary concept of her own responsibility. She knew that she was one of the guilty parties in the grizzly scene she'd just fled but wasn't yet ready or able to make a full accounting of her own transgressions.

What she did not know, what would later prove to be a failure of imagination, was that the worst was not yet over.

Susan plunged on.

Annie thought they were dead, for sure, when Susan careened over the Ashland Bump, the famously mounded bridge over a canal, just on the Detroit side of the Grosse Pointe border, popular with teenage hotrods showing off their mettle. She feared Susan would crash the Corvette then, as it landed, nose down, spewing sparks and fishtailing to the side. But it was not to be. Susan righted the body of the car through deft handling of the steering wheel. A good Detroit girl knew how to drive.

Annie mistook the significance of this near crash. Once again, she interpreted this as the crescendo. Again, she believed they had come through the worst. Again, she was mistaken.

Susan drove on through the shabby streets of Detroit. Detroit blight, in 1979, was in its early stages. Detroit, like the suburbs that enveloped it, was a city of houses. But these houses did not look like those across the border the girls had so recently crossed. Arson had begun to proliferate and scattered houses were missing. There were corner stores, parking lots, and small factories interspersed with residential stretches. Overall, it looked scruffier and more urban. And darker. The moon had set, the sun had not appeared, and the streetlights were not all functioning.

And then, Susan had her meltdown over the watch.

"I'm sorry, Susan," Annie screamed, hoping to reel her back. "I found it! I didn't know it was yours! I'll give it back. But you have to go faster!"

"I don't know if I can."

"You have to!"

"Stop screaming at me!" The sinews in Susan's neck were straining with the exertion of controlling the car. "I don't think I can."

"They have guns! Do you hear me? *Guns!*"

"Okay!" Susan screamed back at her, "Okay! Okay! Okay!"

Intrepidly, street after street, Susan hurtled deeper into Detroit's east side.

Annie twisted forward and back, sometimes watching their pursuer and sometimes trying to follow Susan's advancing course. Neither girl had any hope of finding the way home from here.

Both girls were concentrated on the most pressing problem, the car that continued to chase them.

Then Susan said the strangest thing.

"Ah!" she gasped. "I don't know the time!"

"Now?" Annie wondered what the hell was the matter with her.

"When we meet in Paris! I don't know the time!"

Annie squinted at Susan in dismay, then something made her turn her head forward. Some shadow of intuition. She saw the Packard Plant first, only a second before Susan did, dark and enormous, hulking before them, as they rounded the last corner. She looked up at the old factory and she wasn't sure if she uttered the command, "Brake!"

Did she say it?

Would it have made any difference?

She saw Susan shift her gaze to look up at the very last moment, the too-late moment, the moment of no return. The mass of the old Packard Plant loomed in front of them. Susan spun the wheel to the left, while furiously pumping the brakes in a futile attempt at stability.

And then the car took over. As though it wanted to fly. As though it were tired of Susan's disorderly driving and wished to show her a better way. It lifted and moved to the side. It jumped in the air. And, just for that second, it *was* smooth sailing.

Then the car hit something immutably hard. Annie could not see that it was a fence post. For, at that same moment, from the force of the impact, she, too, was flying. The car had chosen again. Her Corvette had ejected her, thrust her out, an unworthy passenger on its final journey. But Susan, it had kept.

Simultaneously, one girl was flung to the curb while one girl died in the whirling Corvette, which presently burst into flames.

Then the world went black.

45

If she could lie in utter stillness, ceasing every controllable movement. If she could slow her breath—scoop it so shallow that the oxygen she takes in becomes microscopic, and the carbon dioxide she lets out, immeasurable. If she could render her thoughts pacific—calm like a glass-flat ocean.

Then could she stop this from happening?

But, at last, she knows that she cannot. She could not stop the sliding car then. She can't halt its impact now. After all these years—the warped slow motion of the accident accelerates, and she will finally experience the crash.

Mrs. Ford is at home in bed. It is early on a Sunday morning. How many summer Sundays has she had? It's been eighteen years since she first met Jack. Eighteen summers in Watch Hill. This summer, they shift into memory.

This Sunday morning, like those before it, starts with a lull—after the sun rises and before the hordes arrive for the beach, the carousel, the shops along Bay Street. Before they come to eat ice cream and fudge, clam chowder, and lobster rolls, there is a hush that hangs over the village.

There is a quiet that sits like a low-slung fog on the parking lots, before they admit outsiders to this little slice of Brigadoon. A silence that

208

rings a little—like a bell tone in the distance—before the summer people, those who own the cottages surrounded by wisteria and hydrangea, roses and privet hedges—cottages like Mrs. Ford's—begin their walk to services at the Watch Hill Chapel.

Then the calliope cranks up. The air hisses out of the tubes of the circus instrument—breathy and high—and the show is about to begin. The greatest show on Earth. Step right up, folks! Get your seats! Get your popcorn! Get your peanuts! They enter stage right and stage left—the summer people in their Nantucket Reds and blue blazers, pastel dresses, and pearls—the day trippers nearly naked in their cover-ups and tattoos. They arrive from opposite sides, cross each other on winding paths, and exit in different directions. The tourists head to the beach. The summer people enter the chapel.

The Church is Many as the Waves, but One as the Sea.

In Essentials, Unity: in Non-Essentials, Liberty: in All Things, Charity.

That's what its mottos say. In beautiful blue and gold, against aged walls of wood. But, do they mean it? Charity in *all*? Charity *for* all? Charity for the tattooed visitors? Charity for Mrs. Ford?

She will not go to chapel this morning. She will not join her friends singing hymns—*Amazing Grace* and *Rock of Ages* perhaps. But, there, next to the sea—so placid on a summer morning—she hopes they will remember the furies and fates of winter. She wants their voices to rise high in homage to their seafaring ancestors. She wills them to bargain *For Those at Sea*. She lies motionless in bed, looking out at the lighthouse, dogs on her legs, reciting the words to that hymn:

Eternal Father, strong to save,
Whose arm hath bound the restless wave,
Who bidd'st the mighty ocean deep
Its own appointed limits keep;
Oh, hear us when we cry to Thee,
For those in peril on the sea!

She will not join them afterward, as they gather for refreshments in front of the chapel—facing the dumbfounding beauty of the Atlantic

Ocean—as they nibble their cucumber sandwiches. Had she known that her Sundays were finite, would it have made any difference?

She does not know where she will go or what she will do today or any day going forward. Her housekeeper, Helen, is not at Gull Cottage. Her stepson, Jack Jr., is avoiding her. She is alone in the house, except for her dogs. She is at liberty to construct the day in any manner she wishes. Free to contemplate recent disclosures. She has time to think about where these revelations will lead, what she surely has lost, what decisions she must make, and what consequences lie in store. The creeping inevitability of reckoning is upon her. The gig is up for Annie-Johnston-Nelson-Susan-Bentley-Ford.

She will have to say something to Helen. She does not know what she can say to Jack Jr., whose faith and friendship she may have lost forever. She will not need to say one word to her friends in Watch Hill or New York. The story will travel like wildfire, all on its own, jumping over obstacles like fire over creek beds.

She has had a good run—an extra thirty-five years. She has had the chance to re-invent herself. She has had the opportunity to marry a man she loved. She has had the ability to give to her favorite charities. Hell, she's had the chance to *have* favorite charities. She has had all of these options that the girl born as Susan never had.

But Annie really doesn't think of herself as Annie any more. Nor does she think of herself as the false Susan. She became Susan long ago. Or a version of Susan that was hers.

It has been so long since the summer of 1979. Feelings have been sublimated and facts, she had hoped, were wiped out. Recumbent in bed, her legs pressed down by the weight of her dogs, she finally faces the fact that there is no big cosmic eraser. *She is in peril on the sea.*

She examines the force of her own resolve. In the early years, she willed herself to become Susan, to talk and walk like Susan, to cultivate Susan's interests, to go one better and develop those interests over time, deepening her cultural knowledge.

The French was a sticking point, though; she never could fully master French. That had worried her, but she had learned enough of it to feel that she wouldn't be caught out on that count. In the end, she had been right. French is not what failed her.

She considers what she has done and those she has hurt; those she has lost and those she may still lose. She considers the consequences she may face. She considers the whole sweeping panorama of a life lived in fragmented episodes and broken, disjointed roles, of doors slammed shut in her face and miraculous doors that opened to her touch. As she lies there, tallying collateral damage, she tries to locate herself. No longer Annie, the girl she was born as, and not really the girl born as Susan. Who is she?

And then, like a bobbing cork, physical hunger arises. She thinks about making herself a nice, hot cup of cappuccino with her DeLonghi machine, of taking the dogs out, just to the seawall, to do their business, about multi-grain toast and beach plum jam and sea salt butter.

What does this say about her, she wonders? What kind of a woman, despite the rack and ruin around her, can think about eating breakfast?

The kind of woman that Annie is.

She kicks her legs to wake the dogs, who scramble up the duvet for kisses. She swings her legs around, puts her feet firmly on the floor and heads down to the kitchen.

46

Two bells ring at once. One is the phone. The other, the door. At the exact same moment, they both go off.

"I'll get the phone!" Annie shouts down the stairs. "Helen, would you answer the door?" She doesn't wait for a response.

"Hello?" she says into the receiver.

"It's Jack." His tone is cool and professional. "Do you have a minute?"

"Yes, of course." Annie sits on the edge of her bed. "What is it?"

"I called that FBI agent. He won't tell me much. I think you should be prepared for a charge of homicide."

"I...That could not be farther from the truth!"

"Yes, well, it wouldn't appear that truth-telling is a talent you hold in your repertoire."

"Look, Jack, I'd really like to sit and talk with you about everything that's happened."

"I don't think so. But, there is one thing that's eating at me. Can you tell me something? Truthfully?"

"Yes."

"Did my father know?"

Annie looks around the bedroom, trying to find the words to make Jack feel better. To make him understand that she did—she does—love and value him, despite her years of deceit. She chooses her words carefully. "He knew the important things."

"When? When did he know?"

"I don't know. Long ago. Not so long into our marriage."

"I see. So, it's just me, then? The guy who introduced you to his father? The guy you called last week to help you out of this mess? I'm the only one who didn't know?"

"No, of course not, Jack. No one knew except your father."

"You have crossed every line."

"Jack…"

"I offered you *friendship*! You went on about how that was such an important fucking commodity to you and I gave you that on a platter! And you have betrayed it at every turn! I don't give a shit what you did! I *do* care that you were a fraud from the day I met you!"

"I really am sorry."

There is a very long silence on the line. Annie thinks he may have hung up.

"I don't see a way forward for us," he finally says. "As a family. This is just too much. I don't even know what to call you. I can't come back with you there. Not in that house. I can't continue to work with you."

"I understand."

"You need a lawyer. A criminal lawyer. I suggest you hire one immediately. You're on your own on this one. I can't help you anymore."

And he hangs up the phone.

Annie bows her head to the receiver as the dial tone rings in her ear. Just then, Helen knocks sharply on the bedroom door.

"Yes?" she calls out.

"Someone is at the door, Mrs. Ford."

She hoists herself heavily from the bed. Her body feels like it is increasing in density, her molecules becoming sodden and heavy. Waterlogged. She crosses over and opens the door. "Who is it?"

"A Mr. Sammy Fakhouri, ma'am."

47

Sunday, September 9, 1979
Suburban Detroit

Annie swam deep in a dark ocean. Susan was there too, at a distance. Annie was unable to reach her, no matter how she pumped her legs and arms. She was breathing underwater, though she was not wearing scuba gear. She wondered how she was able to do that. Susan did not wear a tank, either, and appeared to be in trouble. She was not breathing as easily as Annie.

Annie tried to swim like a dolphin, using her torso to propel her, but that worked no better than her extremities. She wished she had a tank of air to give Susan but palpated around her torso and found none.

Sammy swam by and Annie called out to him, asking him to help Susan. He smiled and just kept swimming. Frankie swam by next, with Johnny Buscemi, Danny the Cop, and Vito. They were arguing amongst themselves and paid no attention to Annie.

Suddenly, she was overcome with fear. She examined why she would be afraid of them and could not remember a reason. The point became moot because they were gone from view. Annie looked around to find that Susan was gone, too. Sammy was gone. Frankie was gone. They were all gone.

Annie was alone.

She could not breathe. Whatever magical power she had possessed to enable her to breathe underwater had deserted her. She was gasping, and she was cold. Bone cold. She was far under the surface of this black ocean and she realized that she might not make it to the top. She began to jerk spasmodically.

Then her body metamorphosed into something hard. She couldn't breathe, but she was no longer gasping. She was a solid mass, sinking through icy water, down to the bottom of the sea. She thought she might be a boat. A boat that had shipwrecked on an expedition; maybe in search of whales. She was made of wood and she was damaged and there was no way of righting her direction and propelling herself to the surface.

She contemplated future generations who might find her, lodged in the seabed, covered with barnacles—sharks and scary, pale deep-sea fish swimming in and out of the holes in her sides. Would they find treasure inside her? Annie's mind swam in and out of itself, searching for the ephemeral treasure that she knew she would not find.

Sammy swam back to her and called her name. He repeated it over and over again. Though she was looking right at him and answering him, he did not seem to hear. His eyes bored through her, swam in and out of the holes in her head, just like the fish and the sharks.

Annie rested at the bottom now. The underwater currents shifted glacially, dragging sand along in their path. As centuries passed, it covered her. No fish swam in and out of her holes any more. No sharks chased fish around her hull.

Sammy no longer swam by, nor did Frankie. Or Johnny. Annie wondered if Susan was also buried under the sands of the sea. Her eyes no longer worked, so she could not see her. Her voice was not available, so she could not call out for her.

Only her mind continued, thinking, thinking, thinking. There was nothing else for her to do.

48

Annie opened her eyes. She scanned beige walls and curtains, brown furniture, and wall-to-wall carpeting, and guessed she was in a hotel. She did not remember checking into one and lay there for some time, trying to salvage a memory of where she was and how she'd gotten there. Nothing came to her.

What did come was an overwhelming thirst and a pressing urge to pee. Needing to quickly remedy the latter, she hoisted herself to her elbows and confronted a third sensation—pain. She struggled to pinpoint its source. As she sat up and swung her legs over the side of the bed, it became apparent that it emanated from her entire body.

Annie rested that way for a while, waiting for the throbbing and the dizziness that were sweeping over her to subside. She examined the pajamas she wore. They did not look familiar. In due course, she put her feet to the floor. Standing revealed the next surprise, as her legs nearly buckled under her. She leaned over the mattress to calm a recurrence of vertigo that was now accompanied by nausea. She imagined that she must be sick.

The demands of her bladder trumped all others and forced her to continue forward. Running her hands along the walls, as much for moral support as to steady her wobbly walk, she came to a door, which she opened to discover a closet. Oddly, a few articles of clothing—men's clothes—were hanging inside.

Panic edged into the swirl of emotions overtaking her. She must be in this hotel room with a man. But what man? She had to put that queasy-making thought aside and concentrate on finding a bathroom. The next door proved successful and Annie launched herself onto the toilet.

One bodily function satisfied, the next thing she needed was water. She could use about ten glasses of water. She had not turned on the light in the bathroom before sitting down so, on rising, she moved back to the doorway and felt along the wall for the light switch.

Eureka.

There was the sink, the faucet, and a glass. Annie filled it to the brim, brought it to her lips and cast her eyes up as she began to drink. And there in the mirror, she got her first glimpse of herself, cut, swollen, bruised, and bandaged. Whereupon, she let out a gurgled scream and promptly dropped the glass, shattering it on the bathroom sink and sending shards to the floor.

Seconds after the noise, a man bolted into the room. "Annie?" he said. "Why don't you come and sit down?"

Gingerly, she turned to face him and experienced another shock, in what she feared might be a never-ending parade of them.

"Sammy?"

"Annie, let's go over to the bed." He held out his arms to assist her. She recoiled, and he rephrased. "Come and sit. We can talk. Don't be afraid. Everything will be all right."

At his words, she felt her body slacken. Or maybe she was going to faint. Sammy reached out to grab her and glass crunched beneath his shoes as he carried her across the room. He placed her on the bed with care, yet she couldn't help groaning in pain.

"I'm so sorry," he said.

Tears leaked out of her swollen eyes. "What happened to me? Did Frankie beat me up?"

"You don't remember what happened?" Sammy looked stunned. "I...I'm sorry. I did not consider that you might not remember. I just..."

"Remember what? You're scaring me."

"I'm sorry. Of course, I'll tell you." Sammy examined his feet for a while. "All right. First, can I get you anything? Would you like some water? Some ice for—for anywhere that hurts?"

"I'm very thirsty," she said.

"I'll be right back," Sammy left and returned with a full glass of ice water.

He lifted Annie's head with one hand as he held the glass with the other. As thirsty as she was, she quickly felt nauseated and pushed it away.

"I'll set it here." Sammy placed the glass on a nightstand. "Let me know if you want another sip."

Annie just nodded her head, waiting for him to say something.

"You don't remember anything?" he tried again.

"I remember driving to Frankie's house with Susan. I think she was wearing a nightgown." She saw Sammy wince at that mention. "I was going there to see if Frankie was with someone. A woman."

"Do you recall anything after that? Do you remember getting to Frankie's?"

"I remember his car was there. I felt the hood to see if it was hot." Annie looked up to see Sammy staring at her quizzically. "That's how I can tell sometimes if he's lying. If the hood is hot, it means he's just driven somewhere."

"Oh." He paused. "Do you remember anything else? What about going into the house?"

"Oh, God!" Annie gasped. "I do remember the house. The lights were all on. And there were men there. Lots of men. You were there!"

"Yes."

"What happened there?"

"I...well...how much do you know about Frankie?"

"He's my boyfriend."

"No. I mean, his business."

"The disco? The pizzerias?"

"Look, Annie. There was a meeting that night between the Chaldeans and the Italians. It's all stupid territorial stuff that they were going to pound out. That's why I was there. For my cousin. He couldn't be there. He had to take care of a problem at one of our stores. I try not to get involved. But Jacob asked me to go."

"What are you talking about?"

"How do you think all those drugs funnel through Frankie's Disco? The cocaine? It's all Buscemi and that cop. The Chaldeans want a piece of it and the Italians need us for something else."

"I don't know what you mean."

"Years ago, they walked away from Detroit and we stepped in and bought it. Now gambling is coming."

"Detroit?" It was the only word she could key in on in this jumble of Sammy's story.

"It doesn't really matter. But, that's what that meeting was about— working out who gets what and where."

"I..." She struggled to clear her head. "So, what happened?"

"Jesus." Sammy got up from his seat to pace around the room. He walked over to the window and peeked out of the curtains. He closed them and smoothed them flat. Then, he yanked them open again.

"Sammy. You're making me nervous. What happened?"

"Oh, Annie." He turned and stood still, his arms hanging limp, like a little boy's. "Terrible things have happened."

She felt that flop of her stomach as it summersaulted upside-down. The drop of your insides that you get on waking, when you've managed to fall asleep amidst a shattering loss, and for that instant, you don't remember. But your stomach remembers for you.

"What?" It came out as a whisper.

As he took his first step toward her, as he said the name, "Frankie," and then the name, "Susan," she refused to hear any more.

"Stop." She held up her hands. "Don't come near me! Stop! No! No! No! No! No!"

No.

Up through the roof and into infinity went the word. Following Susan. Following Frankie, as they slipped through Annie's hands like helium balloons—incongruously rising skyward.

In the end, they weighed less than air.

* * *

And, so it was that Sammy Fakhouri, a decent man—a man who barely knew Annie Nelson, who was in love with Susan Bentley, who was on opposite sides in a turf dispute with Frankie Castiglione—had to tell Annie that both were dead.

As Annie sobbed, Sammy recounted events: How he had found Susan in the driveway when he was on his way out. How, with his encouragement, the girls had fled. How he had followed them and flashed his lights to signal them as he flew down the road behind them. He told her how he had arrived seconds after the crash, tried to approach the burning car, tried to grasp its red-hot handle, and finally turned away to pick Annie up from the road. He described how he had called Jacob from a payphone on a burned-out street in Detroit. How Jacob had found them and brought them to this safe house in the middle of a complex in Southfield. He explained how Jacob had called a doctor who made house calls and worked for cash. How the doctor had examined Annie and made the best guesses he could. How, at his instructions, Sammy had kept her hydrated with ice chips and a dampened sponge.

Annie eventually stopped crying and lay with her eyes wide open. Sammy eventually stopped talking and fell asleep on the floor.

And so, the night passed. The first night of Annie's consciousness of the death and destruction around her. Sammy had known for a week and so she excused him for sleeping.

But, as she stared at the ceiling, as she stared at her own self-serving past, she knew that she had no excuses left.

49

Annie looked at the ceiling until the sun came up, and she continued after Sammy arose.

"Would you like some coffee?" He popped his head in the room.

"No," was all she could say.

She gazed at it still, when Sammy returned.

"You have to eat," he said.

"No," she said again.

She rose twice to use the bathroom, whose floor Sammy had dutifully mopped of broken glass. But, again, she went back to bed.

Through the next night, she stared at the ceiling.

"Coffee?" he asked the following morning.

"No," she answered again.

And she regarded the ceiling all day.

But then that evening, Annie's body, that healthy and powerful animal, took issue with her mind. It let her know it was hungry. It let her know it had needs. It let her know that, in a battle of wills, it had always been the strong one.

Finally, Annie obeyed it.

She sat up and noticed her clothes on a chair, resting neat and folded. Sammy must have washed them. She picked up her jeans and her long-sleeved T-shirt—the things she'd been wearing that night—and discovered them sickeningly torn. And, revealed beneath them, lay the remnants of her worldly goods: one gold question mark necklace— gift from her dead boyfriend, one platinum Longines watch—pinched from her dead friend, and one white envelope—taken from Johnny Buscemi. Her possessions were not even hers. She covered them up with the clothes.

Sammy walked into the room.

"You're up! Oh, you don't have to wear those. There are other clothes. I didn't want to throw those away. I washed them. And you had that envelope." He actually blushed. "It was…"

"It was stuffed down the front of my jeans."

"Um. Yes."

"May I have some toast? And coffee?"

Sammy was visibly relieved that one fewer girl would die. "Oh, thank God! Yes, toast! Coffee!" And he ran out of the room.

* * *

"Where did you get this food?" Annie asked as she ate it.

"Don't eat too fast. Jacob leaves it downstairs. We have a spot in the basement. He leaves bags of food and newspapers there and I go down and get them."

"Why are we even here?"

"It just seemed prudent. Until this thing blows over."

"Do people know about what happened?"

"Uh, yes. Can you handle watching the news?"

"I don't know." She was frightened. If she saw it on television, it would become real.

"It's no worse than what you've already learned."

"Okay," she whispered. There was something about Sammy that reassured her.

Sammy clicked the set on and the picture expanded to life. The news was already in progress in the midst of a weather report.

Next, there was an update on the Ayatollah's new government in Iran. When they showed the map on the screen, Sammy pointed a finger. "That's where I come from," he said, moving his finger to the left. "Well. Not so very far from there."

Annie was about to say something when the story they were waiting for began. The television anchor recapped, for the benefit of anyone who'd been living under a rock—or had been unconscious like Annie—the tale of "The Shootout in Grosse Pointe."

But tonight there was a new development.

The newscaster made a mental leap, linking a formerly ignored story of a car crash in Detroit with the killings in Grosse Pointe. The identity of the driver of the totaled car was assumed to be Annie Nelson, girlfriend of Frankie Castiglione. The body of Miss Nelson was burned beyond recognition in the ensuing fire.

One dead girl found in same girl's car. Dead girl's boyfriend murdered a few miles away. All of this occurring on the very same night. Why would identity be questioned? The reporter did not say this, but the meaning was implied.

And the implication of that changed everything.

When Sammy and Annie heard it, when they learned that only Annie was among the casualties, only Annie was tied to the shootout, and only Annie was presumed dead, it was Sammy who hatched the plan for Annie to become Susan.

50

Annie Nelson, who has lived under another name for thirty-five years, stands in the living room of her house in Watch Hill, face-to-face with Sammy Fakhouri. A man she'd last seen in Detroit—at the last moment she'd used her real name. A man she would have bet her fortune on never seeing again.

"Sammy. I…" She finds herself overcome and struggles to find the words. "It's been a long time."

"Yes. It has."

"I mean…I know you were on your way here ten days ago. The FBI visited me."

"I figured they would."

"Are you going to be cryptic? Do I have to pull information out of you?"

"You're still funny, Annie."

"I'm not really joking."

Suddenly, Sammy moves toward her. He awkwardly places his hands on her shoulders and they stand like that for a moment. Then he steps an inch closer to embrace her. Annie stiffens and pulls back, but Sammy clasps onto her firmly. Finally, she lets down her guard and hugs him back. They hold each other for a while.

"You look good," Sammy says. "Almost the same."

"So do you." She lies too. "Hardly different."

"Ah, looks are deceiving. My health is not so good."

"I'm sorry to hear that." Annie disengages herself.

"Yes, blood pressure, cholesterol—you name it."

"And, you're in trouble too."

"I guess we both are," he says.

"You know, I lived my life in trouble, up to a point. I was always in trouble when I was a girl. That awful feeling returns in an instant. Like putting on a pair of old slippers that molded long ago to your feet."

"The comfort of discomfort."

"You still sound like Confucius." She smiles and shakes her head. "But yes. When I got older, I learned about family systems. We end up repeating what we don't understand. Until we finally do. You want a drink?"

"Do you have any mint tea?" Sammy asks.

"Helen?" she raises her voice, but not by much.

"Yes, Mrs. Ford?" Helen appears in a flash. Surely, she was listening at the door.

"Would you make us a pot of mint tea?" Annie turns back to Sammy. "Sit down."

Taking her offer of a seat at the opposite end of the sofa, Sammy looks out at the water. He and Annie remain that way for a few minutes, taking in the panorama—fishing boats and sailboats in the foreground, immense shipping vessels crossing the background—a view that always and never changes.

"Susan would have liked this." Annie gestures at the vista.

"Yes," Sammy replies. "She would have."

"I picture her here. I picture her living my life. Well, living the life I made for her."

"I imagine that is not helpful, Annie."

They lapse into silence, side by side, together with Susan's ghost. Helen returns with the tea tray and Annie busies herself with pouring.

"Honey?"

"No, thank you. Blood sugar."

Annie passes a cup to Sammy and pours one for herself.

"You have done well," Sammy says.

"Yes."

"Tell me about your husband."

"Jack? He died five years ago. Another ghost I live with."

"Good man?"

"Yes, Sammy, he was a very good man. What about you? Have you married?"

"No."

"You would have made a good husband."

"I don't believe I would have made a good husband to anyone."

Annie sets down her cup and studies him. She has not seen this man in decades, and yet some things about him haven't changed: there is a resigned quality to the way he carries himself—a capitulation to fate—as if he has always believed his destiny was beyond his control. She clears her throat. "We need to talk."

"Yes, that's why I came."

"I think it's better if we get out of here." She rises. "Let's walk."

"All right." Sammy sets his cup next to hers.

Annie goes to a kitchen drawer and, bypassing the double lead, selects two single leashes. She connects the dogs and hands one to Sammy. She steers them to the right at the end of her drive and leads them two houses down, to take the turn onto Lighthouse Road.

The skies have clouded over and look ominous to the northeast. Best not to stray too far.

For thirty-five years—and perhaps longer, if she's honest—Annie has lived her life behind a mask, methodically closing an enfilade of interior doors, one after the other, until she is not sure she knows the way back. As they walk, she wonders if this is true of Sammy, as well. Is he like her, unable to find the breadcrumb trail that leads home? Did he, too, almost come to believe his own lies?

"Last time I saw you, you were headed to New York," Sammy says.

They arrive at the end of the road, where it opens onto the green sweep of lawn stretching to the lighthouse. The Atlantic crashes against the rocks and seawall to the left. The calmer waters of the bay gently roll up to the beach of Napatree and the houses with their own seawalls to the right.

Annie leans down and unleashes her dogs, allowing them to run freely.

Darker clouds roll across the sky. Fog is closing in over the point. The lighthouse, immediately in front of them, assumes an unreal appearance, its edges beginning to blur and its light beams to refract through the airborne water droplets of the approaching weather. The mournful sound of the foghorn is next to them now. For the second time this week, Annie thinks of the hymn to lost sailors.

"Yes. I went to New York. I got a job as a receptionist. I put my head down and moved forward.

"A few months after I arrived, there was a transit strike. Early spring of nineteen eighty, but it was very cold. I lived on the Upper West Side, near the Hudson River. I walked to work every day in tennis shoes—in a sea of people in suits and tennis shoes walking for miles to work. And, at night, coming back across Ninety-fifth Street, from Broadway to Riverside Drive, I walked down that concrete canyon into the frigid blast from the river.

"All the windows of my apartment faced a brick wall. My roommate made coffee in a Melitta carafe. The one that looks like an hourglass and you boil water on the stove and pour it through a filter. When she left for work in the morning, she put the whole thing in the refrigerator. So, every other day, we drank yesterday's coffee. That was my life: tennis shoes, the freezing walk, the brick wall view, old coffee."

"It sounds like you were punishing yourself."

"Well." Annie walks to the seawall on the Atlantic side, closer to the rough ocean. "I would have been justified."

She pauses to get a bead on her dogs, now tentatively stepping out onto the big rocks on the bayside.

"Calpurnia! Pliny! Come here!" She waits. Then she calls out a single word, "Cookie!"

At that, both dogs turn and run back to her at a gallop. She produces two dog treats from her pocket. "Magic bullet."

Annie goes on with her story. "It took all of that for me to pull myself together. Every bit of it. That summer, Frankie, the drugs, the accident, Susan's death, the long, dreary years in New York. I did the crash dummy version of growing up. Never took a graceful step in my life."

"What happened with Susan's father?"

Annie lets out a sigh. "He died within the year. I heard that he spent those months in a coma. I think—I pray—he never missed his daughter." She and Sammy both spend a moment on that prayer.

Annie continues, "His lawyer had predeceased him, so my conversations were with a junior partner who'd never met Susan. You'd set up the documents so well that I was able to sign the papers long distance. I had the proper ID to get a notary to sign off on everything.

"The house was sold. The contents were sold separately by one of those tag sale companies. The estate was settled. Susan was the sole beneficiary. It wasn't much, but it gave me a cushion in those early years. I pinched myself every day for a couple years after that, not really believing I'd sailed through it all. Jumping every time the phone rang."

"Forged papers were always my forté," Sammy says with a degree of rueful pride.

"Well, that's certainly among the crimes I could be charged with. But Sammy, how are you walking away? Last I heard you were in FBI custody. Now you're here at the beach and about to travel abroad?"

Sammy, who had been facing the ocean, turns back to her. "Things are not always what they seem."

"You still talk like a fortune cookie. Anyway, look at us. We recognized each other. And Sherry knew me. She knew me right away." Annie decides not to mention Johnny Buscemi.

"Was she your friend?" Sammy asks. "The FBI agents asked me about her, but I don't remember her."

"God, no! She hated me and Susan. After all these years. 'Revenge is a dish best served cold.' Who said that? Was it *Hamlet*?"

"I don't know. *Macbeth*?"

"Well, there's your proof. I'm not actually Susan or I would have known who said that."

"Yes." Sammy turns back to the sea, the wind blowing his once black hair, now splashed with silver, off his face. "Susan would have known."

51

Time: 6:45 p.m.

The air grows leaden. The rain holds off still, but it is coming. Soon, the clouds will burst. The heat of the day shifts in a moment and cold drafts blow in from the ocean.

Sammy and Annie stand at the Atlantic sea wall. They face the old Harkness house. The pop star's guards, in bright yellow slickers, can be seen at lookout points atop the cliff wall, ever vigilant for stalkers. Farther down is the Ocean House, also in yellow, its enormous form resembling a giant Victorian lady in a summer dress.

"Tornado weather," Annie says. "That's what we call this in Michigan. When the day goes from hot to cold in an instant. Usually the sky is green, though. This sky is rather black."

"Do you think we should go back?"

"Are you nervous, Sammy? Scared of a little rain?"

"You want to stand here in the rain, so be it."

Annie spins to face him. "I want to know why you were coming to see me the first time. What did you want from me, Sammy? I haven't seen you for thirty-five years. Why now?"

"That's what I came here today to explain. Don't you want to go inside?"

"No, I don't want to go inside! I want you to tell me right here, right now."

"Fine, I'll tell you now." Sammy resigns himself to the force of her will. "I was coming to ask you for money. I guess that part is obvious. I got myself into a situation that I wanted to get out of and the only way out that I could see required money."

"How did you know how to find me?"

"Come on, Annie. I already knew you started out as Susan Bentley. It wasn't hard to connect a few dots."

Annie turns back to the ocean. The surf is rising. A few intrepid souls in wet suits mount their boards to ride the waves crashing into East Beach. The Ocean House beach attendants run to and fro, folding up lounge chairs, collapsing umbrellas, battening the hatches before the storm.

"What have you gotten yourself into?"

"I can't really say."

"You expect me to give you money and you're not going to tell me what for?"

"The situation has changed since I came here two weeks ago. I'm no longer asking you for anything. Someone is waiting for me right now. This person will pick me up shortly at your house to take me to the airport. I need to go back to Iraq. My window of opportunity, as they say, has closed."

"I can't even follow this."

"You're not meant to follow it."

"You've just ruined my life, Sammy! A life I've spent years constructing!" Annie doesn't come up for air. "*You* put me on that plane to New York. *You* sent me off into the unknown. *You* never tried to find me in the sixteen years when I was alone. And now you're here? And the FBI is all over me? What the hell is this? What's going on?"

"That was not my intention. Remember, I saved your life once. I was coming to you to ask you to help me save mine. Damn it, Annie! I lost as much as you did back then!"

Annie takes a moment to digest what Sammy has just said.

"I'm sorry. I'm not the same self-involved twit you used to know. I really have changed. You got me started on that change in that apartment in Southfield." She reaches her hand out to him. "Remember?"

He softens and takes her hand in his. "Yes. I remember."

52

By the fifteenth day in hiding, Annie's physical condition had dra-
matically improved. Her emotional state was a different matter. She
cried all the time. She, the stoic of her family, now wept at the break of
an egg.

She knew that Sammy cried too. She saw him sometimes, when he
thought he was alone, gazing out the window with tears running down
his cheeks. They didn't gush, like a full-blown sob, they just coursed
slowly along his smooth, olive skin, until they dropped onto his shirt. He
never made a motion to wipe them. Perhaps, he thought if he did that,
she would notice. Sammy's anguish disturbed her even more than her
own. In all her life, she had never seen a man cry.

They stumbled toward a rhythm and stabbed at a semblance of normalcy. All days revolved around the news shows that, more than two
weeks after the shootout, had not ceased to feature that lurid story.
Obsessively, Annie and Sammy watched, searching for a key to the door
out of the apartment in Southfield.

"Sammy!" Annie called from the kitchen, a small, tiled alcove off of
the living room.

Sammy padded in from the bedroom, pulling a shirt over his head.
"I must have fallen asleep." He sniffed the air. "What's that smell?"

"That smell," Annie announced as she carried water glasses to the coffee table, where she had already set out placemats, "is dinner. I really hope you like it!"

"Ah. I'm sure it will be delicious."

"It's almost ready. I just wanted you to be here when I take it out of the oven. I hate for food to get cold."

"My mother is the same way." Sammy plopped on the sofa.

"Is your mom a good cook?" A seed of doubt was entering Annie's mind as she walked back with silverware and napkins.

"My mother is the best cook in the world." Annie deflated as soon as he said it. "Well, I should qualify. My mother is the best Chaldean cook. We eat a very different type of food from you Americans. Dolmas and kibbeh and baba ghannouj."

"I've had food like that in Greektown."

"Right. So, you know what I mean. But my mother's cooking is better than anything you've had there."

Before Annie could call it off, the little egg timer rang. She scurried back to the oven and pulled out a steaming casserole, which she heaped on two plates.

"Well. *Voilà.*" She set the plates before them. "I'm practicing my French while I practice my cooking. That's a lotta practice!"

"Thank you for dinner, Annie. *Merci.*"

"Oh. You're welcome." She sat beside him and held up her water glass. "Well. Here's to the Hindu who does what he kin do way up in those mountains where he must make his skin do!"

Sammy choked on his water. "What did you just say?"

"Just a toast my grandma taught me."

"Your grandmother sounds like an interesting woman."

"She's just a normal grandma."

"Somehow I doubt that."

Annie and Sammy lifted the plates to their knees and turned to face the television. Sammy picked up a fork and a knife, European-style, and prepared his first bite. Annie just used a fork. Detroit-style.

"Mmm." Sammy chewed. "Wow. What is this?"

"Well, I remembered this casserole that everyone makes with green beans, and mushroom soup and these little fried onions. We don't have green beans, so I substituted baked beans. And we don't have mushroom soup, so I thought beef barley was close. And we don't really have fried onions, so I thought Fritos would have the right crunchy contrast." She watched him. "You don't like it, do you?"

"No. I mean yes! You really got the crunchy part right. And the flavors are very...flavorful."

"It's okay, Sammy. I'm eating the same thing." Annie plunked her plate on the coffee table. She took Sammy's from him, as well. "It's terrible. The whole thing. It's not gonna work. I'm not gonna be able to do this. Sammy, I just don't get why I have to pretend to be Susan!"

"Annie, we've talked about all this."

"I know but it just seems so crazy! No one, no one, *no* one will *ever* believe I'm Susan! What? You think if I trot out the word, *voilà*, every once in a while, I suddenly turn into Grace Kelly?"

"Look, I know it seems like a lot. But let's review what happened. You were witness to a very serious event. Many people were killed. But not everyone who was there is dead. There were a number of survivors. Johnny Buscemi is alive. As is Officer Daniel Ravello. I don't know how familiar you are with those two men, but they are extremely powerful and dangerous characters."

"I know Johnny. He's a bad guy."

"That's an understatement. He's not just involved in drugs. And that cop is both his protector and his enforcer. There are rumors that Buscemi is politically connected and may run for office."

"But, how could he? He's a criminal!"

"I'm not from this country. But, where I'm from it happens all the time. Do you think Mr. Buscemi—should he win an election, with that flunky cop Ravello at his side—do you think he'd like to know that you're out there? Knowing what you know about him. Knowing you could identify him as a drug dealer. Not to mention his presence at Frankie's house the night so many people were murdered."

"But I wouldn't say anything!"

"Annie. Listen to yourself. Do you really think that anyone would believe you? You couldn't even control yourself with your boyfriend."

"That's not a very nice thing to say!"

"I just mean that you have a reputation for being hot-headed. You're not seen as a stable girl. You're perceived to be…well, to *use* a great deal of cocaine."

"I…I am?"

"Yes, you are."

"But what about you? You were there too."

"This is the world I live in. I'm part of it and I'll take my chances. Think about it, Annie. This is an opportunity that will never come again. This is your chance to truly erase the past and start over."

Annie slumped back on the sofa and stared at the television screen. She sat like that for a long time. Eventually, she said, "There are some Fritos left in the bag."

"That sounds great." Sammy jumped up to retrieve them.

* * *

And the news played on.

Night after night, they watched, caught up in the collective unconscious, as reporters wove fever dreams. Minutiae of the Italian vs. Chaldean drug mafias were parsed. Details of Chaldean gangs working between Detroit and El Cajon, California were revealed. The Honest Chaldean Grocer was contrasted with the Renegade Chaldean Criminal. Chaldean owners of party stores were queried about these men. The Chaldean Catholic faith was explained, Chaldeans' status in their home country of Iraq was explored, and all things Chaldean became a subject of interest to the reporters of Detroit. Briefly.

In the end, viewers like Annie did not really understand the difference between a Chaldean and a Copt, and a further level of confusion was added with the Maronite Christians, still fleeing civil war in Lebanon, who, at that very moment, were pouring into nearby Dearborn. Locals, much like Annie, enjoyed dining in Detroit's very own Greektown, loved grape leaves and kebabs, and therefore, felt that they understood the cuisines and cultures of the Middle East. Their interest did not extend much farther than that.

In contrast, the Italian American community felt less foreign and the Castigliones were favorite sons. Papa Vito's pizzerias were lauded, the proud history of the family and its contributions to the city were extolled. Dismay was conveyed that the brothers had descended into drug deals when they'd had such a promising start in life. Collectively, Detroit put the veil of charity over their grandfather's early days as the operator of a blind pig—Detroit's special word for a speakeasy.

Human-interest stories abounded. Reporters waxed philosophical. The overarching concept of family honor among Italian Americans was analyzed by TV anchors. Everyone had seen *The Godfather*. The newscasters seemed genuinely sad when they reported that, after ten days, all three Castiglione brothers had perished as a result of the gunfire. Frankie and Vito had died instantly, there in Frankie's living room. But Carmine, the recluse, the accountant, the one who rarely came out at night, took a bullet to the intestines. His death was the grisliest and took days to unfold. Nightly, for over a week, in dark living rooms in front of television sets, Detroit had been rooting for his survival.

No mention was ever made of Johnny Buscemi or Danny the Cop. Their attendance at the scene had been wiped out.

Occasionally, the companion story of the girlfriend who died in the car crash was raised. The reporters did not attempt to account for such a girl. They did not wonder why a pretty girl from a model suburb ended up dead on the side of the road. She was female. She should have known better. She should have kept her legs crossed and her screen door shut. None of this was spoken, but Annie knew that the overall moral of her story was that a girl like that got what a girl like that deserved.

One day, an exclusive appeared in the *Detroit News*, an interview with Sherry Hopkins, waitress at Frankie's Disco. Sherry wished to speak, she said, because she was close with the players involved. She wanted to talk, she said, because she was best friends with the dead girl. She wanted the world to know that she was a player in this play.

Annie read it and scoffed. Sammy paid no attention. Sherry seemed so inconsequential.

53

Thursday, September 27, 1979

No matter how Annie and Sammy scrutinized the coverage, they never found a mention of Susan. They combed every news source, but no item appeared about a vanished college co-ed.

It became evident to them that Susan was not among the missing. As far as the greater world was concerned, one girl died that night and that girl was Annie Nelson. Overworked Detroit cops had no reason to dispute the identity of a dead girl found alone in her own car—especially given what had transpired at her boyfriend's house that night.

Susan's father would not question her whereabouts, either. Annie knew he hardly got out of bed anymore, didn't talk on the phone, was rarely even awake. Susan had told Annie she had already said her good-byes to him and planned to drive back to school before he woke the next day. She said she'd packed her car and left it in the garage.

It was strangely simple, this way, for Annie to get out of town. To avoid the Italians and Chaldeans who might associate her with the deal turned deadly and wish to eliminate her as a witness. To shake off her old self and, in one fell swoop, obliterate the loathsome person she had become.

As they developed their plan, Sammy and Annie first had to confront the existence of Susan's beloved *Le Car*, ticking like a time bomb in her garage. Annie knew that no one else parked there—the nurse parked on the street. But eventually—even if not right away—someone would open the garage door and discover it, sitting packed and abandoned by its owner.

Sammy knew a guy who took care of unwanted cars for a price. His clients were generally insurance frauds, but the process was the same. Once they got the car out of Susan's garage, it would go to a chop shop, one of the many scattered in city and suburb, alike, and it would never be seen again. Sammy's cousin took care of the rest.

Faithful Jacob called the apartment once a day. He and Sammy established a series of rings and hang-ups, in patterns that varied from one call to the next. On one of those calls, Sammy gave the location of the car.

Jacob reported that the operation had unfolded like clockwork, in the dead of night, on Susan's quiet street. Two men, dressed in black, had walked from the corner, up the driveway, and through the gate. Silently, they traversed the property and opened the garage door. One man shifted the little car to neutral and steered, as the other pushed it out to the road. There, they started the engine and drove away.

Arranging Susan's leave of absence from college was easy. A quick call to the operator gave them the number of Lake Erie College. As Susan, Annie asked for the registrar's office. Miss Marjorie Ainsworth got on the line herself. She'd tried to call Susan's house, she said, and never received an answer. She said she was worried and asked Annie a series of questions.

Yes, Annie answered, her father was still ailing. Yes, she replied, she needed to care for him. Yes, she responded, she planned to return. A leave was all that was required—maybe only the fall, maybe the entire year. And that is exactly what was granted.

With Jacob's help, Sammy took care of the documents. Driver's license and passport were easily falsified since the entire contents of Susan's car—of Susan's life—were spread on the floor in front of them, neatly delivered by Jacob. It was all there, coldly tidy, in labeled banker's boxes that Susan had packed before she died.

Sammy and Annie felt squeamish as they rifled through Susan's life. Letters to her father were crisply bound with a pale pink ribbon. Ballet slippers were boxed next to leotards. A soft blue leather diary exposed her inner life, a matching phone book contained her worldly ties—doctors, dentist, lawyer. It was a veritable roadmap to Susan's identity.

The journal also contained a thought or two about Annie. Annie had sobered up enough by this point to see the veracity of Susan's words. Sitting on the floor of the apartment in Southfield, an apartment whose location she didn't even know, she saw herself reflected in the clear-eyed writing of her friend.

It was not a flattering picture.

Susan wrote in the self-important way of the literary college student experimenting with her own voice—the voice she'd used to explain *profiteroles* and Paris to Annie.

It was the last page that got to Annie—that pierced any remaining trace of armor that she had constructed against the truth. Annie felt a creeping sadness permeate her as she read Susan's final thoughts, written the night of Wednesday, September 5th. The night that Annie would wake her and drag her out of the house.

Weds. 9/5/79
10 p.m.

Summer is over. In many ways, it never actually started. And yet it's time to go. It makes me think of that funny old song my father always sang when I was a girl:

> *"Get out the way for old Dan Tucker,*
> *He's too late to get his supper.*
> *Supper's over and dinner's cookin',*
> *Old Dan Tucker's just standin' there lookin'."*

Did I think that song was funny when I was young? I can't remember. Now I think I'm the one who's always standing there looking.

Not like Annie. She never stands by to watch anything. I don't think she observes one single thing that doesn't revolve around herself. She never even said goodbye.

I don't understand what that friendship meant in my life. She seemed so warm and funny at first. The drugs explain a lot of it, but I also misjudged her. Is that the lesson for me? Choose my friends more wisely?

I don't know why I followed Annie to work at Frankie's Disco. I don't know why I left Winkleman's. I don't know if she ever even really liked me. Maybe she just didn't want to go to Frankie's alone. Maybe she just wanted an audience. Maybe I'll write about it someday: My Summer of Slumming!

I don't know what will happen to her but she's not going back to college. She says she is, but I don't think so. I think she uses cocaine all the time now. And that boyfriend is scary. I'm glad I'm leaving tomorrow, for all of the obvious reasons.

Not for my dad, though. I am afraid to leave my dad.

And not for Sammy. What did THAT all mean? I like him so much. I thought that something special was happening between us. I thought we might even have a future. But then he said that thing about meeting in Paris a year from now. It's depressing but, if all else fails, I'll hold onto it.

And that was it.

The end of the journal. The end of Susan.

Annie sat on the floor, journal in one hand and her unholy loot in the other: necklace, watch, and the sealed white envelope she had taken from Johnny's drawer. Like Justicia, blindfolded and holding the scales of justice in her hands, Annie could see clearly that both sides rendered her guilty.

She set down the objects, stumbled to the bathroom, and vomited.

54

The wind picks up, forcing Annie and Sammy to shout. The dogs bark and race after leaves and debris that dance across the lawn. The beaches are empty. The surfers have hauled their boards back to their cars. The beach staff have chained up the furniture and disappeared into the hotel. Sammy and Annie are alone, except for the almost human presence of the lighthouse. It sounds its horn and revolves its light— warning them to steer clear of the rocks, to lash themselves to the wheel.

The sky is darkest above, slightly lighter below, lending an unnatural glow to these forlorn stragglers.

"Why do you have to go back to Iraq?"

"I have some work to do there. Something I was hoping to avoid."

"Are you involved in this endless war? Are you a soldier or something?"

"Or something. Look, Annie, I'm a Chaldean. Remember you learned all about the Chaldeans back in that apartment? It's a hell of a time to be a Chaldean in Iraq. ISIS is slaughtering us and I'm working to help my people. That's more or less what I'm doing."

"Which is it, Sammy? More or less?"

242

"Let's say more. But I came to see you because I wanted to do less. And one thing led to another and now I'm hooked back into doing more. And you, my friend, have been exposed. I'm sorry for that."

"You and me both."

"Annie, listen to me. We worked so hard to bring you back—to re-create your life. We did such a good job. Why would I want to undo it?"

"Fine, I believe you, but I'm still faced with the consequences. I've been meeting with the FBI. They're pushing me up against a wall. They're asking me to do things that I'm not sure I'm able to do."

"Like what?"

"Like testify against someone. Publicly! Look, Sammy, this is an old world here. Watch Hill is a small town. This is not New York or Los Angeles where you can go to jail for two years and still get the best table at your favorite restaurant when you get out. My husband created something here. Something of meaning.

"Everything I have—everything Susan Ford has—is part of Jack Ford's legacy. And it—I—am intricately tied up with my stepson. We run a company together, we share this house. We're both members of this community. We're linked in every way. And, right now, he's reeling from the news that I'm not the woman he thought I was. *Literally*! I don't know if he'll ever be able to understand or forgive that. And if the whole hideous past were to come out in court records? In newspapers? On television? I wouldn't know how to put the pieces of Mrs. Ford's life together again."

"I am sorry." They both grow quiet. "Testify against whom?"

"You know what? I've answered every one of your questions and you've answered none of mine. What's going on with *you*, Sammy? Why did the FBI arrest you, then let you go?"

"I cannot give you details, but please put two and two together."

"We're back to the *Inscrutable East*! Can you please stop talking in riddles?"

"You're an intelligent woman. Why do you think the FBI would let me go?"

"I have no idea."

"Think, Annie. Think."

Annie stares at him for a long while, then slowly says, "You work for the CIA?"

"That would be a fair assessment."

"But, if you're a CIA agent, how could you be arrested?"

Sammy hesitates, then he says, "I'm an involuntary volunteer."

Annie blinks. "Am I supposed to understand that? Is that the explanation?"

"I'm not formally recognized as an agent. There is no record of me. I don't even exist. The FBI would have no access to my status."

"Is this what you've been doing all these years?"

"No. It's not. About three years ago, the CIA stopped me inside the border of Iran, doing something I wasn't supposed to do, and they made me an offer I couldn't refuse."

"I still don't understand."

"Annie, I was dealing in guns. Smuggling. From Iran to my contacts in Iraq. I can't make it any plainer than that. They detained me and threatened to lock me away if I didn't work for them. That's how it works with the CIA."

"I'm learning that's how it works with the FBI, too."

"When I was on my way to you last week, the FBI picked me up without knowing any of this. Then, I called my contact at the CIA and he had me released."

"But you came here for money to get out? To run away?"

"I did. But that was a mistake. I see that now. I would retract it if I could. I came here today to apologize."

"What will they do to you?"

"Look, it was selfish of me to think I could just walk away. There are things going on over there—this war—it is bigger than me. Than any of us."

55

The rain comes in sheets. Annie, Sammy, and both dogs are instantly soaked. Annie re-leashes the dogs and, grasping Sammy's hand, leads them off Lighthouse Point and back up Lighthouse Road.

"This way!" Annie yells, as she pulls Sammy and the dogs across a neighbor's property. "This is a shortcut."

On they run over an unbroken string of manicured lawns as the rain engulfs them. Without warning, lightning splits the sky into vertical slices as it cracks down to the sea. The thunder that follows is immediate and deafening. The dogs startle. Cal manages to slip out of her collar and dashes back in the direction from which they've come.

"Shit!" Annie shouts, "Can you pick up Pliny? I have to get Cal! She's old and gets confused!"

"I'm not going to let you go back there alone!" Sammy says as he hoists the remaining dog into his arms.

"No, you have to get him into the house. And I have to get Cal! *Right now!*"

Sammy persists, barely audible, though he is shouting over the raging storm. "You take this dog back and I'll get the one that's run away."

"She won't come to you!" Annie yells, "Sammy, I've got to go. We're wasting time!"

And with that, Annie retraces the route to the lighthouse.

Another clap of lightning and peal of thunder cause her to look back at Sammy. The piercing noise has made Pliny yelp and leap from Sammy's arms. The dog plops on the wet grass and starts to run in an entirely different direction.

Annie hesitates, about to run back, but then Sammy just manages to step on Pliny's leash to stop him in his tracks. He walks his hands carefully up the leash to the body of the dog and picks him up again.

Annie sprints, slips, and stumbles back to the lighthouse to find her other dog.

The wind and rain have reached a fever pitch. She knows, from the strength of the storm that it won't last long. She's lived through many of these summer tempests that cartwheel across the sea. She is sure that this very moment is its peak, and in no more than fifteen minutes, it will be wreaking havoc over Stonington and Mystic to the west, leaving Watch Hill with a stunning sunset. Maybe even a rainbow. In the meantime, she needs to find her dog, who knows no such thing and is scared to death.

"Calpurnia!" Her voice doubles back into her face as she shouts directly into the wind. She makes a 180-degree turn. "Cal!"

There is no way that her little Calpurnia will come out from whatever cover she's found. Annie prays that she didn't stray back to the rocks, which are currently being pummeled by surging waves, slamming down and retreating with suction force.

"Cookie!" she cries at the top of her lungs. "Cookie! Cookie!"

As Annie calls out that ridiculous word, she starts to cry. The tears and the rain cover her face, as she runs and yells, "Cookie! Cookie! Cookie!" like some demented Muppet mantra. Annie careens around the hill calling for her dog, looking under the industrial garbage bin, peeking behind rocks, confronting the notion that her entire life has been an exercise in foolishness.

Here, now, at the lighthouse, in the storm—her dog missing, jail looming, Sammy, Johnny, and the FBI all coming at her from different angles—her own foolishness is brought home to her. Able to run no more, at the end of the line, she sits on the grass and cries harder. She had been unwise to stay out on the point so long. She'd been thoughtless to expose her dogs to danger.

Long ago, she'd been a selfish girl doing reckless things that got her friend and her boyfriend killed. She'd been stupid to hide out, then, in fear of Johnny Buscemi. She'd been rash to go along with Sammy's ridiculous plan. Dreaming to think she had really escaped Fate, that she had truly made a new life and a new person out of herself—neither Susan nor Annie but another entity entirely.

As she sits in the rain watching it all melt before her eyes, she sees, for the first time, that she is a foolish person chasing futile dreams.

Swept up in the drama of the storm, Annie buries her head in her hands and cries louder. No one can hear her. No one can see her.

Just as she had predicted, the storm soon blows off to the west. Little Calpurnia has crept back and is sitting at her feet. Annie absently reaches out to stroke her sodden fur, but her mind is focused on the impossible choices she needs to make.

And make today.

56

Annie huddles on the ground with her dog on her lap—both of them soaked to the bone. She looks up to see Sammy slogging toward them. He is no dryer than they are.

The sun glows red out of the western sky, its beams changing colors as they bounce off the beads of water still saturating the air. Black clouds are visible, farther along, to the left of the setting sun. It is a Turner sky, dark and light, hopeful and hopeless, hellish and heavenly. Chiaroscuro.

"Shall I pick you up and carry you home?" Sammy is nothing, if not gallant.

"I thought you said you weren't well."

"Never too ill to rescue a damsel in distress."

"I appreciate the thought, but a piggy back ride won't save me at this juncture." Annie wipes her face and looks up at him. "And we don't want to have to call nine-one-one if your heart goes. We're both kind of fugitives of justice."

"Madame, you have become quite practical." Sammy reaches out a hand to offer Annie assistance in rising.

"I suppose I have," she says as they begin the trip back to her house. "And who ever would have expected practicality from the likes of me?"

"You have surprised me more than once."

When they arrive at the door of Gull Cottage, they nearly smack into Helen. She wears rubber boots and a rain slicker and is determinedly on her way out. "Mrs. Ford! You are very wet!"

"Yes, Helen, I am very wet."

"I was coming to look for you." Helen eyes Sammy suspiciously.

"Well, I'm back," Annie says, but she can see that this does not satisfy Helen.

"You need dry clothes. Him too."

"Yes. Yes," Annie says but she does not move.

Helen and Sammy wait awkwardly.

"Follow me," Helen commands Sammy.

Sammy seems grateful for some direction and the chance to get out of his wet clothes. He grabs his suitcase and follows Helen as Annie slowly mounts the stairs.

57

Tuesday, October 9, 1979
Suburban Detroit

Today was the day when Sammy would cut and color Annie's hair, advancing her transformation from brunette Annie Nelson to blond Susan Bentley. Sammy had sent Jacob to purchase scissors and hair dye, stressing that it shouldn't be too blond—not Marilyn Monroe, just regular blond—more like Farah Fawcett. Jacob listened patiently without comprehending. In the end, he purchased ten boxes of varied Clairol blonds and left them at their clandestine pickup spot in the basement. Sammy and Annie stood in the bathroom studying the boxes, debating which blond was most like Susan's blond.

"Should I be ash blond or honey blond?"

"How about honey?"

"What about strawberry blond?"

"Not with your skin tone."

"Really, Sammy?" Annie smiled. "Listen to you! I've never met a man who knew about skin tone."

"I think the last guy you dated was a caveman." The lighthearted mood was broken. "I'm sorry, Annie. That wasn't funny."

"It's okay. I know you were just trying to make me laugh."

Annie's face had improved. Her bruises had faded from black and blue to yellow and green. Sammy teased her that these new colors made her look like a walking science experiment, a Petri dish growing mold for penicillin. Even in their current circumstances, they laughed. Despite the deaths and their cloudy future, Annie and Sammy were young and very much alive.

"I think we should cut your hair first and then dye it. That way, we're not dying all the hair we're just going to cut off."

"How short was Susan's hair?" Annie held both hands to her skull like a helmet. "I hate short hair."

"Well, my dear, you don't really have any choice." Sammy picked up the scissors.

Annie was wearing one of Sammy's shirts, a white button down, and nothing else but panties. They had wrangled one of the kitchen stools into the bathroom, so Annie could sit up high and see herself in the mirror. Sammy said it was a mistake. He thought he was better able to make a detached decision away from Annie's scrutiny. He feared she would balk.

But Annie had prevailed and there they were—crammed tightly into the tiny bathroom—Annie on her stool and Sammy standing next to her. They talked to each other—as hairdresser and client do—looking not at each other face to face, but at each other's faces in the mirror. Annie had grown used to the look of her abrasions and was no longer self-conscious at her own image.

They had considered placing a photograph of Susan in the bathroom, one they had found in her boxes. But it was too unbearably sad to have Susan's face staring back at them as they further obliterated her from the face of the earth. They knew what she looked like. They could do this without visual aids.

"Move your hands, please, mademoiselle." Sammy picked up a lock of Annie's chestnut hair. She had worn it long her entire life and was rather vain about it. In fact, she regarded it as one of her best features. Small price to pay, she recognized. Not remotely the sacrifice Susan had made.

Annie gritted her teeth, closed her eyes and surrendered. "Do it," she said.

Snip. They had begun. Snip. He took another strand. Snip. It was getting easier. Annie opened one eye to see half of her head looking a little scruffy. Both eyes popped open.

"I think it's uneven!" Her arms flew up to grab at Sammy's wrists.

Sammy deftly dodged. "Just give me a minute here. I'll even it out at the end."

"That's what my mother said when she cut my bangs when I was little! She kept evening it until I looked like Mamie Eisenhower!"

"Was that bad? I don't remember what Mamie Eisenhower looked like."

"Trust me, it was awful."

"Okay, I'll be careful."

Sammy cut while Annie critiqued.

"Why don't you close your eyes again?" Sammy requested. "You're making me nervous. If I make a mistake it's because you made me nervous."

"Don't blame me for your mistakes!"

"I haven't made any yet. Close your eyes and be quiet. I'm concentrating."

Annie tried, but soon was peeking out from under her eyelashes. "I look like Joan of Arc."

"I thought you had your eyes closed!"

"I'm seeing with my mind's eye that I must look like Joan of Arc."

"I'll give you Joan of Arc." And Sammy tickled her a little. Just a little.

And so, they continued in the tiny bathroom of the apartment, the safe house, in Southfield. For today, they had mostly forgotten what had brought them here. For today, they were a boy and a girl, in close proximity in a very small room.

"Now for the color!" Sammy suddenly announced, much to Annie's surprise.

"That's it? That's my haircut?"

"Well, I'll clean it up after it's blond."

It was the coloring process that nudged Sammy and Annie over the line. It was a messy, wet, sticky undertaking that involved water and splashing and spilling. It was the hair dye that got all over Sammy's T-shirt, which caused him to lift it over his head and toss it aside. It was the water that soaked the front of Annie's shirt that made her cold and itchy. It was Annie who told Sammy to turn away while she unbuttoned it to take it off. It was Annie who asked Sammy to hand her a towel to wrap around her nakedness. It was Sammy, turning back to her, who did not hand it over. It was Sammy who stood staring, just staring, at Annie.

It was Annie who moved toward Sammy, the ever-so-short distance that separated them and kissed him with her bruised and tender lips. It was Annie and Sammy who fell on each other with all of the hunger, pain and loss they had experienced in the past thirty days. It was Sammy and Annie who made love on the bathroom sink, with Annie's hair all over the bathroom floor.

It was Sammy who whispered the name, Susan, softly in Annie's ear, not meaning to hurt her, hoping she hadn't heard. It was Annie who cried afterwards and Sammy who tried to soothe her. It was Sammy and Annie who were sealed in a pact of survival. It was the two of them who would escape, would go on, would put this summer and its deaths behind them.

It was Annie and Sammy who would live.

58

Wednesday, October 31, 1979

"Trick or Treat!"

Annie jumped out at Sammy from behind the front door, causing him to spring a foot in the air and drop the paper bags he'd been carrying from the pickup spot in the basement. Canned goods, oranges, apples and pears spilled all over the floor. Intent on stopping the rolling foodstuff, Sammy did not at first observe that she had fashioned herself a Halloween costume.

"Jesus Christ, Annie!" he blurted from all fours. "You scared the life out of me. Don't scare the guy you're hiding out with, okay? You could get yourself hurt."

Sammy continued to crawl around on the floor, cramming items back into bags. When he finally looked up, she saw him register the black leotard and tights that she'd pilfered from Susan's dance wardrobe. His eyes traveled down to the black tail hanging from her behind and up again to the two black ears that she'd made with Susan's construction paper. His eyes finally landed on the black whiskers and nose that she'd drawn on her face with eyebrow pencil.

"You look like a cat," he said.

"Yes, goddamn it! I'm a cat! It's goddamn Halloween and I'm a goddamn cat!" and she flounced out of the room, slamming the bedroom door behind her.

Sammy and Annie had been holed up in the apartment in South-field for nearly eight weeks. Caught in the unreality of their life in isolation from the world, they found themselves playing house in more ways than one.

Every day, Annie read Susan's books. Sammy couldn't bear to. Five times a week, Sammy taught Annie French. The cruel punch line that French lessons were delivered via Sammy instead of Susan was not lost on Annie.

Together, Sammy and Annie created a schedule of lessons for Annie, lessons in becoming Susan. The material was all there, in the boxes, on the floor—the guide to becoming the girl.

"Annie." She heard him gently knock. "Annie, I'm sorry. I forgot it was Halloween. May I come in?"

Annie was lying on the bed, crying, and did not answer.

Sammy turned the knob. "Annie, don't cry. I'm sorry."

She looked up at him, as he looked down at her, and they did what they did all the time now. Every night and every day. They slowly undressed and made love. Her body was nearly healed but the pattern was established. He touched her with trepidation. She lightly touched him back. No force was used between them—like bodies of ether, the skin of one slipped across the skin of the other.

"Annie, I need to tell you something," Sammy said afterward, as he twisted little strands of her hair.

"That sounds ominous." She leaned up on her elbows. "First, I need you to tell me about you and Susan."

"Oh, I...I don't think that's a very good idea."

"Please, Sammy. I loved her too. I know I had a piss poor way of showing it. It's just...I don't know why I acted the way I did." Annie sat up fully. "But I loved her too."

Sammy hoisted himself up to sit. He looked at the wall, not at Annie. He remained still for a good, long while, before he answered.

"I picture her that last night when she was wearing the nightgown, just like Wendy in *Peter Pan*. I saw that play once, in London. She walked

255

around the car and the light from the streetlamp caught her hair and the nightgown and everything was iridescent and shining back at me.

"And I picture her smiling. I know she was not actually smiling. But it helps me to imagine her that way. Because the other image that rises up in my head, the one I cannot shake off, is what expression was on her face at the end."

Annie said nothing.

"I saw myself in Susan," Sammy continued, "a younger version of myself. We dreamed a similar dream of beauty and art and sweet, sad moments. Melancholy. That's a good word for it. I saw a strain of melancholy in Susan that I have within myself. The difference was, I thought she could get out. I'm trapped by responsibility, habit, clan—but I thought she could get out."

Sammy turned to look at Annie, the flesh-and-blood girl who was next to him on the bed.

"But you're different, Annie. You don't have a melancholy bone in your body. You're strong and fierce. You're the most alive person I've ever met. And, now that you're off of drugs"—he winked at her—"you're becoming tolerably nice."

Annie did not know if she regretted asking the question. It was clear that Sammy loved Susan but there was another thing, as well—some sort of misalignment with the two of them. Maybe a man like Sammy and a woman like Susan could not really be together. Maybe she, Annie, would be a better fit for Sammy. Maybe there was a real future for them, outside of the four walls of this apartment.

Annie could not help but fantasize.

She stood up with the sheet wrapped around her. Her cat face was smudged, but still there. She went into the bathroom and returned with a washcloth. "What did you want to tell me?"

"It's almost time to go, Annie. My cousin says they've stopped looking for anyone who might have survived that night. Jacob will arrange your ticket to New York and my ticket to Baghdad. I'll go there for a few months. He'll bring us to the airport."

Annie sat down with a plop, on the floor, right where she'd been standing, the air rushing out of her in an audible whoosh. "Now?"

"I think he means in a few weeks. Not right now."

Sammy rose and moved to Annie, wearing nothing but the skin God gave him. "We still have a few weeks."

And, again, because that is what they did in those days, in that apartment, they made love on the floor. Because it made them feel alive.

Because it kept their dead at bay.

59

Thursday, November 22, 1979

The time had come to say goodbye. Sammy's cousin, Jacob, had picked Thanksgiving Day to send them packing, to end their idyll, to flush them out of the womb in which they'd been living for two and a half months. Perhaps he'd reckoned that all the thugs would be home with their families, saying grace at the table for the bounty that lay before them. Not looking for the girl who got away. The girl who was dead, after all.

Annie thought it was particularly insensitive to send her away on her favorite holiday. She realized that she and Sammy would not have been roasting a turkey. But why did Jacob have to choose this day to send her off into the abyss?

When she was a child, Thanksgiving was the one holiday they'd spent at Grandma Annie's. Christmas, they had to have at her house, with her mother and stepfather presiding over the whole sorry spectacle. On Christmas, there was always a fight. Something would go wrong. Her mother would burn the roast, or the lights on the tree would stop working; something would trigger what inevitably came next—her stepfather getting angry and picking a fight.

Thanksgiving at her grandmother's house was happy. Her stepfather behaved better there.

As a little girl, Annie would stand at the kitchen storm door and draw pictures with her fingers in the condensation. Little ice-crystal flowers were clustered in the corners of the glass, but the center was steamed over from the heat of the roasting turkey and the boiling potatoes and the baking pies. Annie would draw pictures and write words and Grandma Annie, no matter how busy she was getting that meal on the table, would always take a moment, here and there, to walk over and say something nice.

Now, here she was—unable to see her grandmother or have one last Thanksgiving or hear a single kind word—being hustled into Detroit Metropolitan Airport by a couple of Chaldeans.

They sat in the car, Annie, Sammy, and Jacob, in front of the terminal. Annie's flight was first; Sammy had a hellish series of connections that wouldn't begin for several hours. Annie was almost late, but she wanted a minute alone with Sammy to say goodbye. She had been alone with him for so long now that she barely remembered how to talk to another person.

She did not know how she would survive in New York, how she would make it on her own. She had never before done it. Sammy had given her money and she had selected some of Susan's clothes, a few books, Susan's address book and her journal. Sammy had told her about a place, the Barbizon Hotel for Women, that he said would be a good place to start. She had that address in her purse.

"Consider the name of this town," Jacob spoke suddenly, startling her out of her daydream. Annie and Sammy both looked at the sign at which Jacob was pointing. Detroit Metropolitan Airport, it informed them, existed in Romulus, Michigan.

"You think about the legend of the founding of Rome," Jacob continued. "The twins, Romulus and Remus. The miracles that took place to keep them alive as babies—suckled by a wolf, fed by a woodpecker, raised by shepherds. And then, Romulus—the stronger one—killing Remus in the end. What parallels do you think the founding fathers meant to draw?"

"Jacob," Sammy said to his cousin. "This is probably not the moment. Can you give us a minute?"

"What?" Jacob looked from Sammy to Annie. "Oh. Sure."

He exited the car.

"Listen, Annie—" Sammy began.

"I always know when someone starts with, 'Listen, Annie,' it's gonna be bad." Annie's eyes were filling with tears.

"No, it's not bad. It's been really great these past months. I really…I really care about you." That was the way to say it when you didn't want to use the "L" word.

"I care about you, too." Annie wasn't going to use the "L" word if he wasn't.

"Listen, Annie—" Sammy said it again, then he laughed. "We both need to go do what we planned to do now. We need to focus on making new lives. You're ready. You've worked really hard and you can do this. I know it. I believe in you."

"Thanks, Sammy," she said. "It means a lot to me to hear you say that."

Jacob knocked on the car window, which made them both jump. "Annie, you have to go now."

"Okay," she said to Jacob outside the window. "Okay," she said as she looked at Sammy.

She kissed him softly and started to go. And then she hesitated and turned back to face him.

"I'm still not used to your hair. It takes me by surprise," he said, as he smoothed a little piece of it.

"Yeah. I think it'll take a while." Annie reached around her neck and took off the gold chain, the one with the question mark at the end, the one she had asked him about at the racetrack in a lifetime before this one.

"Here, Sammy." She placed it over his head. "You take it. It'll bring you luck."

"Will it? I hope so."

"I know so! C'mon, Sammy. We've been through so much. You've helped me in ways I can't even begin to thank you for. Don't you fall down on me now!" And Annie knew then that she was stronger than Sammy. After all those weeks of depending on him, it was clear to her now. She was the strong one—Romulus to his Remus. She did not know if he knew it yet, but she knew.

"Here," Sammy said. "I have something I want you to have, as well."

Annie's heart inexplicably soared, and her imagination leapt ahead of her.

Sammy reached into his waistband and pulled out a gun—his .38 caliber Smith & Wesson. He placed it in Annie's hand. "You may need this someday. Be careful though. It's not a toy. You'd better put it in your suitcase."

Annie looked down at the gun and reeled back her fantasy. "Thanks, Sammy. I can't say any man has ever given me a gun before."

"Really, Annie. Be careful."

"I will. You too."

And they gave each other one last kiss.

Annie stepped out of the car and softly closed the door. She zipped the gun into her bag and walked into the terminal, suitcase with the gun in one hand, purse with the sealed white envelope in the other.

She never turned back to look at Sammy. That, she could not bear.

60

Monday, August 18, 2014
Watch Hill
Time: 8:21 p.m.

Annie stands in the doorframe, observing Sammy. He is seated before a roaring fire, sipping tea from the tray that Helen put out. He looks very much like he belongs. He wears white jeans and a navy V-neck sweater. His feet are bare. The wheel of destiny turns on tiny pivots; an *nth* of a degree in either direction establishes a trajectory. Could Annie have made a life with Sammy? The wheel turned long ago, and the question became moot.

"Did you make the fire?"

"Like a good Iraqi Boy Scout."

"You have Boy Scouts over there?"

"Arrogant American."

Annie has changed into black jeans and a black sweater. Her feet, like Sammy's, are bare. Helen clears her throat. She is standing in the other doorway, the one closest to the kitchen.

"I made soup today. Split pea. Do you want some now?"

"No, thank you, Helen. You can go. I'll warm it up later."

Helen looks at Sammy. "You want me to stay, Mrs. Ford?"

"It's okay, Helen. I'm fine."

Helen gives both of them one last look before leaving for the night. Annie does not move from the doorway.

"Helen doesn't like me," Sammy says.

"I think she smells trouble. But I guarantee you she cannot, in her wildest dreams, conceive of how much trouble you actually are. She probably just thinks you're an old lover."

"Well. Rather astute, I'd say."

"That's it, isn't it? I know you know the story of the blind men feeling the elephant. You probably told it to me first. They each feel a portion of the animal and draw conclusions about the whole. They're not wrong, per se, but they're not fully right."

"And there, my dear, lies the rub."

"You've picked up more idiomatic expressions since I last saw you."

"And you've picked up more Eastern philosophy."

"I've applied myself over the years."

The dogs, after their adventure in the storm, have collapsed in two heaps in front of the fire. One is snoring—Calpurnia. Pliny is in the middle of a dream, his little face and paws twitching.

"He must be chasing a rabbit," Sammy says.

"I hope he catches it."

"Yes. I hope so too." Sammy puts down his cup. "My contact will be here soon."

"Are you going to go with him?"

"Do I have a choice? Sometimes I think maybe it's all just scripted and we delude ourselves into thinking we have free will."

"Oh God, Sammy—I couldn't bear that! It's so fatalistic."

"No, of course not. You are an American woman, Annie, through and through. You're the best they have."

"I'm not the best of anything, Sammy." She reddens in spite of herself and changes the subject. "Do you think about Susan?"

"Every day."

"Do you ever think about me?"

"Also, every day."

"Why did you say you wouldn't have made a good husband?"

"Well, after I think about Susan and after I think about you, what time do I have left? What energy?"

"Oh, Sammy—I don't think love is measured out that way. I was able to find love with Jack, even after all that happened."

"That's lucky for you."

"Yes," Annie says. "Yes, I've always had luck."

"Ah, but Annie, that's the difference between us. After many years in the desert—and I don't mean that metaphorically—I finally understand myself a little. You have made your luck. Luck appears, and you charge in after it. I don't do that. I pull back. I pulled back with Susan. I pulled back with you. That's what I do. Then that luck is gone. A life is gone."

Annie smiles sadly at her friend, but she doesn't deny the truth of his words. "Follow me. I want to show you something." She turns from her post in the doorway and heads for the stairs. Remarkably, the spent dogs stay where they are. Sammy places both hands on his thighs and pushes himself up. "Where to?"

Annie leads Sammy upstairs. They go down a hall, around a corner, up a step and into her bedroom where the lighthouse is framed dead center in the glass of the large double doors.

"Wow. What a view to wake up to."

"Yes, it's extraordinary. Jack saw everything in terms of framing views. When you explore this house, you see interior windows everywhere. It kind of alarmed me when I first came here; I felt like I might be looked at when I wasn't looking back. You can imagine my concern."

"It's a lot to take in, this house."

"It's a reflection of my husband. I think that's what a haunted house is; Jack inhabits the very bricks and mortar of this house. Up here, by the sea, with the lighthouse and the fog and the waves that crash on the rocks, I feel like I'm here with Jack. Like *The Ghost and Mrs. Muir.*"

"I don't belong here. I shouldn't have come. I'm terribly sorry, Annie." He smiles in the same heart piercing way that he did as a youth. The beautiful smile of a sad man, a man the right kind of woman could rescue. Annie can't help but fantasize, if only for a moment.

She turns to resume walking. She leads Sammy through the master bathroom, with its own sweeping view of sea, sky, and lighthouse. She turns precipitously out a different door and down a short hall. Through another door, they enter a small, windowless space. At the far side, she presses a spring-paneled wall, which pops open to her touch. An enormous safe is revealed.

"Sammy, I've decided to leave." Annie has started to cry again—not sobs, like before, but tears are running down her face. She forcefully wipes them and gives one good sniff, pulling herself together.

"There's nothing for me here. With Jack and with my stepson, I was part of this place, and it was part of me. I belonged. I hadn't felt like I belonged to anything for so many years, not since I was a little girl. I lost that for a long time—or I threw it away. But I found it again with Jack. And I won't get to keep that now. Not here. Not as Mrs. Ford."

"I am so very sorry, Annie. I would undo my actions, if I could."

"Well. We don't have an undo button, do we?" She turns back to the safe and reaches for it. Then she pauses. "Sammy, do you remember a girl called Diane Englund? She was a waitress at Frankie's that summer."

"I don't know. What did she look like?"

"Irish. Dark hair, pale skin, freckles. Younger than the rest of us."

"Maybe. I'm not sure."

"You know the necklace I gave you all those years ago?"

"Yes, of course. I've kept it with me always. But it wasn't returned to me when I collected my possessions this morning."

"No, it wouldn't be because it's a piece of evidence in the disappearance of that girl, Diane. She was working at Frankie's when Susan and I arrived. Susan really liked her. And, one day, she just wasn't there anymore. The FBI thought you had something to do with what happened to her."

"What *did* happen to her?"

Annie turns back to the safe and rotates the tumbler—to the left, to the right, to the left—like a game of Russian Roulette. She halts mid-turn. "Look, Sammy—I went back to their office on Friday to clear your name.

That's when they made me their offer—just like the CIA made to you. I have to hurry now. There isn't much time."

She spins the wheel again and the door clicks open. There, on the shelves, are stacks and stacks of money: hundred-dollar bills, bound in neat bundles, side by side, in piles.

Sammy's breath leaves his lungs in a small burst. "How much is in there?" he asks.

"Two million. With care, it'll be enough. I'm asking you to come with me."

A pained expression crosses Sammy's face. "Oh God, Annie. Eleven days ago, I was coming to ask you just that. I was ready to ditch it all—to travel to Canada on *foot* just to get out of the hellhole I'd been living in."

"So, what's different now?"

"Like I said—I'm not like you! Sure, I've made plans. But, I've always let them go. You asked what I was doing all those years? The same damned thing I was doing the last time I saw you—a little forging, a little gun running, a little bookmaking.

"I was finished, though. My trip to Mehran was to be my last. But then, the CIA picked me up there—in broad daylight—right in the middle of Iran. They took me back across the border into Iraq and made their proposition: work for them or rot in jail."

"So we're in exactly the same predicament! And I'm offering you the way out. Precisely what you came looking for. You let me go at that airport all those years ago. Are you going to let me walk out the door now?"

"Oh, Annie. Everything is simpler for you."

"That's a patronizing thing to say!"

"I don't mean it like that. I admire everything about you."

Annie stomps away from him and begins stuffing money into cloth bags—nice, normal travel bags. She puts a few stacks to the side.

"What's that for?" Sammy asks.

"For Helen. She's worked with me for years. I want to leave her in good shape for the future. Plus, I can't bring my dogs; I have to leave them with her." Annie is moving quickly. "C'mon, Sammy. Change your clothes. We'll move around better in dark clothes."

Annie shuts the door of the safe and studies the two duffle bags on the floor. "This will be heavy but manageable," she says and hoists one with each arm. "Look, Sammy. This is it; now or never. I'm leaving everything I've worked thirty-five years to create. I'm leaving my dogs, for God's sake! I thought I'd escaped, but it's all caught up with me. I've cried. I've mourned. And now, I'm taking the situation into my own hands.

"And, you can choose, Sammy! You chose to get in that taxi and give my address, and you can do it again. You can get off the fucking fence you've been living on your entire life and choose!" Annie looks at him, out of breath. Then she adds, more softly, "Now, are you coming with me? Or are you going back to Baghdad?"

61

Time: 8:50 p.m.

Bang, bang, bang.

Three knocks come from downstairs. Someone is at the front door of Gull Cottage.

"Annie, that's my contact. He's here to take me to the airport."

"I can't tell you what to do, Sammy. It's not any good if I tell you; you have to make this decision for yourself. But I'm walking down the back stairs and out the back door and I'm doing it now." Annie goes into the bathroom and starts throwing toiletries into a small bag. She moves to a desk in the bedroom, where she stuffs the extra money, Helen's money, into a large envelope on which she writes her name and a short note. She scrawls a few words to Jack Jr. as well, taking a moment to carefully prop up both envelopes against a framed photograph—a smiling photo of herself and Jack Sr.

She stops to look at it. Suddenly, she flips the frame around, unfastens it, and pulls out the picture. "This was our wedding day," she says. She places the photo carefully in one of her bags and re-props the letters on the empty frame.

She crosses back to the bedside table, opens it, and retrieves the gun, Sammy's old .38, which she holds up in the air to show Sammy.

"Remember this?"

Bang! Bang! Bang!

268

The knocking grows louder.

Annie places the gun into her smallest bag. Then she ceases her rapid motion and studies Sammy intently.

"Listen, Sammy," she begins. "Sit with me for a minute. I have something to tell you."

"Someone once told me that if a person begins a sentence with 'listen,' she is about to give you bad news."

"I'm about to give you some news, but I hope you won't find it bad."

"I think I'll take it standing up," he says.

"Sammy, I insist." Annie pulls him over to the foot of the bed, where she sits with him, face to face. "When I left you in Detroit that day—that Thanksgiving, and I went to New York—well, I found out I was pregnant. I didn't know it right away, not for a few months. My body had been so messed up by the cocaine that summer that I hadn't had periods for a while. So I wasn't paying attention until it became pretty obvious. Anyway, there it was: I was pregnant, and there was nothing to do but have the baby. I gave her up for adoption."

Sammy turns away from Annie and faces the windows on the water. He sits rigidly still, appearing to barely breathe.

"Are you okay?" she asks him.

He blinks as though a flashbulb has gone off. Then he blinks several times more. He rubs his eyes. He pinches his nose. He turns back to Annie. "Her?" he asks, and his voice catches like a teenage boy's.

"Yes, a girl. She was beautiful, Sammy. Dark hair, dark eyes."

Sammy turns back to the water. "Do you know anything about her?"

"I know a little. I've looked into the records in recent years. I'd like to see her."

"She is alive and well?"

"She is."

"Where does she live?"

"She lives in Detroit."

Sammy looks sucker-punched by this detail.

"I requested that she go to a family in Michigan."

Bang! Bang! Bang!

269

"Annie, what am I supposed to do with this information now? That man is pounding on your door to take me back to Iraq!"

"I don't know, Sammy. The choice is yours." Annie hoists the three bags over her shoulders. "I'm leaving now."

"Wait!"

"Are you coming?"

Sammy goes to the desk where Annie has left the envelopes. He grabs the pen and scribbles on a scrap of paper. "Take Jacob's number. He'll be able to help you. It's not enough, I know. I'm sorry."

"I'm sorry too. For everything." Annie stands in the doorway, holding her bags. She makes no motion to leave. Finally, she says, "I have one more thing to tell you."

62

Tuesday, June 24, 1980
New York

It was a stifling summer day—too hot to be pregnant, groused Annie. Though she really needed to start thinking of herself as Susan, even when she was alone.

Sweat ran down her face, down every part of her body. It gathered under her breasts and atop her enormous belly as she waddled her way west on 95th Street. At least there was a breeze from the Hudson River. She'd been allowed to leave work early today, so that was one good thing—although she had nowhere to go, no one to see, and nothing to do. She was eight months pregnant with a child who would never be hers. She'd signed the adoption contract last month, so this life that was growing inside of her would not stick around for company. Well, at least her medical bills would be paid.

She opened the heavy front door of her building, pressed for the elevator, and waited as it cranked down to the lobby. She really had to pee. The baby was pressing on her bladder and she could not make it a full hour without running to a bathroom, wherever she was. Most restaurants took pity on her, considering her bulk, and let her use their restrooms, even if she couldn't afford to eat there.

Once in the apartment, she made a beeline for the bathroom. Her roommate was away in Ohio visiting family. They'd found each other on a grocery-store notices board—two Midwestern loners adrift in New York. She was a singularly uncurious girl and did not question the pregnancy. Annie had made a cursory explanation of her intentions and the subject was promptly dropped. The two of them never became friendly. At least she was someone to help with the rent.

The evening stretched in front of her, like every evening before it and those, she imagined, that would follow. It wasn't even six and it wouldn't be dark for hours. Was this the longest day of the year? It hardly mattered. She would not be able to see the lingering daylight from this apartment as it existed in perpetual gloom. She crossed to the kitchen, flipped on a light, and was shocked by the cockroaches that scurried across the floor.

"Shit!" She backed out of the room as fast as she could.

She sat in the one faded chair, opposite the faded sofa, and tried to fold her knees up under her in case any cockroaches migrated out there. It was no easy task at her size.

She thought about what she had resolved to do. Knowing her roommate would be away, she had made her decision to open the white envelope. She would finally look at its contents, take responsibility for her actions, and acknowledge all that she had done that led up to the situation she found herself in now. Then, she would say a prayer and burn the pictures in the kitchen sink.

A ritual to mark her transition to a new life.

It was time. Her due date was in a few weeks and she wanted to do this before the baby was born. She wanted to come home from the hospital and have nothing of the old life in her possession—to render herself an empty vessel both physically and psychically.

She peeked into the kitchen again to scan for the cockroaches. They were nowhere to be seen.

She crossed over to the hall closet and reached to the top shelf for the box in which she stored her papers. Taking it down, she dug through it to retrieve the old purse that had traveled with her across lifetimes and found it at the bottom of a pile. Inside of it, she found the white envelope.

She walked back to the kitchen and located the big box of matches. Their stove did not work without matches, which was another unsettling thing about New York. In Warren, you could just turn a stove on and it would work. You didn't have to stick your head inside, like you were gassing yourself, to find some pilot light while you held a lit match.

She paused in front of the sink to compose herself, to find that centered place that she had known so well, as a little girl at St. Mary Magdalen Church. She closed her eyes and breathed in and out. She had not touched cocaine or alcohol since the night of September 5th of last year. She was learning to calm herself without help now.

Ready.

She pried open the envelope, then hesitated. Maybe it was enough to simply remember what happened that night with Johnny, what happened that whole gruesome summer. Maybe she didn't need to look at the actual, physical proof of her own fall from grace.

But no.

That was not what she had decided to do. She would face it. She would reckon with herself. And she would begin the process of atonement.

She took the pictures out. She held them in front of her face. She squinted to see better.

Something was not right.

They were not photos of her at all.

The photographs were of young Diane—the sweet, freckled waitress from Frankie's, the one who stopped coming to work in the middle of the summer.

But here she was, in these pictures!

She was naked, just as Annie had been in the photos that Johnny had taken of her. Diane was wearing nothing but the gold question mark necklace.

How had she gotten that necklace? When had these photos been taken?

Annie's head swam, and her hands began to shake. Her stomach, already pressed so high in her chest by the baby, felt like it would exit through her mouth.

She stumbled back to the chair and leaned in toward the lamp. In a few of the pictures, Diane could have been smiling, but it wasn't clear. Her lips were stretched back a little, but the expression was more of a wince. Her brows were furrowed. Her eyes were half closed and rolled back.

In most of the pictures, however, her eyes were open wide and staring. Her head hung at an unnatural angle and her neck looked dark and smudged. Bruised.

OhGodohGodohGodohGodohGodohGodohGodohGodoh GodohGod—

Diane appeared to be dead.

63

Friday, August 15, 2014
Boston

DelVecchio drummed his fingers on the glass—the porthole of the door to their little cubicle—as he looked out into the hallway of the FBI offices. As though the blank white walls out there might hold the answer to all of his questions.

Annie knew that the answer he was seeking did not lie in the hallway.

She sat at the table, face-to-face with Provenzano, knowing full well that the answer rested in her. It lay on the table in the pile of pictures she had brought to show them. Pictures of the dead Diane.

It lay in what they were going to ask her to do about it.

"Thank you, Mrs. Ford, for returning to talk to us. Are you comfortable?" asked Provenzano, working to soften her.

"As comfortable as I expect to be," she said, unable at that moment to imagine actual comfort.

"Good. Like I said, we're glad you called us. Glad you came back. We always encourage cooperation as best for everyone involved; we believe you'll find that to be true. So, let's get started. First of all, how much do you know about Congressman Buscemi?"

"Just what I've told you," Annie answered. "He wasn't a congressman when I knew him."

"Well, he's been a congressman for a long time. And we've been after him for longer," DelVecchio said.

"For drug dealing?"

"That's the tip of the iceberg. Buscemi stopped directly dealing drugs when he ran for congress. Obviously. But his ties to his former associates run deep. Did you know a cop by the name of Daniel Ravello?"

"Yes. He was always with a group that hung out at Frankie's—with Johnny Buscemi, in particular. And he was with Johnny again when I saw him in New York last week."

"Ravello's no longer a police officer. He's Buscemi's chief aide and has been since Buscemi took office. These affiliates of Buscemi's are involved in all sorts of unsavory matters: racketeering, extortion, prostitution, book making, drugs, arms trafficking. The list goes on. Ravello has kept Buscemi's name out of it all. He's kind of the clean-up guy," DelVecchio said. "But we believe, strongly, that Buscemi has a finger in all of those pies."

"These pictures"—Provenzano jumped in, gesturing at the grisly show-and-tell on the table—"combined with your testimony regarding your first-hand personal experience with Buscemi, could be the key that locks Buscemi away. Remember Al Capone: after everything he did, our guys got him on tax evasion."

"Wait." She thinks she might vomit. "I would have to testify?"

"We're asking you to do two things. First, we want you to meet with Johnny Buscemi. Immediately," Provenzano said. "We'll provide a contact number for him—his cell phone so that he picks it up himself. You'll organize a meeting at your house in Watch Hill."

"Why would he come to my house?" Annie was reeling.

DelVecchio answered. "You'll tell him you have the photos. You'll tell him you have the necklace that Diane Englund was wearing in the pictures on the night she was killed. You'll offer to give him those items in exchange for his silence about you. As you've said, he saw you in New York last week. So he knows you're alive—and he can guess at how much you have to hide. It's pretty tidy. Everyone has something to gain here."

"There's something I don't understand," she said. "I got that necklace from Frankie Castiglione. Not from Johnny Buscemi. How did Frankie get it? Who killed Diane?"

"Does it matter? If you lie down with dogs, you get up with fleas," DelVecchio crudely responded. "Only she's not getting up. Ever again. Somebody killed her and it sure as hell looks like Buscemi, from what you've told us."

Provenzano took it from there. "Look, Mrs. Ford, we need to nail this guy. Castiglione is dead. He's out of our reach. We don't know which of them killed her. Maybe all of them. But this guy has gotten away with way too much for way too long. People have died, and you've given us the first tangible proof of it. And we need you to take him down. We'll be very close by. We'll fit you with a wire, so we'll be able to hear everything that goes on. We can be next to you very quickly should something go wrong."

"Do you even know how much can go wrong?" she asked. "Johnny Buscemi is a violent man. You can see that from those pictures. What if he decides to kill me?"

"He's also a United States Representative. We doubt that he'll hurt you."

"That seems pretty easy for you to say, from wherever you're hiding— in the bushes or in the closet or somewhere! He may be a congressman, but I'll be backing him into a pretty uncomfortable corner."

"We understand that, Mrs. Ford. That's why we'll be nearby."

"Then what?"

"You'll show him the photographs and the necklace. Get him to talk. Is that understood? You have to get him to talk."

64

It was early Monday morning, but Annie had been awake for hours. She sat in one of the Adirondack chairs near the seawall, holding a piece of paper. Her coffee cup was next to her, as usual, resting on the arm of her chair. Her dogs slept at her feet.

Mrs. Ford's favorite way to begin her day.

It was too early for the shot signaling the raising of the flag at the Watch Hill Yacht Club. The sun had barely risen, and a mist hovered over the ocean. The beauty of it pierced her, cut a hole right through her. Or maybe it just shone a spotlight on the hole that she had never been able to fill.

She looked down at the paper, at the phone number written there by Agent Provenzano, and laid her hand on her cellphone, sitting on the opposite arm of her chair. There was no use procrastinating. It was not as though she had many options. Susan, had she been alive, would have made the call by now. Susan would have called him on Friday, after leaving the FBI office. Susan would not have let this fester all weekend.

But she was not now and never had been Susan.

She picked up the phone and stabbed in the digits.

"Hello," said a melodious male voice on the other end of the line—a bit gravelly from sleep, but still a very nice voice.

"It's Annie Nelson." She sat up straighter to fortify herself against him. "I have that envelope I took from you—I think that's what you were talking about in New York. I also have the necklace. The unusual one that Diane was wearing in the photos you took of her."

"Well, well," he said in his most sarcastic tone. "Good morning, little girl."

"Come to my house in Watch Hill. Tonight, at midnight. The town will be dead by then, so no one will see you come or go. You have time to catch a flight into Providence and it's a forty-five-minute drive from there."

"I don't think so, little girl. I think I'd rather have you come see me in Detroit."

Annie dropped the register of her voice as low as she possibly could. "First of all, don't you ever—and I mean *ever*—call me that again. I am *not* your little girl. Is that clear?" She did not wait for an answer. "Secondly, I kind of have you by the balls here, Johnny. I'm not coming to Detroit. If you want the pictures and the necklace—if you want to keep those balls—you'll meet me where I want to meet."

"All grown up now, aren't you?"

"Cut the crap. Are you coming or not?"

"What's your address?"

65

Monday, August 18, 2014
Time: 8:58 p.m.

"What else do you need to tell me?" Sammy is ashen. "Is it about the baby?"

"No." Annie sets her bags on the floor and walks over to the window. She looks at the lighthouse making its revolutions as though this were a normal day, an average day, a day of no special consequence.

"It's about Diane," she continues. "That waitress I mentioned before. Johnny killed her. Or, someone killed her—I don't know who—but Johnny was involved. That necklace I gave you, the one that Frankie gave me, it belonged to her. I didn't know that then.

"And now, the FBI are threatening me with jail for all sorts of crimes. They read me a list that could put me away for a very long time, everything from identity theft to murder and a dozen things in between. They've made me an offer: They'll let it all go if I do something for them. Two things, in fact." She looks at her watch. "The first is that, in three hours, I'm supposed to meet with Johnny Buscemi. I called him early this morning and he's on his way here now. They want me to wear a wire. Set him up.

"And maybe I would have been able to do that. Maybe it would have felt good. But there's a second part. I would have to publicly testify against him. Sammy, I did some things back then that I'm not proud of.

Ugly things, and most of them, with him. And it turns out now that it's all wrapped up in Diane's death.

"But, to bring him down, I'd end up bringing the whole house down with me. The house my husband built. I don't want to do that! I don't want to destroy the names and reputations of my husband and stepson. It's not fair to them.

"I'm not Susan Ford, as much as I wanted to be. She's not even real. I made her up. And I'm certainly not Susan Bentley. She died a long time ago. I'm Annie Nelson. I lost *her* so many years ago that I think it's time to find her."

"Jesus Christ, Annie. You're really playing with fire here."

"Look, it's pretty simple: if I go now, I can leave Susan Ford intact—crystallize her here. She can disappear—off into the fog of the Atlantic."

Bang! Bang! Bang! The knocking at the door resumes.

Sammy looks at her. "You've made up your mind?"

"I have."

"You have always amazed me, Annie."

"You sure as hell never showed me that."

"I'm not as expressive as you are."

"That's putting it mildly. Are you coming?"

"I can't. Not now."

66

Annie goes down the back stairs and exits a small door at the side of the house. She does not pass through the living room. She cannot face her dogs, sleeping there, trusting that their world has not changed.

For an instant, the thought of leaving her dogs doubles her over in pain. She has made too many departures for one person; she's spent too many years alone. Precipitously, she sits on the steps with her head between her knees, willing the pain away.

It would be so easy. She could turn around right now, wake her dogs and walk with them back up those stairs. Back up to her life. But she reminds herself that that life has vanished. Susan Ford is already gone.

She collects herself and continues.

She moves down a narrow alley, past an old stone fountain, and around the back of the gatehouse toward the road. She lifts the latch on a picture-book white wooden gate and closes it softly behind her.

She looks both ways.

No cars are parked on the road.

She walks down Bay Street, the heart of Watch Hill. She passes the carousel, its horses still, the newspaper kiosk closed; passes the entrance to the public beach; passes St. Clair Annex, its ice cream window selling cones to the after-dinner crowd. She passes the Olympia Tea Room, alive with summer revelers. She nears the boats bobbing in the bay.

Here, she stops. She sets down her bags and takes one last look at all that she is giving up. Here is Venus, Jack's magnificent yacht, a seventy-four-foot-long wooden beauty nearly a hundred years old, its varnished surfaces gleaming in the lamplight.

She takes her laptop out of her bag and lets it slide, with the slightest plop, into the water of the bay. Then she takes out her iPhone and iPad and does the same. The noise they make is even softer. She looks down to see that the ripples they made are already dying.

And then she says the words she was never able to say to her husband when he left her on an April afternoon: "Goodbye, Jack."

"Hello, little girl."

Annie's knees buckle. The voice is right next to her, a whisper in her ear. She turns, expecting to see Johnny Buscemi, and looks straight into the face of Danny Ravello.

"The boss told me to say that to you. He said you'd know what it meant."

"I-uh—" Annie scrambles to collect her thoughts. "What are you doing here?"

"You didn't really think the congressman would come here himself, did you?"

"I-I guess I did."

"That wouldn't be too smart, would it?"

"I don't know what you mean."

"Huh. The boss said you were pretty sharp. I thought you might pick up the thread a little faster."

"Look, I'm not quite sure why you're here. I have some personal business with Johnny Buscemi and I don't really see what that has to do with you."

"Lemme make it real clear: He sent me to pick up the package you called him about."

"Well, I don't have that package with me. I was expecting Johnny a bit later. I was taking a stroll."

"With your luggage?"

Annie can't help but look over her shoulder at the three bags she wishes she still had in her hands, sitting in a row on the seawall.

"Looks to me like you're going somewhere."

"I—" Annie's mind is completely blank. She cannot think of one single thing to say or do. The resourcefulness that had been her stalwart companion throughout many lives—and just as many crises—has deserted her.

She reckons this man will kill her, right here, right now, on Bay Street, right in the middle of Watch Hill. He could shoot her with a silenced gun and push her in the water. She racks her memory to try to come up with famous Watch Hill murders of the past, some nefarious grouping that she is surely about to join in the seedy underbelly of this perfect town.

She casts her eyes to the heavens above and thinks to utter a little prayer, put in one last ask. This time, she will ask for grace. If she is going to go, tonight, at the hands of Danny Ravello, she would like to do it with dignity. She knows she did not enter this world with much of that comely commodity, but maybe she can redeem herself now. Go down with her tiara on.

"Come on." Ravello grabs her forearm, which snaps her out of her trance. "Let's march. Let's go get that package."

"Ow! You're hurting me!" Annie's spunk materializes at the first touch of his hand. And then she drops her tone to threaten him in return. "Let go of me."

"I don't think so."

"At least let me get my bags."

"Fine." He shoves her, just a little, over to the seawall.

And then, as Annie is bending to hoist her duffels over her arms and looking around for an exit, she hears the distinct Locust Valley Lockjaw of Cecilia Thatcher.

"Susan!"

There stands Cecilia, resplendent in pink Jack Rogers, a green Lilly Pulitzer shift, a cable-knit sweater, and a headband. With her is her husband, Tom, and their basset hound, Daphne. "We missed you at the cookout last week! Aren't you a naughty girl to go off at the last minute!"

Cecilia Thatcher waggles a finger at Annie, while casting meaningful glances in the direction of Danny Ravello. She waits for the socially correct number of seconds to allow Mrs. Ford to introduce her companion.

Annie says nothing.

Cecilia shakes her head, almost imperceptibly, at this breach of etiquette. "Cecilia Thatcher!" she finally says, as she thrusts her right hand toward Ravello. "And, this is my husband, Tom!"

God, she is irritating. But Annie is ready to kiss her feet right now.

"Uh, Ravello," he says, as he grudgingly produces his hand.

"Oh! *Italiano! Piacere di conoscerti!*" Cecilia laughs in a flirtatious way as she keeps ahold of his big mitt in her two little hands. "I studied Italian back at Pembroke! Oops! Now I'm giving away my age!"

Annie has finally regained her equilibrium. In one move, she leaps onto the seawall, and hops over the gate to the dock.

"Susan!" Cecilia's mouth drops open.

Annie bolts full speed down the length of the pier.

Ravello yanks his hand away from Cecilia. He grabs her by the shoulders and thrusts her to the side, to clear his own path after Annie. He fumbles to opens the gate. Finally, he gives it a good kick, splintering its pickets in all directions, and sets off down the long pier.

Annie bypasses Venus and sprints to the end of the dock. She works to untie two ropes attaching a much smaller boat—a little inflatable Zodiac.

Danny Ravello advances steadily toward her.

Annie throws both lines aboard the Zodiac and jumps on after them. She reaches under the console to grope for the key—it should be hanging there on its little floating donut.

Ravello is getting closer.

Annie locates the key and tries shoving it into the ignition. She drops it onto the deck.

"Shit!" she mutters.

Ravello rounds the corner, where the dock flares out in a T. He is steps from the Zodiac now.

Annie finds the key, wiggles it into place and turns it. The engine sputters and coughs.

Ravello grabs onto the side of the Zodiac.

And now Annie prays. A quick, silent prayer: *Hail Mary, full of Grace, the Lord is with Thee*…. She turns the key once more and, finally, the engine starts.

Just as Danny Ravello puts one foot on board, she retrieves her gun and points it straight at him.

"Get your ass off my boat," she says in her lowest voice, "or I will shoot you."

"I really don't think you'll do that. I have a gun aimed right at you."

And he does. It looks like a big one.

In a flash, Annie tosses her gun to the deck of her boat. She grabs the wheel, revs the engine and drops Danny Ravello into the drink.

His gun sinks like a stone.

Annie easily avoids his splashing grasp as she speeds out into the dark harbor of Watch Hill. She maneuvers through the boats at anchor in the bay. It is high summer, and the harbor is filled with vessels. At the moment when she could continue straight, to follow along Napatree Point and on by the side of Sandy Point, to leave the harbor and enter the sea, she makes a different choice.

There, she takes a sharp turn to the right and motors quietly up the Pawcatuck River. Half an hour later, she turns the wheel toward a private, residential dock on Margin Street in Westerly. She cuts the engine and jumps off, making sure she has her bags and her gun. She kicks the boat back into the current.

She watches it float down the river toward Watch Hill. She imagines it floating out to Fisher's Island Sound, drifting on past the lighthouse and into the open ocean of the Atlantic.

Free.

She thinks about her dogs, asleep in front of the fire. She pictures them dozing there all night, Calpurnia and Pliny, enjoying the dying embers, dreaming their doggie dreams. Snoring. She hopes they will not wake until Helen comes in at eight the next morning.

She pictures the FBI agents, knocking at her door at right about this moment. She pictures Sammy already in a car, almost at the airport, or wherever it is they are taking him. She imagines Danny Ravello, fishing himself out of the bay.

She pictures them all crisscrossing each other tonight, all over the little village of Watch Hill.

67

Time: 10:47 p.m.

Annie arrives at the Westerly Train Station just before the 10:54 p.m. arrival of the 178 Northeast Regional from New York. The last train in either direction to stop here tonight. She arrives on foot. She has walked the final stretch from the dock, through the streets of downtown Westerly. She pauses a moment, in the shadows, to catch her breath. Station wagons and SUVs are parked, trunks open, ready for family members' bags. Two taxis wait, as well, for anyone who might be in need of their services.

The elegant Westerly Train Station was rebuilt in 1912 in the Spanish Colonial Revival style. Stucco walls, a terra cotta tile roof supported by wooden rafter tails, and arching colonnades always make Annie think more of California than New England. It is a beautiful station and creates a picturesque welcome to travelers, arriving in search of a sandy beach by the sea.

Annie slips onto the platform, unremarkable in her dark clothes and bags, another traveler at the train station. When the train pulls in, she merges with the disembarking crowd, exiting to the parking lot in the clump of arriving passengers. Anyone who is later asked if they had seen her at the station would not remember anything unusual. Just the regular passengers with their regular luggage, getting off of the regular train.

Annie separates from the group and jumps into a taxi. She asks to be taken to the Mohegan Sun Casino.

"Why didn't you get off at New London?" the driver barks.

"I must have slept through it and the conductor didn't remind me," Annie explains. "I just woke up and am so glad I haven't gone too far."

"That'll be fifty bucks," he says, which seems a bit steep.

"Is cash all right?" Annie asks, sweetly.

And they're off.

68

Tuesday, August 19, 2014
Connecticut
Time: 12:45 a.m.

Annie looks around, a bit dazed by the five thousand slot machines of the Mohegan Sun Casino. The faux logs and ersatz birch bark of the Native American décor make a surreal backdrop to the clanging machinery. The sheer number of slot machines is formidable. Five thousand people can drink, smoke, and lose their money at any one time, twenty-four hours a day. A tax on the poor, Jack had always called it.

Two casinos cluster in close proximity in northeastern Connecticut—only forty minutes away from Watch Hill—Foxwoods and the Mohegan Sun. Annie has chosen the Mohegan Sun with a roll of the metaphorical dice. There is zero chance that any of the wealthy denizens of Watch Hill will be present to recognize Mrs. Ford walking through its cavernous spaces at one o'clock in the morning. None of her friends will be here to see her, dressed in black and carrying her luggage, on her way back from the ladies' room and looking for the bus stop.

The Long Lucky Bus is departing shortly. One of several bus lines that ply I-95 in the summer, New York to Boston and all casino stops in between, it will be her lucky coach tonight. Her bus ticket to New York will cost less than her cab fare from Westerly to the casino. Her ticket to New York is buyable with cash, requires no identification, and comes with a pizza coupon.

Annie sits in the waiting room, holding her bags on her lap, trying not to doze, to keep her attention focused on the glass double doors. She ignores the three other lonely souls in the waiting room, those whose money and luck have run out. Others, those who still have cash in their pockets or room on their credit cards, gamble until the last minute. But, eventually, they join her group.

Like the pilgrims in *The Canterbury Tales*, Annie and her fellow wanderers board the bus. Should they choose to share their stories, like those 14th century travelers did, to pass the time, to amuse each other, to win a free dinner (though they all have their pizza coupons), Annie wonders what those stories might contain. Would her own tale be the most interesting? Would she possess more secrets than the average person? Or is she, as she half suspects, given what she's seen of human nature thus far, just one among many, not that special and not that different. These people, catching a bus at a casino in the middle of the night must surely have tales to tell.

Annie selects a seat in the back and keeps her bags with her. She tucks one tightly under her feet and keeps the other two on her lap. Should she sleep, which she both longs for and fears, she needs to be able to feel any movement of those bags. The bags carry everything she has to start a new life. Except for Jacob's number, which she has tucked into her pocket.

The bus begins to roll. The motion and the darkness have a soporific effect, and, for the first time, Annie realizes she is exhausted. She does not want to think about her little dogs. She does not want to think about the men in her life—not Jack or Jack Jr. or Johnny or Sammy. And, certainly not Danny Ravello. She does not want to think of the women either. Those she has abandoned—Susan, her grandmother—even Diane, in a way, when she held onto those pictures for so many years. And, of course, her daughter. The biggest abandonment of all.

She does not want to think, and she does not want to feel. She will close her eyes, safe on the bus at this miniscule moment in time. She will rest, knowing that this much of her plan has been successfully carried out.

The spinning of the bus wheels, for now, eclipses the spinning of her mind.

69

Time: 2:55 a.m.

The Long Lucky bus heaves its bulk to the right, off the highway and into a rest stop. Tires squeal and brakes hiss as the bus comes to a lumbering stop.

"Fifteen minutes!" the driver announces.

Annie hesitates then remembers her bladder—one of the disadvantages of advancing age. She could use the bathroom on the bus, but she might as well go here. It is probably cleaner inside. She collects her load and trudges off to the ladies' room.

Mindful of the time, she leaves the stall and tucks her bags tightly between her feet to wash her hands. She has to pick up all three bags with her dripping hands to make her way over to the hand dryer, on the wall near the door.

It is then that she notices someone watching her. Glancing up, Annie makes eye contact with the woman before she can catch herself.

"Look at you." The woman could be any age, forty, fifty, sixty. She is dressed in stretchy pants and a printed blouse. Medium height. Nondescript in every way. "Win some money?"

Annie bitterly regrets leaving the safety of the bus.

"Who, me?" Annie smiles widely then tones it down a notch. That smile was too big. She looks like the Cheshire cat, grinning in the bathroom. "Nah, I just have my clothes and things."

"Want me to carry one of those bags for you? Your clothes look pretty heavy."

"No thanks." Annie tries to make the hoisting of the bags look effortless. Her hands are still wet, but she needs to get out of there. "Not heavy at all. Well, goodnight."

"Oh, I'm going with you. We're on the same bus."

Shit.

Shit. Shit. Shit.

Annie gets back on the bus and into her seat and tucks her bags in around her.

She is determined to stay awake. She only has an hour to go. She cannot afford to sleep now, with that leering woman on board. She stares straight ahead. She should have bought coffee. Her eyes start to flutter. Her head droops and snaps up a few times. Then one last head drop, and she is gone.

And then she has it—the precious kernel of a memory—just what she has been searching for since this entire nightmare began. Her comfort thought, the one that makes her believe in miracles. It comes to her effortlessly in a dream, as the bus flies down the highway.

She met Jack on July 14, 1996. Bastille Day. It was a sultry Sunday night in New York. She had gone with a group of friends to Florent, in the Meatpacking District, for a little French celebration. They were a ragtag lot, this being July and this being New York.

At that point, more than sixteen years into her life as a new person, she had come to think of herself as Susan. The vestiges of Annie were fuzzy around the edges, dreamlike. The remnants of the real Susan, or the old Susan, for she thought of herself as very real, were equally ephemeral. In all those years, she had never once run into anyone who had known either person back in Michigan. There were occasional days, though not very often, when she did not think once of that summer of 1979.

She was of an age at which many of her peers were married with children. Those friends were not out on a Sunday night. They may have been in the country or they may have been in the city, but they were definitely not in a bar. This group that she was with was composed of the footloose ones, the commitment-phobes, the die-hards.

Chief among these friends was young Jack Ford Jr. They both worked in real estate, she for a little boutique firm—a job Jack Jr. had helped her land—and he for his eminent father and namesake.

Jack Jr. was gregarious and funny, and everyone loved to be with him. The two of them had spent a lot of time together since they'd met in the subway three years before. He was the life of any party and she usually said yes when he invited her out. But she had been vigilant about maintaining a physical wall between them. Jack was a ladies' man and she no longer had a tolerance for that sort of arrangement. She believed that their friendship was actually a relief for them both.

It was already late. Champagne was flowing, in honor of the French Revolution. They hadn't had their main course yet. The words to *la Marseillaise* could be heard in the corner being mangled by some men who should have been cut off hours ago. "*Allons enfants de la patrie*" was as far as they could go, so they repeated it ad infinitum.

Jack had stepped away. When he came back to the table, he announced that one more would be joining their group. He'd just spoken to his father, who happened to be in the city and who happened to say yes to his son's invitation to join them.

"Move over, Susan, and my dad can sit next to you," Jack said to her. She was glad for the rest of her life that she did so.

Jack Ford Sr. walked into Florent, the way he walked into any place, with quiet confidence. He was not a swaggerer, but he was no shrinking violet, either. Jack exuded a peaceful acceptance that he belonged wherever he went, which made him both likeable and a little bit intimidating.

And then there was the way he dressed. This was the Meatpacking District, so the color black was *de rigueur*. Black on black, shades of black, variations of black, a black shot with a black chaser. Jack walked in like he'd just stepped off a Hinckley yacht—pink pants, a green and white checked shirt, navy blazer, yellow socks and a sky-blue sweater thrown around his shoulders. He was a cacophony of color.

She laughed out loud when she saw him, so utterly charmed was she by his originality. It was that quality that she perceived first, that she fell in love with and of which she remained forever in awe. Jack was 100 percent Jack, through and through. Plop him down in Paris, Shanghai, LA, or Abidjan, and he would dress the same, talk the same, be the same.

She, Susan, who wasn't really even Susan, who had lived her life as a chameleon, was amazed and impressed. She, who had always been whatever she needed to be to get by, felt, for the first time, that she was in the presence of someone with whom she might be able to be herself. It was a gut reaction she had not felt in years and years. Not since her Sundays at St. Mary Magdalen Church with Grandma Annie.

Jack homed in on her, focusing his pale blue eyes with laser-like intensity. He barely listened when his son introduced him to the table and he waited, not very patiently, for his son to shut up so that he could talk to this woman. Jack was a man who knew what he wanted and, at that moment, she was it.

For the first night of what was to become many, they talked for hours of life in all of its iterations. History was his interest. Movies were hers. In the sixteen years that had passed since Annie had taken on Susan's enthusiasms, they had fused with her own. Books, religion, and dogs, they both loved them.

Jack had a passion for boats, antique wooden boats. He collected them. There, their experiences differed. She did not elaborate on her own boating history back in Michigan.

For a man of his age and generation, Jack was extraordinarily talkative. She knew many younger men who did not have Jack's communication skills. Jack loved women who laughed at his jokes. Fortuitously, she found him very funny.

Jack asked her if she'd been to Watch Hill, where he'd just finished building a house. She had not. She visited him at that house, Gull Cottage, over Labor Day and they were married by the end of the year. It was a first marriage for Susan, a second for Jack.

After their dreamy snow globe wedding in New York, Jack and Susan piled into his old Jaguar and drove through the snow—up to Watch Hill, to Gull Cottage, his creation, the house that would always remind Susan of Jack—for their first night as husband and wife.

Later, as they were sharing a glass of wine and the little picnic of cheese and bread their friends had packed, Jack was uncannily prescient.

"Here's to new beginnings." He held his glass up to hers. "We are not children. We both have lived full lives before we met. Complicated lives that helped to shape us and lead us to each other. May we honor the past but also keep it behind us. It is with great hope that I look to our future together. A little secret about me—I always need something to look forward to. Little surprises along the way."

She smiled as she raised her glass to her husband. "I'll do my best to surprise you."

70

Time: 3:00 a.m.

Annie burrows deep into the memory of Jack. It is always like this when she dreams about him. She feels herself waking and harnesses every ability she has to propel herself back into the dream. Her powers, of course, are insufficient. She floats up to consciousness against her will—no matter how many mental weights she ties around her imagination to keep herself below the surface—and finds herself in a world without Jack. It is always a brutal splash of cold water in the face.

This time, she senses Jack next to her, touching her, and feels like her trick might be working. The sensation is so real.

Fuck. The sensation *is* so real.

Annie snaps open her eyes to look straight into the face of the woman from the rest stop. She immediately reels her head back and whacks it hard on the window of the bus. Her right hand flies up to hold her head while her left-hand edges toward her littlest bag.

"I was having a very pleasant dream." Annie recovers some composure. "I wish you hadn't disturbed me."

"Good morning, sunshine!" The woman clearly thinks that line is the pinnacle of wit for she laughs heartily.

"You're very close to me right now and you're making me uncomfortable."

"I just thought you might need a friend. You look a little out of place here. Like you don't belong."

"You can't even imagine the kinds of places I belong."

"Look." The woman gets an A for effort. "I can tell you have a pile of money there. I didn't see you gambling tonight, but I was at the slots. You must have been at the big boy tables. Wontcha just share some with little ol' me?" She says this in a cutesy voice.

"I do not have money in these bags." Annie enunciates every syllable. "And I am asking you for the final time to move to another seat."

"I have a lot of friends in the city. They might even be at the Port Authority when we get there."

Annie lifts her left hand from the bag. She points Sammy's little .38 directly into the woman's obnoxious face. "Lady," she says in her lowest, most menacing voice, "you are fucking with the wrong blonde."

In the face of such persuasion, the woman slides back and moves to a different seat.

And, with that, Annie is fully Annie again.

71

Disconsolately, she stared at the news on the hospital television.

On the world stage, the important milestone that occurred on this day did not happen in New York City. On this hot summer Sunday, when much of the city was deserted by those who had the means to desert it, when she, who went by the name of Susan Bentley, was giving birth to a baby girl in the maternity ward of Roosevelt Hospital—on this same day, the deposed Shah of Iran, Mohammad Reza Pahlavi, the last and final ruler in a 2500-year lineage going back to the coronation of Cyrus the Great, died of cancer in Cairo.

She, the new mother, and the dying old man had little in common save their shared status as exiles, living on the run, far from their homes and their people.

In Iran, the ancestral home of the Shah, his replacement, the Ayatollah Khomeini, had returned triumphantly the year before, in February 1979.

Iraq, the country next door, also had a new ruler. Saddam Hussein had taken the office of president on July 16, 1979, during the very summer when Susan and Annie, Sammy and Frankie were marking their days at a disco in Warren. She knew that only Sammy had paid attention to it at the time.

She thought about her baby, born on this day in New York, who carried the surname of a dead woman, a woman with whom she had no blood ties. Baby Girl Bentley was not aware of events playing out in the Middle East. She was not aware of her own genetic links to that region. She was not aware of war or peace, of human bonds, intact or broken, of love or loss, of forgiveness or redemption as she cried in her bassinet and was comforted by a nurse, a stranger, with a baby bottle.

The woman whose name she bore lay in a grave in Michigan. The woman whose name was etched in stone above that grave—she—Annie, or whoever she was—right now lay in a bed at Roosevelt Hospital, down the hall from the nursery where the baby girl cried.

The baby's father—she imagined Sammy sitting in a café in Baghdad—was unaware of her birth. Was he right now planning his return to the US, hoping to escape the drumbeats of war that Annie, even now, could hear?

And, for that brief moment—inspired by new life or induced by morphine—she grasped the whirling swirl of the cosmos. She saw that the world turned then as it turns now and would continue to turn ever after. Human bodies came together and moved apart, but no connections were ever truly severed. As it was in the beginning, is now, and ever shall be, world without end. And, then that clarity left her.

72

Annie is home. The scene of her childhood. The scene of the crime. She has been in Detroit for a week. Her first task was to find Jacob. They met at Our Lady of Perpetual Help, a Chaldean Catholic church in Warren. She remembers this church as St. Sylvester. She had friends who were parishioners there, who were baptized there, who made their First Communions there. And now it is Chaldean.

Documents secured, identity changed again, she moves on. She thanks Jacob; tells him that Sammy is well. She does not say more. She does not know how much Jacob knows about his cousin's life and work. Jacob does not ask questions, does not inquire about her need for an identity switch, the second in her life. He delivers the docs and takes the cash. They hug awkwardly and say goodbye.

At two o'clock in the afternoon she walks into a different church, farther west, the Shrine of the Little Flower. A stunning example of Art Deco architecture, with a soaring tower and a chapel in the round, it stands as a monument to the highest ideals of Christianity.

She gets down on her knees. In the chapel dedicated to St. Therese of Lisieux, Annie lowers her head in prayer. Next to her lies a bouquet of white roses, a symbol of the saint. She lights a candle. She says a novena.

She leaves the church and crosses the wide expanse of Woodward Avenue, taking two lights to do it. The first light gets her to the median strip, the second light to the corner beyond and the entrance to Roseland Cemetery. Five white stone pillars stand tall, each topped by an urn of stone flowers. She enters the little gatehouse on the right, gives a name, requests a map and sets off onto the cemetery grounds.

It is some distance onto the property, after a few stops, to recalibrate her directions in consultation with the map, but she finds what she is looking for. A double headstone in pale grey granite faces away from her. She must walk around it to read its inscription:

Annie Wales Johnston	*Annie Johnston Nelson*
Born October 9, 1902	*Born May 11, 1958*
Died July 26, 1980	*Died September 6, 1979*

Across the bottom of the stone, in what must have cost her mother and stepfather a fortune—money that she has trouble imagining them spending—are the words:

Holy Mary, Mother of God, Pray for Us Sinners,
Now and at the Hour of Our Death.
Amen.

She mentally fills in the rest of the prayer—her favorite. She realizes, as she does so, that her parents did not pay for those words. Her grandmother must have had the stone created when she died—when Susan died—and was buried by Annie's family. Her grandmother must have had Annie's name inscribed to the right, leaving room for herself on the left. She must have taken money from her savings, money that would never go to her dead granddaughter, her favorite, the child who had broken her heart and hastened her own death.

She drops to her knees on the cold, hard ground, feeling the weight of what she has done to her grandmother—the woman who loved her completely. The woman she completely deserted. She holds up the bouquet of roses, raises it to her forehead, then places it on the ground. She reaches out to touch the gravestone. It is then that she stops short. She looks at the date of her grandmother's death; one day before a little girl was born in Roosevelt Hospital in New York City.

And she glimpses a moment of clarity once more.

She gets up, wipes the dirt off her knees, and strides down the cemetery road.

73

Saturday, September 20, 2014

*S*peramus meliora; resurget cineribus. We hope for better things; it will arise from the ashes.

Detroit, the phoenix, the city that has burned and burned again, is rising from the ashes, fulfilling the prophecy of its motto.

At the corner of Canfield and Cass, an area where, twenty years before, bodies in Dumpsters would not raise an eyebrow, Annie—her hair dark once more—waits in a trendy restaurant. She has only a cup of tea and keeps her attention riveted out the window. It has taken her a long time—long in all measurable ways—to get to this place and she does not want to miss her moment.

Across the street is a Bikram yoga studio, also trendy. Annie keeps her eyes trained on the studio's door. Presently, it opens.

A group of young people emerges. Dressed in yoga clothes, carrying eco-water bottles and towels, they spill outside. They laugh and talk, then split up, singly and in pairs, walking to their cars or down the block together.

One among them is a tall, dark beauty. There is something about her walk—an awkwardness that isn't quite graceful but is appealing nonetheless. Sure enough, she trips, just a little, on the sidewalk. The young man by her side reaches out to take her elbow and steady her. It is clear to an impartial observer that she does not need saving. But Annie can see that the man is not impartial.

Annie throws a twenty on the table and leaves the restaurant. She steps out onto the pavement and is about to cross the street when another woman emerges from the yoga studio, holding a bag, and calls out, "Susan!"

The heads of the older woman and the younger woman turn in unison at the name.

"Did I forget something?" the younger woman responds.

"Your bag!"

"Oh, thanks!" The younger woman laughs. "I don't know where my head is! What would I have done without this today?" She skips back to take the bag from her helpful friend.

Annie smiles to herself as she remembers scrawling a name on a birth certificate in a hospital long ago.

Susan.

The adoptive family kept the name.

She steps off the curb to meet her daughter.

Just then, a car rounds the corner and cuts her off, blocking her passage across the road. It is a bland-looking car—American, like most of the cars in Detroit.

She stops in her tracks to study it. Champagne, she would call that color. But then, it is gone, rounding the next corner before she can get a proper look.

She turns to scan the opposite sidewalk. Her daughter is still there.

Once more, she looks back in the direction in which the car just disappeared. It is probably nothing. Jitters, she thinks. It isn't even likely. No one would find her here. She has covered her tracks so well.

Just then, a hand grabs onto her upper arm, the hand of someone behind her.

She closes her eyes reflexively. For just one second, she does not want to know if it is Johnny or Danny or the FBI who has tracked her to this spot.

"Wait!" she says to the specter. "Just give me a minute. Please. I'll go wherever you want me to go. Just give me a minute more."

She opens her eyes and studies her daughter, working hard to commit her face to memory. A sense of futility hits her. She will never meet her. She will never be able to explain to her the way things happened and why. She will never get to hear her daughter's triumphs and tears and growing-up stories. This is all she will ever have of her. Just this vision on a street in Detroit on a random autumn day. She uses every ounce of her being to savor it. To memorize it. To store it.

"Okay," she finally surrenders. "I'm ready. Do what you have to do."

"Then let's go meet our daughter," the voice behind her says. A voice with a very slight accent.

She spins to look at Sammy.

"I'm off of the fence," he says. He shrugs and smiles a very white smile. She'd never noticed how white his teeth were. "I'm ready to make a commitment."

She has to admit that she's surprised. In fact, she is utterly speechless.

"I'm sorry," he continues. "There's so much I'm sorry for that I'll just give a blanket apology. And, I'll probably just keep apologizing."

"Well," she finally says. "I owe so many apologies myself. I probably have you beat."

"We could make it a competition. Shall we start right now?"

This makes her smile. "I think we have something better to do." She holds out her hand to him. He takes it.

Together, they cross the street.

The End

Acknowledgments

This book would not have been possible without the support and encouragement of a village of family, friends and colleagues. First, to my Teacher, I send gratitude and love abounding. A very special thank you to the late Gene Wilder—the earliest of the early encouragers—and to Jan Kardys and Barbara Ellis of the Unicorn Writers' Conference. Enormous thanks to my agent, Mollie Glick, and to Anthony Ziccardi, Maddie Sturgeon, Emi Battaglia, Devon Brown, Ellis Levine, Molly Lindley Pisani, Becky Ford, Cassandra Tai-Marcellini, Lydia MacLear, Lindley Pless, May Wuthrich, Saskia Maarleveld, Jenn Hansen-de Paola, Sam Huss, and Nikki Sinning, the most talented team of professionals.

I am deeply thankful to my very own personal posse of the brightest and most generous friends and family, listed alphabetically, because there is no other fair way to count them: Chuck Adams, Cyndy Anderson, Susie Baker, Mary Randolf Ballinger, Nancy Bolitho, Charlie Bommarito, Tom Bommarito, Peter Bundy, Cilla and Hillary Bercovici, Jeanne McWilliams Blasberg, Sean Byrne, Bob Callahan, Murph Carmody, Darby Cartun, Patricia Chadwick, Lillian Clagett, Jenny Clark, Tania Clark, Harriette Cole, Michael Cooper, Sarah Cooper, Trudy Coxe, Ian Cron, Kelly Cunningham, Chantal Curtis, Freddie Davis, Lucy Day, Brigitte Stacey Dennett, Melissa Devaney, Lauren DiStefano, Djuana Dolan, Lily Downing and David Yudain, Jean Doyen de Montaillou and Michael Kovner, Diane Eichenbaum, Kathy Eldon, Deborah Foreman, Icy Frantz, Tony Fulgenzio, Missy Gagarin, Marcia Geller, Mitch Giannunzio, Valerie Gibala, Kathie Lee Gifford, Anne Goodrich, Bill Goodrich, Kathy Goodrich, Cee Greene, Louisa Greene, Claire Tisne Haft, Myrna Haft,

Julie Hardinge, Melinda Hassen, Hilary Hatfield, Mary Ann Henry, Nina Holden, Daniel Hostettler, Kim Hubbard, Toni Hudson, Medvis Jackson, Whitney Kershaw, Jennifer and Dan King, Alexandra and Cody Kittle, Laurette and Kit Kittle, Sheila Kotur, Mary Kramer, Anharad Lewellyn, Laura Lewis, Tim Lewis, Kamie Lightburn, Patricia Lovejoy, Barbara Lusk, Layng and Linda Martine, Jessica McShane, Heidi McWilliams, Christopher Meigher, Leigh Rappaport Michaelessi, Barbara Miller, Warren Miller, Scott Mitchell, Iliana Moore, Lansing Moore, Linda Munger, Jan Ogden, Joan Patton, Annie Philbrick, Justine Picardie, Tim Plaza, Pliny Porter, Tess Porter and Danny Forrester, Brian Posler, Carrie Pryor, Amy Steele Pulitzer, Katherine Pushkar, Annie Rehlander, Kirk Reynolds, Victor Rivera, Andrea Robinson, Jane Rosenman, Alice Ross, Carmina Roth, Amanda Royce, Chuck Royce, Sharon and Chad Royce, Wesley Royce and Patrick Conlisk, Leah Rukeyser, Salvador Salort-Pons, Chelsea Schelter, Sue Goodrich Schelter, Betsy Schwengel, Ammanda Seelye Salzman, Adrianne Singer, Max Sinsteden, Vicky Skouras, Joanne Sloneker, Robin Springborn, Susan Sterling, Robert Sturnialo, Alease Fisher Tallman, Ken Tigar, Julia Nimfa Timber, Ben Tomek, Elaine Ubina, Brooke Warner, Jack Weatherford, Jennifer Weier, Kim Whalen, Tina Whitman, Jessica Wick, and Beatriz Williams. A special shout out to the most mysterious group of writers that I am privileged to be among.

And—finally—kisses and cookies to Paige, Georgina and Puck, some helpers, some hinderers—you know who you are.